Thomas Fuller

Good Thoughts in Bad Times and other Papers

Thomas Fuller

Good Thoughts in Bad Times and other Papers

ISBN/EAN: 9783337399207

Printed in Europe, USA, Canada, Australia, Japan

Cover: Foto ©Andreas Hilbeck / pixelio.de

More available books at **www.hansebooks.com**

Good Thoughts

in

Bad Times

and

Other Papers

By THOMAS FULLER, D. D.

BOSTON
TICKNOR AND FIELDS
1863

TO

WILLIAM CULLEN BRYANT,

THE LIFE-LONG DEFENDER OF IMPARTIAL LIBERTY,

THIS EDITION OF

FULLER'S GOOD THOUGHTS IN BAD TIMES

IS DEDICATED

BY THE PUBLISHERS.

PREFACE.

THE author of this book lived and wrote in stirring times. A chaplain in the army during the great civil war in England, he collected, when on his marches and countermarches through the country, materials for his admirable works. He was born in 1608, and died in 1661, so that much of his fifty-four years of life was spent among no very peaceful scenes. He followed the army with a loyal heart and courageous spirit, and wrought earnestly to mitigate the violence of hostile parties. Possessed of extraordinary abilities, the king sought him out, and invited the eloquent minister to preach before him. One of the wittiest and wisest divines who have ever ascended the pulpit, he has left behind him a fame second to none who have laboured to elevate and make their fellow-creatures better. Those who heard him preach in his little church in the Strand hung upon his persuasive lips with eager delight, and it was said by a contemporary, that even the windows and sextonry of his small chapel were crowded as if bees had swarmed to his mellifluous discourse.

Whether he lifted up his voice in the tabernacle or in the garrison, he was ever the same earnest advocate of whatsoever he thought was just and true. Once during the war he so animated the troops to a vigorous defence, that they fought the besiegers to the abandonment of their enterprise with the loss of more than a thousand men.

He wrote many books that will always be read and remembered. "Next to Shakespeare," said Coleridge, "I am not certain whether Thomas Fuller, beyond all other writers, does not excite in me the sense and emulation of the marvellous; the degree in which any given faculty or combination of faculties is possessed and manifested, so far surpassing what we would have thought possible in a single mind, as to give one's admiration the flavour and quality of wonder. Fuller was incomparably the most sensible, the least prejudiced great man, in an age that boasted of a galaxy of great men. In all his numerous volumes on so many different subjects, it is scarcely too much to say that you will hardly find a page in which some one sentence out of every three does not deserve to be quoted by itself as a motto or as a maxim."

Fuller's best-known writings are " The History of the Holy War," " The Holy and Profane State," " The Church History of Britain," " The History of the Worthies of England," and " Good Thoughts in Bad Times." His religion was of a practical kind, and his personal piety ever commended itself as springing from a clean heart. Though a warm advocate of the monarchical form of government, he held the rights of the people in sacred respect. "A Commonwealth and a King," said he, "are no more contrary than the trunk or body of a tree and the top branch thereof : there is a republic included in every monarchy."

An anecdote recorded of Fuller, in Basil Montague's " Selections," illustrates the goodness of his heart as well as his ready wit. Dr. Fuller had an extraordinary memory. He could name in order the signs on both sides the way from the beginning of Paternoster Row at Ave-Maria Lane to the bottom of Cheapside. He could dictate to five several amanuenses at the same time, and each on a different subject. The Doctor making a visit to the Committee of Sequestrators sitting at Waltham, in Essex, they soon fell into a discourse and commendation of his great memory; to which he replied, "'Tis true, gentlemen, that fame has given me the report of a memorist, and if you please, I will give you an experiment of it." They all accepted the motion, and told him they should look upon it as an obligation, praying him to begin. "Gentlemen," says he, "I will give you an instance of my memory in the particular business in which you are employed. Your worships have thought fit to sequester an honest but poor cavalier parson, my neighbour, from his living, and committed him to prison; he has a large family of children, and his circumstances are but indifferent; if you will please to release him out of prison, and restore him to his parish, *I will never forget the kindness while I live!*"

Fuller died just as his earthly prospects began to look brightest. A bishopric was about to have been granted him, when the chancel of his church at Cranford was opened to receive his remains. The Latin inscription over his body has the rare merit of telling the truth concerning the sleeper below, for he is certainly one of the most illustrious, as well as one of the most original, writers of our language. He is never barren or tedious, and his imagination follows in rank that of Taylor and others among the great names in English literature. One of his biographers says, "He was a kind husband, a tender

father to his children, a good friend and neighbour, and *a well-behaved, civilized person in every
respect.*" He used to call the buzzing polemics
that were rife in his time "insects of a day,"
and he had all the liberal attributes of a great and
noble character. He was, as we learn from several authentic accounts, of a joyous temperament
and boundless good-nature ; endowed with that
happy buoyancy of spirit which, next to religion
itself, is the most precious possession of man.
Untiring humour seemed the ruling passion of
his soul. Quaintly and facetiously he thought,
wrote, and spoke, preferring ever a jocose turn
of expression even in his gravest discourses.
With a heart open to all innocent pleasures, and
purged from the "leaven of malice and unchar-
itableness," it was as natural that he should be
full of mirth as it is for the grasshopper to chirp,
or bee to hum, or the birds to warble in the
spring breeze and the bright sunshine. "Some
men," says he, in his Essay on Gravity, "are of
a very cheerful disposition ; and God forbid that
all such should be condemned for lightness. O,
let not any envious eye disinherit men of that
which is their portion in this life, comfortably
to enjoy the blessings thereof!"

He is described as a person whose physiogno-
my was an index to his natural character. He
had a fine robust frame, light flaxen, curling

hair, bright blue smiling eyes, and a frank,
hearty manner. He loved the walks of common life, and was never weary of gossip with
the country people. His sympathy went out
to meet those who were oppressed, and his large
nature embraced all mankind. He will always
be honoured and loved, for he had "genuine
veneration for all that is divine, and genuine
sympathy for all that is human."

This volume of Good Thoughts in Bad
Times is reprinted now in this country because
there is much in it of a nature relevant to our
own disturbed state. Fuller wrote and practised
that he might eradicate error and implant the
loftiest virtues in the heart of man. His mission
was incomparably the highest God vouchsafes
to mortals, and in peace and war he wrote and
spoke such wisdom as time treasures for the
benefit of the world. In our own days of trial
it will be well to remember such words as these,
which he penned when his own land was
plunged in dangers manifold. " Music is sweetest near or over rivers, where the echo thereof
is best rebounded by the water. Praise for pensiveness, thanks for tears, and blessing God over
the floods of affliction, makes the most melodious music in the ear of Heaven."

Boston, January, 1863.

Contents.

CONTENTS. xiii

Good Thoughts in
Bad Times.

To the Right Honourable

THE LADY DALKEITH,

Lady Governess to her Highness the
Princess Henrietta.

MADAM, —

IT is unsafe in these dangerous days for any to go abroad without a convoy, or, at the least, a pass ; my book hath both in being dedicated to your Honour. The Apostle saith, Who planteth a vineyard, and eateth not of the fruit thereof ? **1 Cor. ix. 7.** I am one of your Honour's planting, and could heartily wish that the fruit I bring forth were worthy to be tasted by your judicious palate. Howsoever, accept these grapes, if not for their goodness, for their novelty : though not sweetest relished, they are soonest ripe, being the first fruits of Exeter press, presented unto you. And if ever my ingratitude should forget my obligations to your Honour, these black lines will turn red, and blush his unworthiness that wrote them. In this pamphlet your Ladyship shall praise whatsoever you are pleased but to pardon. But I am tedious, for your Honour can spare no more minutes from looking on a better book, her infant Highness, committed to your charge. Was ever more hope of worth in a less volume? But O! how excellently will the same, in due time, be set forth, seeing the paper is so pure, and your Ladyship the overseer to correct the press ! The continuance and increase of whose happiness here, and hereafter, is desired in his daily devotions, who resteth

Your Honour's in all

Christian service,

THOMAS FULLER.

Good Thoughts in Bad Times.

PERSONAL MEDITATIONS.

I.

ORD, how near was I to danger, yet escaped! I was upon the brink of the brink of it, yet fell not in; they are well kept who are kept by thee. Excellent archer! Thou didst hit thy mark in missing it, as meaning to fright, not hurt me. Let me not now be such a fool as to pay my thanks to blind Fortune for a favour which the eye of Providence hath bestowed upon me. Rather let the narrowness of my escape make my thankfulness to thy goodness the larger, lest my ingratitude justly cause, that, whereas this arrow but hit my hat, the next pierce my head.

II.

LORD, when thou shalt visit me with a sharp disease, I fear I shall be impatient; for I am choleric by my nature, and tender by my temper, and have not been acquainted with sickness all my lifetime. I cannot expect any kind usage from that which hath been a stranger unto me. I fear I shall rave and rage. O whither will my mind sail, when distemper shall steer it? whither will my fancy run, when diseases shall ride it? My tongue, which of itself is a fire, sure will be a wild-fire when the furnace of my mouth is made seven times hotter with a burning fever. But, Lord, though I should talk idly to my own shame, let me not talk wickedly to thy dishonour. Teach me the art of patience whilst I am well, and give me the use of it when I am sick. In that day either lighten my burden or strengthen my back. Make me, who so often, in my health, have discovered my weakness presuming on my own strength, to be strong in sickness when I solely rely on thy assistance.

James iii. 6.

III.

LORD, this morning my unseasonable visiting of a friend disturbed him in the midst of his devotions: unhappy to hinder another man's goodness. If I myself build not, shall I snatch the axe and hammer from him that doth? Yet I could willingly have wished, that, rather than he should then have cut off the cable of his prayers, I had twisted my cord to it, and had joined with him in his devotions; however, to make him the best amends I may, I now request of thee for him whatsoever he would have requested for himself. Thus he shall be no loser, if thou be pleased to hear my prayer for him, and to hearken to our Saviour's intercession for us both.

IV.

LORD, since these woful wars began, one, formerly mine intimate acquaintance, is now turned a stranger, yea, an enemy. Teach me how to behave myself towards him. Must the new foe quite justle out the old friend? May I not with him continue some commerce of kindness? Though the amity be broken on his side, may I not preserve my counterpart entire? Yet how can I be kind to him, without being cruel to myself and thy cause? O guide my shaking hand, to draw so small a line straight; or rather, because I know not how to carry myself towards him in this controversy, even be pleased to take away the subject of the question, and speedily to reconcile these unnatural differences.

V.

LORD, my voice by nature is harsh and untunable, and it is vain to lavish any art to better it. Can my singing of psalms be pleasing to thy ears, which is unpleasant to my own? yet though I cannot chant with the nightingale, or chirp with the blackbird, I had rather chatter with the swallow, yea, rather croak with the raven, than be altogether silent. Hadst thou given me a better voice, I would have praised thee with a better voice. Now what my music wants in sweetness, let it have in sense, singing praises with understanding. Yea, Lord, create in me a new heart (therein to make melody), and I will be contented with my old voice, until in thy due time, being admitted into the choir of heaven, I have another, more harmonious, bestowed upon me.

Isaiah xxxviii. 14.

Psalms xlvii. 7.

Ephes. v. 19.

VI.

LORD, within a little time I have heard the same precept in sundry places, and by several preachers, pressed upon me. The doctrine seemeth to haunt my soul; whithersoever I turn, it meets me. Surely this is from thy providence, and should be for my profit. It is because I am an ill proficient in this point, that I must not turn over a new leaf, but am still kept to my old lesson: Peter was grieved because our Saviour said unto him the third time, Lovest thou me? But I will not be offended at thy often inculcating the same precept: but rather conclude, that I am much concerned therein, and that it is thy pleasure, that the nail should be soundly fastened in me, which thou hast knocked in with so many hammers.

John xxi. 17.

VII.

LORD, before I commit a sin, it seems to me so shallow, that I may wade through it dry-shod from any guiltiness: but when I have committed it, it often seems so deep that I cannot escape without drowning. Thus I am always in the extremities: either my sins are so small that they need not my repentance, or so great that they cannot obtain thy pardon. Lend me, O Lord, a reed out of thy sanctuary, truly to measure the dimension of my offences. But O! as thou revealest to me more of my misery, reveal also more of thy mercy: lest if my wounds in my apprehension gape wider than thy tents, my soul run out at them. If my badness seem bigger than thy goodness, but one hair's breadth, but one moment, that is room and time enough for me to run to eternal despair.

2

VIII.

LORD, I do discover a fallacy, whereby I have long deceived myself. Which is this: I have desired to begin my amendment from my birthday, or from the first day of the year, or from some eminent festival, that so my repentance might bear some remarkable date. But when those days were come, I have adjourned my amendment to some other time. Thus, whilst I could not agree with myself when to start, I have almost lost the running of the race. I am resolved thus to befool myself no longer. I see no day to to-day, the instant time is always the fittest time. In Nebuchadnezzar's image, the lower the members, the coarser the metal; the farther off the time, the more unfit. To-day is the golden opportunity, to-morrow will be the silver season, next day but the brazen one, and so long, till at last I shall come to the toes of clay, and be turned to dust. Grant, therefore, that to-day I may hear thy voice. And if this day be obscure in the calendar, and remarkable in itself for nothing else, give me to make it memorable in my soul thereupon, by thy assistance, beginning the reformation of my life.

Daniel II. 33.

Psalm xcv. 7.

IX.

LORD, I saw one, whom I knew to be notoriously bad, in great extremity. It was hard to say whether his former wickedness or present want were the greater; if I could have made the distinction, I could willingly have fed his person, and starved his profaneness. This being impossible, I adventured to relieve him. For I know that amongst many objects, all of them being in extreme miseries, charity, though shooting at random, cannot miss a right mark. Since, Lord, the party, being recovered, is become worse than ever before, (thus they are always impaired with affliction who thereby are not improved,) Lord, count me not accessary to his badness, because I relieved him. Let me not suffer harm in myself, for my desire to do good to him. Yea, Lord, be pleased to clear my credit amongst men, that they may understand my hands according to the simplicity of my heart. I gave to him only in hope to keep the stock alive, that so afterwards it might be better grafted. Now, finding myself deceived, my arms shall return into my own bosom.

X.

LORD, thy servants are now praying in the church, and I am here staying at home, detained by necessary occasions, such as are not of my seeking, but of thy sending; my care could not prevent them, my power could not remove them. Wherefore, though I cannot go to church, there to sit down at table with the rest of thy guests, be pleased, Lord, to send me a dish of their meat hither, and feed my soul with holy thoughts. Eldad and Medad, though staying still in the camp (no doubt on just cause), yet prophesied as well as the other elders. Though they went not out to the spirit, the spirit came home to them. Thus never any dutiful child lost his legacy for being absent at the making of his father's will, if at the same time he were employed about his father's business. I fear too many at church have their bodies there, and minds at home. Behold, in exchange, my body here and heart there. Though I cannot pray with them, I pray for them. Yea, this comforts me, I am with thy congregation, because I would be with it.

Numb. xi. 26.

XI

L ORD, I trust thou hast pardoned the bad examples I have set before others, be pleased also to pardon me the sins which they have committed by my bad examples. (It is the best manners in thy court to heap requests upon requests.) If thou hast forgiven my sins, the children of my corrupt nature, forgive me my grandchildren also. Let not the transcripts remain, since thou hast blotted out the original. And for the time to come, bless me with barrenness in bad actions, and my bad actions with barrenness in procreation, that they may never beget others according to their likeness.

XII.

L ORD, what faults I correct in my son, I commit myself: I beat him for dabbling in the dirt, whilst my own soul doth wallow in sin: I beat him for crying to cut his own meat, yet am not myself contented with that state thy providence hath carved unto me: I beat him for crying when he is to go to sleep, and yet I fear I myself shall cry when thou callest me to sleep with my fathers. Alas! I am more childish than my child, and what I inflict on him I justly deserve to receive

from thee: only here is the difference: I pray
and desire that my correction on my child may
do him good; it is in thy power, Lord, to
effect that thy correction on me shall do me
good.

XIII.

L ORD, I perceive my soul deeply guilty
of envy. By my good will I would
Numb. xl. have none prophesy but mine own Moses. I
28.
had rather thy work were undone, than done
better by another than by myself: had rather
that thine enemies were all alive, than that I
should kill but my thousand, and others their
ten thousands of them. My corruption repines
at other men's better parts, as if what my soul
wants of them in substance she would supply
in swelling. Dispossess me, Lord, of this bad
spirit, and turn my envy into holy emulation.
Let me labour to exceed them in pains, who
excel me in parts: and knowing that my sword,
in cutting down sin, hath a duller edge, let
me strike with the greater force; yea, make
other men's gifts to be mine, by making me
thankful to thee for them. It was some comfort to Naomi, that, wanting a son herself, she
Ruth iv. brought up Ruth's child in her bosom. If my
16.
soul be too old to be a mother of goodness,

Lord, make it but a dry-nurse. Let me feed, and foster, and nourish, and cherish the graces in others, honouring their persons, praising their parts, and glorifying thy name, who hath given such gifts unto them.

XIV.

LORD, when young, I have almost quarrelled with that petition in our Liturgy, Give peace in our time, O Lord; needless to wish for light at noonday; for then peace was so plentiful, no fear of famine, but suspicion of a surfeit thereof. And yet how many good comments was this prayer then capable of! Give peace, that is, continue and preserve it; give peace, that is, give us hearts worthy of it, and thankful for it. In our time, that is, all our time: for there is more besides a fair morning required to make a fair day. Now I see the mother had more wisdom than her son. The Church knew better than I how to pray. Now I am better informed of the necessity, of that petition. Yea, with the daughters of the horseleech, I have need to cry, Give, give peace Prov. in our time, O Lord. xxx. 15.

XV.

LORD, unruly soldiers command poor people to open them their doors, otherwise threatening to break in. But if those in the house knew their own strength, it were easy to keep them out, seeing the doors are threatening-proof, and it is not the breath of their oaths can blow the locks open. Yet silly souls, being affrighted, they obey, and betray themselves to their violence. Thus Satan serves me, or rather, thus I serve myself. When I cannot be forced, I am fooled out of my integrity. He cannot constrain, if I do not consent. If I do but keep possession, all the posse of hell cannot violently eject me: but I cowardly surrender to his summons. Thus there needs no more to my undoing but myself.

XVI.

LORD, when I am to travel, I never use to provide myself till the very time; partly out of laziness, loath to be troubled till needs I must; partly out of pride, as presuming all necessaries for my journey will wait upon me at the instant. (Some say this is scholars' fashion, and it seems by following it I hope to approve myself to be one.) However, it often comes to pass that my journey is finally stopped, through the narrowness of the time to provide for it. Grant, Lord, that my confessed improvidence in temporal, may make me suspect my providence in spiritual matters. Solomon saith, Man goeth to his long home. Short Eccles. preparation will not fit so .long a journey. O xii. 5. let me not put it off to the last, to have my oil to buy, when I am to burn it. But let Matth. me so dispose of myself, that when I am to xxv. 10. die, I may have nothing to do but to die.

XVII.

LORD, when in any writing I have occasion to insert these passages, God willing, God lending me life, etc., I observe, Lord, that I can scarce hold my hand from encircling these words in a parenthesis, as if they were not essential to the sentence, but may as well be left out as put in. Whereas, indeed, they are not only of the commission at large, but so of the quorum, that without them all the rest is nothing; wherefore hereafter I will write those words fully and fairly, without any enclosure about them. Let critics censure it for bad grammar, I am sure it is good divinity.

XVIII.

LORD, many temporal matters, which I have desired, thou hast denied me; it vexed me for the present that I wanted my will; since, considering in cold blood, I plainly perceive, had that which I desired been done, I had been undone! Yea, what thou gavest me, instead of those things which I wished, though less toothsome to me, were more wholesome for me. Forgive, I pray, my former anger, and now accept my humble thanks. Lord, grant me one suit, which is this, deny me all suits which are bad for me: when I petition for what is unfitting, O let the King of heaven make use of his negative voice. Rather let me fast than have quails given with intent that I should be choked in eating them.

Numb.
xi. 38.

XIX.

LORD, this day I disputed with myself, whether or no I had said my prayers this morning, and I could not call to mind any remarkable passage whence I could certainly conclude that I had offered my prayers unto thee. Frozen affections, which left no spark of remembrance behind them! Yet at last I hardly recovered one token, whence I was assured that I had said my prayers. It seems I had said them, and only said them, rather by heart than with my heart. Can I hope that thou wouldst remember my prayers, when I had almost forgotten that I had prayed? Or rather have I not cause to fear that thou rememberest my prayers too well, to punish the coldness and badness of them? Alas! are not devotions thus done in effect left undone? Well Jacob advised his sons, at their second going into Egypt, Take double money in your hand; peradventure it was an oversight. So, Lord, I come with my second morning sacrifice: be pleased to accept it, which I desire, and endeavour to present with a little better devotion than I did the former.

Gen. xliii. 12.

XX.

LORD, the motions of thy Holy Spirit were formerly frequent in my heart; but, alas! of late they have been great strangers. It seems they did not like their last entertainment, they are so loath to come again. I fear they were grieved, that either I heard them not attentively, or believed them not faithfully, or practised them not conscionably. If they be pleased to come again, this is all I dare promise, that they do deserve, and I do desire they should be

Ephes. iv. 30.

Rev. iii.
20.

well used.   Let thy Holy Spirit be pleased, not only to stand before the door and knock, but also to come in.   If I do not open the door, it were too unreasonable to request such a miracle to come in when the doors were shut, as thou

John xx.
19.

didst to the apostles.   Yet let me humbly beg of thee, that thou wouldst make the iron gate of

Acts xii.
10.

my heart open of its own accord.   Then let thy Spirit be pleased to sup in my heart; I have given it an invitation, and I hope I shall give it room.   But, O thou that sendest the guest, send the meat also; and if I be so unmannerly as not to make the Holy Spirit welcome, O let thy effectual grace make me to make it welcome.

XXI.

LORD, I confess this morning I remembered my breakfast, but forgot my prayers. And as I have returned .no praise, so thou mightst justly have afforded me no protection. Yet thou hast carefully kept me to the middle of this day, intrusted me with a new debt before I have paid the old score. It is now. noon, too late for a morning, too soon for an evening sacrifice. My corrupt heart prompts me to put off my prayers till night; but I know it too well, or rather too ill, to trust it. I fear, if till night I defer them, at night I shall forget them. Be pleased, therefore, now to accept them. Lord, let not a few hours the later make a breach; especially seeing (be it spoken not to excuse my negligence, but to implore thy pardon) a thousand years in thy sight are but as yesterday. I promise hereafter, by thy assistance, to bring forth fruit in due season. See how I am ashamed the sun should shine on me, who now newly start in the race of my devotions, when he like a giant hath run more than half his course in the heavens.

XXII.

LORD, this day casually I am fallen into a bad company, and know not how I came hither, or how to get hence. Sure I am, not my improvidence hath run me, but thy providence hath led me into this danger. I was not wandering in any base by-path, but walking in the highway of my vocation; wherefore, Lord, thou that calledst me hither, keep me here. Stop their mouths, that they speak no blasphemy, or stop my ears, that I hear none; or open my mouth soberly to reprove what I hear. Give me to guard myself; but, Lord, guard my guarding of myself. Let not the smoke of their badness put out mine eyes, but the shining of my innocency lighten theirs. Let me give physic to them, and not take infection from them. Yea, make me the better for their badness. Then shall their bad company be to me like the dirt of oysters, whose mud hath soap in it, and doth rather scour than defile.

XXIII.

LORD, often have I thought with myself, I will sin but this one sin more, and then I will repent of it, and of all the rest of my sins together. So foolish was I, and ignorant. As if I should be more able to pay my debts when I owe more: or as if I should say, I will wound my friend once again, and then I will lovingly shake hands with him; but what if my friend will not shake hands with me? Besides, can one commit one sin more, and but one sin more? Unclean creatures went by couples into the ark. Grant, Lord, at this instant I may break off my badness: otherwise thou mayest justly make the last minute wherein I do sin on earth to be the last minute wherein I shall sin on earth, and the first wherein thou mightst make me suffer in another place.

Gen. vii. 2.

XXIV.

L ORD, the preacher this day came home to my heart. A left-handed Gibeonite with his sling hit not the mark more sure than ^{Judges xx.} he my darling sins. I could find no fault with _{16.} his sermon, save only that it had too much truth. But this I quarrelled at, that he went far from his text to come close to me, and so was faulty himself in telling me of my faults. Thus they will creep out at small crannies who have a mind to escape; and yet I cannot deny but that that which he spake (though nothing to that portion of Scripture which he had for his text) was according to the proportion of Scripture. And is not thy word in general the text at large of every preacher? Yea, rather I should have concluded, that, if he went from his text, thy goodness sent him to meet me; for without thy guidance it had been impossible for him so truly to have traced the intricate turnings of my deceitful heart.

XXV.

L ORD, be pleased to shake my clay cottage before thou throwest it down. May it totter awhile before it doth tumble. Let me be summoned before I am surprised. Deliver

me from sudden death. Not from sudden
death in respect of itself, for I care not how
short my passage be, so it be safe. Never
any weary traveller complained that he came
too soon to his journey's end. But let
it not be sudden in respect of me.
Make me always ready to receive
death. Thus no guest comes
unawares to him who
keeps a constant
table.

SCRIPTURE OBSERVATIONS.

I.

LORD, in the parable of the four sorts of ground whereon the seed was sown, the last alone proved fruitful. Matth. xiii. 8. There the bad were more than the good: but amongst the servants two improved Matth. xxv. 18. their talents, or pounds, and only one buried them. There the good were more than the Luke xix. 20. bad. Again, amongst the ten virgins, five were wise and five foolish: there the good and bad Matth. xxv. 2. were equal. I see that concerning the number of the saints in comparison to the reprobates, no certainty can be collected from these parables. Good reason, for it is not their principal purpose to meddle with that point. Grant that I may never rack a Scripture simile beyond the true intent thereof, lest, instead of sucking milk, I squeeze blood out of it.

II.

L ORD, thou didst intend from all eternity to make Christ the heir of all. No danger of disinheriting him, thy only son, and so well deserving. Yet thou sayest to him, Psalm ii. 8. Ask of me and I will give thee the heathen for thine inheritance, &c. This homage he must do for thy boon, to beg it. I see thy goodness delights to have thy favours sued for, expecting we should crave what thou intendest we should have; that so, though we cannot give a full price, we may take some pains for thy favours, and obtain them, though not for the merit, by the means of our petitions.

III.

L ORD, I find that Ezekiel in his prophecies is styled ninety times, and more, by this appellation, Son of man; and surely not once oftener than there was need for. For he had more visions than any one (not to say than all) of the prophets of his time. It was necessary, therefore, that his mortal extraction should often be sounded in his ears, Son of man, lest his frequent conversing with visions might make him mistake himself to be some angel. Amongst other revelations it was therefore needful to reveal him to himself, Son of man, lest seeing many visions might have made him blind with spiritual pride. Lord, as thou increasest thy graces in me, and favours on me, so with them daily increase in my soul the monitors and remembrancers of my mortality. So shall my soul be kept in a good temper, and humble deportment towards thee,

IV.

LORD, I read how Jacob (then only accompanied with his staff) vowed at Bethel, that if thou gavest him but bread and raiment, Gen. xxviii. 20 - 22. he would make that place thy house. After his return, the condition on thy side was overperformed, but the obligation on his part wholly neglected: for when thou hadst made his staff to swell, and to break into two bands, he, after his return, turned purchaser, bought a field in Gen. xxxiii. 19. Shalem, intending there to set up his rest. But thou art pleased to be his remembrancer in a new vision, and to spur him afresh, who tired in his promise. Arise, go to Bethel, and make Gen. xxxv. 1. there an altar, &c. Lord, if rich Jacob forgot what poor Jacob did promise, no wonder, if I be bountiful to offer thee in my affliction what I am niggardly to perform in my prosperity. But O! take not advantage of the forfeitures, but be pleased to demand payment once again. Pinch me into the remembrance of my promises, that so I may reinforce my old vows with new resolutions.

V.

LORD, I read when our Saviour was examined in the high-priest's hall, that Peter stood without, till John (being his spokesman to the maid that kept the door) procured his admission in. John meant to let him out of the cold, and not to let him into a temptation: but his courtesy in intention proved a mischief in event, and the occasion of his denying his master. O let never my kindness concur in the remotest degree to the damage of my friend. May the chain which I sent him for an ornament never prove his fetters. But if I should be unhappy herein, I am sure thou wilt not punish my good-will, but pity my ill-success.

John xviii. 16.

VI.

LORD, the Apostle saith to the Corinthians, God will not suffer you to be tempted above what you are able. But how comes he to contradict himself, by his own confession in his next epistle? where, speaking of his own sickness, he saith, We were pressed out of

1 Cor. x. 13.

2 Cor. i. 8.

measure above strength. Perchance this will be expounded by propounding another riddle of the same Apostle's: who, praising Abraham, saith, That against hope he believed in hope. ^{Rom. iv.} That is, against carnal hope he believed in ^{18.} spiritual hope. So the same wedge will serve to cleave the former difficulty. Paul was pressed above his human, not above his heavenly strength. Grant, Lord, that I may not mangle and dismember thy word, but study it entirely, comparing one place with another. For diamonds can only cut diamonds, and no such comments on the Scripture as the Scripture.

VII.

LORD, I observe that the vulgar translation reads the Apostle's precept thus: Give ^{2 Peter i.} diligence to make your calling and election sure ^{10.} by good works. But in our English Testaments these words, by good works, are left out. It grieved me at the first to see our translation defective; but it offended me afterwards to see the other redundant. For those words are not in the Greek, which is the original. And it is an ill work to put good works in, to the corruption of the Scripture. Grant, Lord, that, though we leave good works out in the text, we may take them in in our comment. In that

3

exposition which our practice is to make on this precept in our lives and conversations.

VIII.

Matth. 1.
7, 8.

LORD, I find the genealogy of my Saviour strangely checkered with four remarkable changes in four immediate generations.

1. Roboam begat Abia; that is, a bad father begat a bad son.

2. Abia begat Asa; that is, a bad father a good son.

3. Asa begat Josaphat; that is, a good father a good son.

4. Josaphat begat Joram; that is, a good father a bad son.

I see, Lord, from hence, that my father's piety cannot be entailed; that is bad news for me. But I see also, that actual impiety is not always hereditary; that is good news for my son.

IX.

LORD, when in my daily service I read David's Psalms, give me to alter the accent of my soul according to their several subjects. In such psalms, wherein he confesseth his sins, or requesteth thy pardon, or praiseth for former, or prayeth for future favours, in all these give me to raise my soul to as high a pitch as may be. But when I come to such psalms wherein he curseth his enemies, O there let me bring my soul down to a lower note. For those words were made only to fit David's mouth. I have the like breath, but not the same spirit to pronounce them. Nor let me flatter myself, that it is lawful for me, with David, to curse thine enemies, lest my deceitful heart entitle all mine enemies to be thine, and so what was religion in David prove malice in me, whilst I act revenge under the pretence of piety.

X.

LORD, I read of the two witnesses, And Rev. xi. 7. when they shall have finished their testimony, the beast that ascendeth out of the bottomless pit shall make war against them, and shall overcome them, and kill them. They could not be killed whilst they were doing, but when they had done their work; during their employment they were invincible. No better armour against the darts of death than to be busied in thy service. Why art thou so heavy, O my soul? No malice of man can antedate my end a minute, whilst my Maker hath any work for me to do. And when all my daily task is ended, why should I grudge then to go to bed?

XI.

Matth.
xvii. 1.

L ORD, I read at the transfiguration that Peter, James, and John were admitted to behold Christ; but Andrew was excluded.

Mark v.
37.

So again at the reviving of the daughter of the ruler of the synagogue, these three were let in,

Mark xiv.
33.

and Andrew shut out. Lastly, in the agony the aforesaid three were called to be witnesses thereof, and still Andrew left behind. Yet he was Peter's brother, and a good man, and an apostle: why did not Christ take the two pair of brothers? Was it not pity to part them? But methinks I seem more offended thereat than Andrew himself was, whom I find to express no discontent, being pleased to be accounted a loyal subject for the general, though he was no favorite in these particulars. Give me to be pleased in myself, and thankful to thee, for what I am, though I be not equal to others in personal perfections. For such peculiar privileges are courtesies from thee when given, and no injuries to us when denied.

XII.

L ORD, St. Paul teacheth the art of heavenly thrift, how to make a new sermon of an old. Many (saith he) walk, of whom I have told you often, and now tell you weeping, ^{Phil. iii.} that they are enemies to the cross of Christ. ^{18.} Formerly he had told it with his tongue, but now with his tears; formerly he taught it with his words, but now with weeping. Thus new affections make an old sermon new. May I not, by the same proportion, make an old prayer new? Lord, thus long I have offered my prayer dry unto thee, now, Lord, I offer it wet. Then wilt thou own some new addition therein, when, though the sacrifice be the same, yet the dressing of it is different, being steeped in his tears who bringeth it unto thee.

XIII.

LORD, I read of my Saviour, that when he was in the wilderness, then the devil ^{Matth. iv.} leaveth him, and behold angels came and min- ^{11.} istered unto him. A great change in a little time. No twilight betwixt night and day. No purgatory condition betwixt hell and heaven, but instantly, when out devil, in angel. Such is the case of every solitary soul. It will make company for itself. A musing mind will not stand neuter a minute, but presently side with legions of good or bad thoughts. Grant, therefore, that my soul, which ever will have some, may never have bad company.

XIV.

LORD, I read how Cushi and Ahimaaz ran a race, who first should bring tidings of victory to David. Ahimaaz, though last setting forth, came first to his journey's end; not that he had the fleeter feet, but the better brains, to choose the way of most advantage. For the text saith, So Ahimaaz ran by the way of the plain, and overran Cushi. Prayers made to God by saints fetch a needless compass about. That is but a rough and uneven way. Besides one steep passage therein, questionable whether it can be climbed up, and saints in heaven made sensible of what we say on earth. The way of the plain, or plain way, both shortest and surest, is, Call upon me in the time of trouble. Such prayers, though starting last, will come first to the mark.

2 Sam.
xviii. 23.

XV.

LORD, this morning I read a chapter in the Bible, and therein observed a memorable passage, whereof I never took notice before. Why now, and no sooner, did I see it? Formerly my eyes were as open, and the letters as legible. Is there not a thin veil laid over thy word, which is more rarefied by read-

ing, and at last wholly worn away? Or was
it because I came with more appetite than before? The milk was always there in the
breast, but the child till now was not hungry
enough to find out the teat. I see the oil of
thy word will never leave increasing whilst
any bring an empty barrel. The Old Testament will still be a New Testament to him who
comes with a fresh desire of information.

XVI.

L ORD, at the first Passover God kept touch
with the Hebrews very punctually; at
the end of the four hundred and thirty years, Exod. xii
41.
in the self-same day it came to pass, that all
the hosts of the Lord went out of the land of
Egypt; but at the first Easter God was better
than his word. Having promised that Christ
should lie but three days in the grave, his
fatherly affection did run to relieve him. By
a charitable synecdoche, two pieces of days were
counted for whole ones. God did cut the Rom. ix.
28.
work short in righteousness. Thus the measure of his mercy under the law was full, but
it ran over in the gospel.

XVII.

LORD, the Apostle dissuadeth the Hebrews from covetousness, with this argument, because God said, I will not leave thee nor forsake thee. Yet I find not that God ever gave this promise to all the Jews, but he spake Josh. i. 5. it only to Joshua when first made commander against the Canaanites; which, without violence to the analogy of faith, the Apostle applieth to all good men in general. Is it so that we are heirs apparent to all promises made to thy servants in Scripture? Are the characters of grace granted to them good to me? Then Gen. xlv. will I say, with Jacob, I have enough. But 23. because I cannot entitle myself to thy promises to them, except I imitate their piety to thee, grant I may take as much care in following the one, as comfort in the other.

XVIII.

Gen. i. 11. LORD, I read that thou didst make grass, herbs, and trees the third day. As for Gen. i. 16. the sun, moon, and stars, thou madest them on the fourth day of the creation. Thus at first thou didst confute the folly of such who maintain that all vegetables, in their growth, are enslaved to a necessary and unavoidable dependence on the influence of the stars. Whereas plants were even when planets were not. It is false that the marigold follows the sun, whereas the sun follows the marigold, as made the day before him. Hereafter I will admire thee more, and fear astrologers less; not affrighted with their doleful predictions of dearth and drought, collected from the complexions of the planets. Must the earth of necessity be sad, because some ill-natured star is sullen? as if the grass could not grow without asking it leave. Whereas thy power, which made herbs before the stars, can preserve them without their propitious, yea, against their malignant aspects.

XIX.

LORD, I read how Paul, writing from Rome, spake to Philemon to prepare Philemon, ver. 22. him a lodging, hoping to make use thereof; yet we find not that he ever did use it, being martyred not long after. However, he was no loser, whom thou didst lodge in a higher mansion in heaven. Let me always be thus deceived to my advantage. I shall have no cause to complain, though I never wear the new clothes fitted for me, if, before I put them on, death clothe me with glorious immortality.

XX.

LORD, when our Saviour sent his Apostles abroad to preach, he enjoined them in one Gospel, Possess nothing, neither shoes nor staff. But it is said in another Gospel, And he commanded them, that they should take nothing for their journey, save a staff only. The reconciliation is easy. They might have a staff, to speak them travellers, not soldiers; one to walk with, not to war with; a staff which was a wand, not a weapon. But O! in how doleful days do we live, wherein ministers are not, as formerly, armed with their nakedness, but need staves and swords too to defend them from violence.

Matth. x 10.
Mark vi. 8.

XXI.

LORD, I discover an arrant laziness in my soul. For when I am to read a chapter in the Bible, before I begin it, I look where it endeth. And if it endeth not on the same side, I cannot keep my hands from turning over the leaf, to measure the length thereof on the other side; if it swells to many verses, I begin to grudge. Surely my heart is not rightly affected. Were I truly hungry after heavenly food, I would not complain of meat. Scourge, Lord, this laziness out of my soul;

make the reading of thy word not a penance, but a pleasure unto me; teach me, that as amongst many heaps of gold, all being equally pure, that is the best which is the biggest, so I may esteem that chapter in thy word the best that is the longest.

XXII.

LORD, I find David making a syllogism, in mood and figure, two propositions he perfected.

18. If I regard wickedness in my heart, Psalm lxvi. the Lord will not hear me.

19. But verily God hath heard me, he hath attended to the voice of my prayer.

Now I expected that David should have concluded thus:

Therefore I regard not wickedness in my heart.

But far otherwise he concludes:

20. Blessed be God, who hath not turned away my prayer, nor his mercy from me.

Thus David hath deceived, but not wronged me. I looked that he should have clapped the crown on his own, and he puts it on God's head. I will learn this excellent logic; for I like David's better than Aristotle's syllogisms, that, whatsoever the premises be, I make God's glory the conclusion.

XXIII.

Prov. xxx. 9.

LORD, wise Agur made it his wish, Give me not poverty, lest I steal, and take the name of my God in vain. He saith not, lest I steal, and be caught in the manner, and then be stocked, or whipped, or branded, or forced to fourfold restitution, or put to any other shameful or painful punishment. But he saith, Lest I steal, and take the name of my God in vain: that is, lest, professing to serve thee, I confute a good profession with a bad conversation. Thus thy children count sin to be the greatest smart in sin, as being more sensible of the wound they therein give to the glory of God, than of all the stripes that man may lay upon them for punishment.

XXIV.

LORD, I read that when my Saviour dispossessed the man's son of a devil, he

Mark ix. 25.

enjoined the evil spirit to come out of him, and enter no more into him. But I find,

Luke iv. 13.

that when my Saviour himself was tempted of Satan, the devil departed from him for a season. Retreating, as it seems, with mind to return. How came it to pass, Lord, that he who expelled him finally out of others did not propel him so from himself? Sure it does not follow, that because he did not, he could not do it. Or that he was less able to help himself, because he was more charitable to relieve others. No; I see my Saviour was pleased to show himself a God in other men's matters, and but a man in such cases wherein he himself was concerned. Being contented still to be tempted by Satan, that his sufferings for us might cause our conquering through him.

XXV.

LORD, Jannes and Jambres, the apes of Moses and Aaron, imitated them in turning their rods into serpents; only here was the difference: Aaron's rod devoured their rods. That which was solid and substantial lasted, when that which was slight, and but seeming, vanished away. Thus an active fancy in all outward expressions may imitate a lively faith. For matter of language there is nothing what grace doth do, but wit can act: Only the difference appears in the continuance: wit is but for fits and flashes, grace holds out, and is lasting; and, good Lord, of thy goodness, give it to every one that truly desires it.

2 Tim. iii. 8.

Exod. vii. 12.

3 †

HISTORICAL APPLICATIONS.

I.

THE English ambassador some years since prevailed so far with the Turkish emperor, as to persuade him to hear some of our English music, from which (as from other liberal sciences) both he and his nation were naturally averse. But it happened that the musicians were so long in tuning their instruments, that the great Turk, distasting their tediousness, went away in discontent before their music began. I am afraid that the differences and dissensions betwixt Christian churches (being so long in reconciling their discords) will breed in pagans such a disrelish of our religion, as they will not be invited to attend thereunto.

II.

A SIBYL came to Tarquinius Superbus, king of Rome, and offered to sell unto him three tomes of her Oracles : but he, counting the price too high, refused to buy them. Away she went and burnt one tome of them. Returning, she asketh him, whether he would buy the two remaining at the same rate: he refused again, counting her little better than frantic. Thereupon she burns the second tome ; and peremptorily asked him, whether he would give the sum demanded for all the three for the one tome remaining; otherwise she would burn that also, and he would dearly repent it. Tarquin, admiring at her constant resolution, and conceiving some extraordinary worth contained therein, gave her her demand. There are three volumes of man's time ; youth, man's estate, and old age ; and ministers advise them to redeem this time. But men conceive the rate they must give to be unreasonable, because it will cost them the renouncing of their carnal delights. Hereupon one third part of their life (youth) is consumed in the fire of wantonness. Again, ministers counsel men to redeem the remaining volumes of their life. They are but derided at for their pains. And man's estate is

(marginalia: M. Varro, Solinus, Plinius, Halicar, &c.)

(marginalia: Ephes. v. 16.)

also cast away in the smoke of vanity. But preachers ought to press peremptorily on old people, to redeem, now or never, the last volume of their life. Here is the difference: the sibyl still demanded but the same rate for the remaining book; but aged folk (because of their custom in sinning) will find it harder and dearer to redeem this, the last volume, than if they had been chapmen for all three at the first.

III.

Giraldus Cambrensis, and Camden, in the description of that shire.

IN Merionethshire in Wales there be many mountains, whose hanging tops come so close together, that shepherds sitting on several mountains may audibly discourse one with another. And yet they must go many miles before their bodies can meet together, by the reason of the vast hollow valleys which are betwixt them. Our sovereign and the members of his Parliament at London seem very near agreed in their general and public professions; both are for the Protestant religion; can they draw nearer? Both are for the privileges of Parliament; can they come closer? Both are for the liberty of the subject; can they meet evener? And yet, alas! there is a great gulf and vast distance betwixt them which our sins have made, and God grant that our sorrow may seasonably make it up again.

IV.

WHEN John, king of France, had communicated the order of the knighthood of the star to some of his guard, men of mean birth and extraction, the nobility ever after disdained to be admitted into that degree, and so that order in France was extinguished. Seeing that now-a-days drinking, and swearing, and wantonness are grown frequent, even with base beggarly people; it is high time for men of honour, who consult with their credit, to desist from such sins. Not that I would have noblemen invent new vices to be in fashion with themselves alone, but forsake old sins, grown common with the meanest of people.

V.

LONG was this land wasted with civil war betwixt the two houses of York and Lancaster, till the red rose became white with the blood it had lost, and the white rose red with the blood it had shed. At last, they were united in a happy marriage, and their joint titles are twisted together in our gracious sovereign. Thus there hath been a great difference betwixt learned men, wherein the dominion over the creature is founded. Some

4

putting it in nature, others placing it in grace. But the true servants of God have an unquestioned right thereunto : seeing both nature and grace, the first and second Adam, creation and regeneration, are contained in them. Hence their claim is so clear, their title is so true, ignorance cannot doubt it, impudence dare not deny it.

VI.

THE Roman senators conspired against Julius Cæsar to kill him : that very next morning Artemidorus, Cæsar's friend, delivered him a paper (desiring him to peruse it) wherein the whole plot was discovered : but Cæsar complimented his life away, being so taken up to return the salutations of such people as met him in the way, that he pocketed the paper, among other petitions, as unconcerned therein ; and so, going to the senate-house, was slain. The world, flesh, and devil have a design for the destruction of men ; we ministers bring our people a letter, God's word, wherein all the conspiracy is revealed. But who hath believed our report ? Most men are so busy about worldly delights, they are not at leisure to listen to us, or read the letter ; but thus, alas ! run headlong to their own ruin and destruction.

Plutarch in Julius Cæsar.

VII.

IT is reported of Philip the Second, king of Spain, that besieging the town of St. Quintin, and being to make a breach, he was forced with his cannon to batter down a small chapel on the wall, dedicated to St. Lawrence. In reparation to which saint, he afterwards built and consecrated unto him that famous chapel in the Escurial in Spain, for workmanship one of the wonders of the world. How many churches and chapels of the God of St. Lawrence have been laid waste in England by this woful war? And, which is more (and more to be lamented), how many living temples of the Holy Ghost, Christian people, have therein been causelessly and cruelly destroyed? How shall our nation be ever able to make recompense for it? God of his goodness forgive us that debt which we of ourselves are not able to satisfy.

VIII.

IN the days of King Edward the Sixth, the lord protector marched with a powerful army into Scotland, to demand their young queen Mary in marriage to our king, according to their promises. The Scotch refusing
Sir John Heywood in the Life of Edward the Sixth.

to do it, were beaten by the English in Mus-
selborough fight. One demanding of a Scot-
tish lord (taken prisoner in the battle), " Now,
sir, how do you like our king's marriage with
your queen?" "I always," quoth he, "did like
the marriage, but I do not like the wooing,
that you should fetch a bride with fire and
sword." It is not enough for men to propound
pious projects to themselves, if they go about
by indirect courses to compass them. God's
own work must be done by God's own ways.
Otherwise we can take no comfort in obtain-
ing the end, if we cannot justify the means used
thereunto.

IX.

A SAGAMORE, or petty king in Vir-
ginia, guessing the greatness of other
kings by his own, sent a native hither, who
understood English; commanding him to score
upon a long cane (given him of purpose to
be his register) the number of Englishmen,
that hereby his master might know the strength
of this our nation. Landing at Plymouth, a
populous place (and which he mistook for all
England), he had no leisure to eat, for notch-
ing up the men he met. At Exeter the difficulty of his task was increased; coming at last to
London (that forest of people) he broke his

cane in pieces, perceiving the impossibility of his employment. Some may conceive that they can reckon up the sins they commit in one day. Perchance they may make hard shifts to sum up their notorious ill deeds: more difficult it is to score up their wicked words. But O how infinite are their idle thoughts! High time, then, to leave off counting, and cry out, with David, Who can tell how oft he offend-eth? Lord, cleanse me from my secret sins. ^{Psalm xix. 12.}

X.

MARTIN DE GOLIN, master of the Teutonic order, was taken prisoner by the Prussians, and delivered bound to be be-headed. But he persuaded his executioner (who had him alone) first to take off his costly clothes, which otherwise would be spoiled with the sprinkling of his blood. Now the prisoner, being partly unbound, to be unclothed, and finding his arms somewhat loosened, struck the executioner to the ground, killed him afterwards with his own sword, and so regained both his life and liberty. Christ hath overcome the world, and delivered it to us to destroy it. But we are all Achæans by nature, and the Babylonish garment is a bait for our covetousness: whilst, therefore, we seek to take the plunder of this world's wardrobe, we let go the mastery we had formerly of it. And too often that which Christ's passion made our captive our folly makes our conqueror.

XI.

Camd.
Britan. in
Kent.

I READ how Pope Pius the Fourth had a great ship, richly laden, landed at Sandwich in Kent, where it suddenly sunk, and so, with the sands, choked up the harbour, that ever since that place hath been deprived of the benefit thereof. I see that happiness doth not always attend the adventures of his Holiness. Would he had carried away his ship, and left us our harbour. May his spiritual merchandise never come more into this island, but rather sink in Tiber than sail thus far, bringing so small good and so great annoyance. Sure he is not so happy in opening the doors of heaven, as he is unhappy to obstruct havens on earth.

XII.

Gualterus
Mappæus
de nugis
Curiallum.

JEFFRY, Archbishop of York, and base son to King Henry the Second, used proudly to protest by his faith, and the royalty of the king his father. To whom one said, You may sometimes, sir, as well remember what was the hon-

esty of your mother. Good men when puffed
up with pride, for their heavenly extraction
and paternal descent, how they are God's sons
by adoption, may seasonably call to mind the
corruption which they carry about them. I
have said to the worm, Thou art my mother. Job xvii.
14.
And this consideration will temper their souls
with humility.

XIII.

I COULD both sigh and smile at the simplicity of a native American, sent by a
Spaniard, his master, with a basket of figs, and
a letter (wherein the figs were mentioned), to
carry them both to one of his master's friends.
By the way, this messenger ate up the figs, but
delivered the letter, whereby his deed was discovered, and he soundly punished. Being sent
a second time on the like message, he first took
the letter (which he conceived had eyes as well
as a tongue) and hid it in the ground, sitting
himself on the place where he put it ; and then
securely fell to feed on his figs, presuming that
that paper which saw nothing could tell nothing. Then, taking it again out of the ground,
he delivered it to his master's friend, whereby
his fault was perceived, and he worse beaten
than before. Men conceive they can manage

their sins with secrecy; but they carry about them a letter, or book rather, written by God's finger, their conscience bearing witness to all their actions. But sinners being often detected and accused, hereby grow wary at last, and, to prevent this speaking paper from telling any tales, do smother, stifle, and suppress it, when they go about the committing of any wickedness. Yet conscience (though buried for a time in silence) hath afterwards a resurrection, and discovers all, to their greater shame and heavier punishment.

Rom. ii. 15.

XIV.

JOHN COURCY, Earl of Ulster, in Ireland, endeavoured fifteen several times to sail over thither, and so often was beaten back again with bad weather. At last he expostulated his case with God in a vision, complaining of hard measure; that, having built and repaired so many monasteries to God and his saints, he should have so bad success. It was answered him, that this was but his just punishment, because he had formerly put out the image of the Trinity* out of the cathedral church of Down, and placed the picture of

Annal. Ilibern. in anno 1204; and Camden's Brit., p. 797.

---

* Lawfully, I presume, to apply a Popish vision to confute a Popish practice.

St. Patrick in the room thereof. Surely God will not hold them guiltless who justle him out of his temple, and give to saints that adoration due alone to his divine majesty.

.

XV.

THE Libyans kept all women in common. But when a child was born, they used to send it to that man to maintain (as father thereof) whom the infant most resembled in his complexion. Satan and my sinful nature enter common in my soul in the causing of wicked thoughts. The sons by their faces speak their sires. Proud, wanton, covetous, envious, idle thoughts, I must own to come from myself. God forgive me, it is vain to deny it, those children are so like to their father. But as for some hideous, horrible thoughts, such as I start at the motion of them, being out of the road of my corruption (and yet which way will not that wander?) so that they smell of hell's brimstone about them: these fall to Satan's lot to father them. The swarthy blackness of their complexion plainly shows who begot them; not being of mine extraction, but his injection.

XVI.

MARCUS MANLIUS deserved exceedingly well of the Roman state, having valiantly defended their Capitol.   But afterward, falling into disfavour with the people, he was condemned to death.   However, the people would not be so unthankful as to suffer him to be executed in any place from whence the Capitol might be beheld.   For the prospect thereof prompted them with fresh remembrance Livius, lib. of his former merits.   At last, they found a low vi. cap. 20. place in the Petiline grove, by the river gate, where no pinnacle of the Capitol could be perceived, and there he was put to death.   We may admire how men can find in their hearts to sin against God.   For we can find no one place in the whole world which is not marked with a signal character of his mercy unto us.   It was said properly of the Jews, but is not untrue of all Christians, that they are God's vineyard. Mark xii. And God fenced it, and gathered out the stones 1. thereof, and planted it with the choicest vine, and built a tower in the midst thereof; and also digged a wine-press therein; which way can men look, and not have their eyes met with the remembrance of God's favour unto them? Look about the vineyard, it is fenced; look without it, the stones are cast out; look within it, it is planted with the choicest vine; look above it, a tower is built in the midst thereof; look beneath it, a wine-press is digged. It is impossible for one to look any way, and to avoid the beholding of God's bounty. Ungrateful man! And as there is no place, so there is no time for us to sin, without being at that instant beholden to him; we owe to him that we are, even when we are rebellious against him.

XVII.

A DUEL was to be fought, by consent of both kings, betwixt an English and a French lord. The aforesaid John Courcy, Earl of Ulster, was chosen champion for the English; a man of great stomach and strength, but lately much weakened by long imprisonment. Wherefore, to prepare himself beforehand, the king allowed him what plenty and variety of meat he was pleased to eat. But the monsieur (who was to encounter him) hearing what great quantity of victuals Courcy did daily devour, and thence collecting his unusual strength, out of fear, refused to fight with him. If by the standard of their cups, and measure of their drinking, one might truly infer soldiers' strength by rules of proportion, most vast and valiant achievements may justly be expected from some gallants of these times.

Annal. Hibern. in anno 1204; and Camden's Brit., p. 797.

XVIII.

I HAVE heard that the brook near Lutterworth, in Leicestershire, into which the ashes of the burnt bones of Wickliffe were cast, never since doth drown the meadow about it. Papists expound this to be, because God was well pleased with the sacrifice of the ashes of such a heretic. Protestants ascribe it rather to proceed from the virtue of the dust of such a reverend martyr. I see it is a case for a friend. Such accidents signify nothing in themselves but according to the pleasure of interpreters. Give me such solid reasons, whereon I may rest and rely. Solomon saith, The words of the wise are like nails, fastened by the masters of the assembly. A nail is firm, and will hold driving in, and will hold driven in. Send me such arguments. As for these waxen topical devices, I shall never think worse or better of any religion for their sake.

Eccles. xii. 11.

XIX.

Plutarch in the Life of Alexander the Great.

ALEXANDER the Great, when a child, was checked by his governor Leonidas for being over-profuse in spending perfumes: because on a day, being to sacrifice to the gods, he took both his hands full of frankincense, and cast it into the fire: but afterwards, being a man, he conquered the country of Judæa (the fountain whence such spices did flow), and sent Leonidas a present of five hundred talents' weight of frankincense, to show him how his former prodigality made him thrive the better in success, and to advise him to be no more niggardly in divine service. Thus they that sow plentifully shall reap plentifully. I see there is no such way to have a large harvest as to have a large heart. The free giving of the branches of our present estate to God, is the readiest means to have the root increased for the future.

XX.

THE poets fable, that this was one of the labours imposed on Hercules, to make clean the Augean stable, or stall rather. For therein, they said, were kept three thousand kine, and it had not been cleansed for thirty years together. But Hercules, by letting the river Alpheus into it, did that with ease which before was conceived impossible. This stall is the pure emblem of my impure soul, which hath been defiled with millions of sins for more than thirty years together. O that I might by a lively faith, and unfeigned repentance, let the stream of that fountain into my soul, which is opened for Judah and Jerusalem. It is impossible by all my pains to purge out my uncleanness; which is quickly done by the rivulet of the blood of my Saviour.

XXI.

THE Venetians showed the treasure of their state, being in many great coffers full of gold and silver, to the Spanish ambassador. But the ambassador, peeping under the bottom of those coffers, demanded whether that their treasure did daily grow, and had a root; for such, saith he, my master's treasure hath: meaning both his Indies. Many men have attained to a great height of piety, to be very abundant and rich therein. But all theirs is but a cistern, not fountain of grace, only God's goodness hath a spring of itself in itself.

XXII.

Justin, lib. xviii. p. 166.

THE Sidonian servants agreed amongst themselves to choose him to be their king who, that morning, should first see the sun. Whilst all others were gazing on the east, one alone looked on the west. Some admired, more mocked him, as if he looked on the feet, there to find the eye of the face. But he first

of all discovered the light of the sun shining on
the tops of houses. God is seen sooner, easier,
clearer in his operatiòns than in his essence.
Best beheld by reflection in his creatures. For Rom. 1. 20.
the invisible things of him, from the creation of
the world, are clearly seen, being understood by
the things that are made.

XXIII.

A N Italian prince, as much delighted with
the person as grieved with the prodigality
of his eldest son, commanded his steward to
deliver him no more money but what the young
prince should tell his own self. The young gallant fretted at his heart, that he must buy
money at so dear a rate, as to have it for telling
it, but (because there was no remedy) he set
himself to task, and being greatly tired with
telling a small sum, he broke off in this consideration. Money may speedily be spent, but
how tedious and troublesome is it to tell it!
And by consequence how much more difficult
to get it! Men may commit sin presently,
pleasantly, with much mirth, in a moment.
But O that they would but seriously consider
with themselves how many their offences are,
and sadly fall accounting them! And if so
hard truly to sum their sins, sure harder sin-

cerely to sorrow for them. If to get their number be so difficult, what is it to get their pardon?

XXIV.

Cottenham.

I KNOW the village in Cambridgeshire where there was a cross full of imagery. Some of the images were such, as that people, not foolishly factious, but judiciously conscientious, took just exception at them: hard by, the youths of the town erected a Maypole, and, to make it of proof against any that should endeavour to cut it down, they armed it with iron as high as any could reach. A violent wind happened to blow it down, which, falling on the cross, dashed it to pieces. It is possible what is counted profaneness may accidentally correct superstition. But I could heartily wish that all pretenders to reformation would first labour to be good themselves, before they go about the amending of others.

XXV.

Plutarch in Theseo.

I READ that Ægeus, the father of Theseus, hid a sword and a pair of shoes under a great stone; and left word with his wife (whom he left with child), that when the son she should bear was able to take up that stone, wield that sword, and wear those shoes, then she should send him to him: for by these signs he would own him for his own son. Christ hath left in the custody of the Church our mother the sword of the Spirit, and the shoes of a Christian conversation, the same which he once wore himself, and they must fit our feet, yea, and we must take up the weight of many heavy crosses, before we can come at them: but when we shall appear before our Heavenly Father, bringing these tokens with us, then, and not before, he will acknowledge us to be no bastards, but his true-born children.

MIXT CONTEMPLATIONS.

I.

WHEN I look on a leaden bullet, therein I can read both God's mercy and man's malice. God's mercy, whose providence, foreseeing that men of lead would make instruments of cruelty, did give that metal a medicinal virtue; as it hurts, so it also heals; and a bullet sent in by man's hatred into a fleshy and no vital part, will (with ordinary care and curing), out of a natural charity, work its own way out. But oh! how devilish were those men who, to frustrate and defeat his goodness, and to countermand the healing power of lead, first found the champing and empoisoning of bullets! Fools, who account themselves honoured with Rom. 1. 30. the shameful title of being the inventors of evil things, endeavouring to out-infinite God's kindness with their cruelty.

II.

I HAVE heard some men, rather causelessly captious than judicially critical, cavil at grammarians for calling some conjunctions disjunctive, as if this were a flat contradiction. Whereas, indeed, the same particle may conjoin words, and yet disjoin the sense. But, alas! how sad is the present condition of Christians, who have a communion disuniting. The Lord's Supper, ordained by our Saviour to conjoin our affections, hath disjoined our judgments. Yea, it is to be feared, lest our long quarrels about the manner of his presence cause the matter of his absence, for our want of charity to receive him.

III.

I HAVE observed that children, when they first put on new shoes, are very curious to keep them clean. Scarce will they set their feet on the ground for fear to dirt the soles of their shoes. Yea, rather they will wipe the leather clean with their coats; and yet, perchance, the next day they will trample with the same shoes in the mire up to the ankles. Alas! children's play is our earnest. On that day wherein we receive the sacrament, we are often

over-precise, scrupling to say or do those things
which lawfully we may.   But we, who are
more than curious that day, are not so much as
careful the next; and too often (what shall I
say?) go on in sin up to the ankles: yea, our
sins go over our heads.

Psalm
xxxviii. 4.

IV.

I KNOW some men very desirous to see the
devil, because they conceive such an apparition would be a confirmation of their faith.
For then, by the logic of opposites, they will
conclude there is a God because there is a devil.
Thus they will not believe there is a heaven,
except hell itself will be deposed for a witness
thereof.   Surely such men's wishes are vain,
and hearts are wicked; for if they will not believe, having Moses and the prophets, and the
apostles, they will not believe, no, if the devil
from hell appears unto them.   Such apparitions
were never ordained by God as the means of
faith.   Besides, Satan will never show himself
but to his own advantage.   If as a devil, to
fright them, if as an angel of light, to flatter
them, how ever to hurt them.   For my part, I
never desire to see him.   And O (if it were
possible) that I might never feel him in his motions and temptations!   I say, let me never see

him till the day of judgment, where he shall stand arraigned at the bar, and God's majesty sit judge on the bench ready to condemn him.

V.

I OBSERVE that antiquaries, such as prize skill above profit (as being rather curious than covetous), do prefer the brass coins of the Roman emperors before those in gold and silver. Because there is much falseness and forgery daily detected, and more suspected, in gold and silver medals, as being commonly cast and counterfeited, whereas brass coins are presumed upon as true and ancient, because it will not quit cost for any to counterfeit them. Plain dealing, Lord, what I want in wealth may I have in sincerity. I care not how mean metal my estate be of, if my soul have the true stamp, really impressed with the unfeigned image of the King of Heaven.

VI.

LOOKING on the chapel of King Henry the Seventh, in Westminster, (God grant I may once again see it, with the saint who belongs to it, our sovereign, there in a well-conditioned peace,) I say, looking on the outside of the chapel, I have much admired the curious

5

workmanship thereof. It added to the wonder, that it is so shadowed with mean houses, well-nigh on all sides, that one may almost touch it as soon as see it. Such a structure needed no base buildings about it, as foils to set it off. Rather this chapel may pass for the emblem of a great worth living in a private way. How is he pleased with his own obscurity, whilst others of less desert make greater show: and whilst proud people stretch out their plumes in ostentation, he useth their vanity for his shelter; more pleased to have worth than to have others take notice of it.

VII.

THE mariners at sea count it the sweetest perfume when the water in the keel of their ship doth stink. For hence they conclude that it is but little, and long since leaked in; but it is woful with them when the water is felt before it is smelt, as fresh flowing in upon them in abundance. It is the best savour in a Christian soul when his sins are loathsome and offensive unto him. A happy token that there hath not been of late in him any insensible supply of heinous offences, because his stale sins are still his new and daily sorrow.

VIII.

I HAVE sometimes considered in what troublesome case is that chamberlain in an inn, who, being but one, is to give attendance to many guests. For suppose them all in one chamber, yet if one shall command him to come to the window, and the other to the table, and another to the bed, and another to the chimney, and another to come up stairs, and another to go down stairs, and all in the same instant, how would he be distracted to please them all. And yet such is the sad condition of my soul by nature, not only a servant, but a slave unto sin. Pride calls me to the window, gluttony to the table, wantonness to the bed, laziness to the chimney, ambition commands me to go up stairs, and covetousness to come down. Vices, I see, are as well contrary to themselves as to virtue. Free me, Lord, from this distracted case; fetch me from being sin's servant to be thine, whose service is perfect freedom ; for thou art but one and ever the same, and always enjoinest commands agreeable to themselves, thy glory, and my good.

IX.

I HAVE observed, that towns which have been casually burnt have been built again more beautiful than before; mud walls, afterwards made of stone; and roofs, formerly but thatched, after advanced to be tiled. The Apostle tells me, that I must not think strange concerning the fiery trial which is to happen unto me. May I likewise prove improved by it. Let my renewed soul, which grows out of the ashes of the old man, be a more firm fabric, and stronger structure: so shall affliction be my advantage.

1 Peter iv. 12.

X.

OUR Saviour saith, When thou doest alms, let not thy left hand know what thy right hand doeth. Yet one may generally observe, that almshouses are commonly built by highway sides, the ready road to ostentation. However, far be it from me to make bad comments on their bounty; I rather interpret it, that they place those houses so publicly, thereby not to gain applause, but imitation. Yea, let those who will plant pious works, have the liberty to choose their own ground. Especially in this age, wherein we are likely, neither in by-ways nor highways, to have any works of mercy, till the whole kingdom be speedily turned into one great hospital, and God's charity only able to relieve us.

Matth. vi. 3.

XI.

HOW wrangling and litigious were we in time of peace! How many actions were created of nothing! Suits we had commenced about a mouthful of grass, or a handful of hay. Now he, who formerly would sue his neighbour for *pedibus ambulando,* can behold his whole field lying waste and must be content. We see our goods taken from us and dare say nothing, not so much as seeking any legal redress, because certain not to find it. May we be restored in due time to our former properties, but not to our former peevishness. And when law shall be again awaked (or rather revived), let us express our thanks to God for so great a gift, by using it not wantonly (as formerly, in vexing our neighbours about trifles), but soberly, to right ourselves in matters of moment.

XII.

ALMOST twenty years since I heard a profane jest, and still remember it. How many pious passages of far later date have I forgotten. It seems my soul is like a filthy pond, wherein fish die soon, and frogs live long. Lord, raze this profane jest out of my memory.

Leave not a letter thereof behind, lest my corruption (an apt scholar) guess it out again;
and be pleased to write some pious meditation
in the place thereof. And grant, Lord, for
the time to come, (because such bad guests
are easier kept out,) that I may be careful not
to admit what I find so difficult to expel.

XIII.

I PERCEIVE there is in the world a good-
nature, falsely so called, as being nothing
else but a facile and flexible disposition, wax
for every impression. What others are so bold
to beg, they are so bashful as not to deny.
Such osiers can never make beams to bear
stress in church and state. If this be good-nature, let me always be a clown; if this be good-
fellowship, let me always be a churl. Give
me to set a sturdy porter before my soul, who
may not equally open to every comer. I cannot conceive how he can be a friend to any,
who is a friend to all, and the worst foe to
himself.

XIV.

HA is the interjection of laughter; Ah is
an interjection of sorrow. The difference betwixt them very small, as consisting

only in the transposition of what is no substantial letter, but a bare aspiration. How quickly,
in the age of a minute, in the very turning of
a breath, is our mirth changed into mourning!

XV.

I HAVE a great friend whom I endeavour
and desire to please, but hitherto all in
vain: the more I seek, the farther off I am
from finding his favour. Whence comes this
miscarriage? Are not my applications to man
more frequent than my addresses to my Maker?
Do I not love his smiles more than I fear Heav-
en's frowns? I confess, to my shame, that
sometimes his anger hath grieved me more than
my sins. Hereafter, by thy assistance, I will
labour to approve my ways in God's presence;
so shall I either have, or not need his friend-
ship, and either please him with more ease,
or displease him with less danger.

XVI.

THIS nation is scourged with a wasting
war. Our sins were ripe; God could
no longer be just if we were prosperous. Blessed be his name that I have suffered my share
in the calamities of my country. Had I poised

myself so politically betwixt both parties, that
I had suffered from neither, yet could I have
taken no contentment in my safe escaping.
For why should I, equally engaged with others
in sinning, be exempted above them from the
punishment? And seeing the bitter cup, which
my brethren have pledged, to pass by me, I
should fear it would be filled again, and returned double, for me to drink it. Yea, I should
suspect that I were reserved alone for a greater
shame and sorrow. It is therefore some comfort that I draw in the same yoke with my
neighbours, and with them jointly bear the burden which our sins jointly brought upon us.

XVII.

WHEN, in my private prayers, I have
been to confess my bosom sins unto
God, I have been loath to speak them aloud;
fearing (though no man could, yet) that the
devil would overhear me, and make use of my
words against me. It being probable, that,
when I have discovered the weakest part of
my soul, he would assault me there. Yet
since, I have considered that therein I shall
tell Satan no news, which he knew not before.
Surely I have not managed my secret sins with
such privacy, but that he, from some circum-

stances, collected what they were. Though the fire was within, he saw some smoke without. Wherefore, for the future, I am resolved to acknowledge my darling faults, though alone, yet aloud; that the devil, who rejoiced in partly knowing of my sins, may be grieved more by hearing the expression of my sorrow. As for any advantage he may make from my confession, this comforts me: God's goodness in assisting me will be above Satan's malice in assaulting me.

XVIII.

IN the midst of my morning prayers I had a good meditation, which since I have forgotten. Thus much I remember of it, that it was pious in itself, but not proper for that time. For it took much from my devotion, and added nothing to my instruction; and my soul, not able to intend two things at once, abated of its fervency in praying. Thus snatching at two employments, I held neither well. Sure this meditation came not from him who is the God of order; he useth to fasten all his nails, and not to drive out one with another. If the same meditation return again when I have leisure and room to receive it, I will say it is of his sending, who so mustereth and marshalleth all good actions, that, like the soldiers in his army, mentioned in the Prophet, Joel ii. 8. they shall not thrust one another, they shall walk every one in his own path.

XIX.

WHEN I go speedily in any action, Lord, give me to call my soul to an account. It is a shrewd suspicion that my bowl runs downhill, because it runs so fast. And, Lord, when I go in an unlawful way, start some rubs to stop me, let my foot slip or stumble. And give me the grace to understand the language of the lets thou throwest in my way. Thou Hosea ii. 6. hast promised, I will hedge up thy way. Lord, be pleased to make the hedge high enough and thick enough, that if I be so mad as to adventure to climb over it, I may not only soundly rake my clothes, but rend my flesh; yea, let me rather be caught, and stick in the hedge, than, breaking in through it, fall on the other side into the deep ditch of eternal damnation.

XX.

COMING hastily into a chamber, I had almost thrown down a crystal hourglass. Fear lest I had, made me grieve as if

I had broken it. But, alas! how much precious time have I cast away without any regret! The hour-glass was but crystal, each hour a pearl; that but like to be broken, this lost outright: that but casually, this done wilfully. A better hour-glass might be bought; but time lost once, lost ever. Thus we grieve more for toys than for treasure. Lord, give me an hour-glass, not to be by me, but to be in me. Teach me to number my days. An hour-glass to turn me, that I may apply my heart unto wisdom. ^{Psalm xo. 12.}

XXI.

WHEN a child, I loved to look on the pictures in the Book of Martyrs. I thought that there the martyrs at the stake seemed like the three children in the fiery furnace, ever since I had known them there, not one hair more of their head was burnt, nor any smell of the fire singeing of their clothes. This made me think martyrdom was nothing. But oh, though the lion be painted fiercer than he is, the fire is far fiercer than it is painted. Thus it is easy for one to endure an affliction, as he limns it out in his own fancy, and represents it to himself but in a bare speculation. But when it is brought indeed, and laid home to us, there must be ^{Dan. iii. 27}

the man, yea, there must be God to assist the man to undergo it.

XXII.

TRAVELLING on the plain (which notwithstanding hath its risings and fallings), I discovered Salisbury steeple many miles off; coming to a declivity, I lost sight thereof; but climbing up the next hill, the steeple grew out of the ground again. Yea, I often found it and lost it, till at last I came safely to it, and took my lodging near it. It fareth thus with us, whilst we are wayfaring to heaven, mounted on the Pisgah top of some good meditation, we get a glimpse of our celestial Canaan. But when either on the flat of an ordinary temper, or in the fall of an extraordinary temptation, we lose the view thereof. Thus, in the sight of our soul, heaven is discovered covered, and recovered; till, though late, at last, though slowly, surely, we arrive at the haven of our happiness.

Deut.
xxxiv. 1.

XXIII.

LORD, I find myself in the latitude of a fever; I am neither well nor ill; not so well that I have any mind to be merry with my friends, nor so ill that my friends have

any cause to condole with me. I am a proba-
tioner in point of my health. As I shall behave myself, so I may be either expelled out of
it, or admitted into it. Lord, let my distemper stop here and go no farther. Shoot thy
murdering pieces against that clay castle, which
surrendereth itself at the first summons. O
spare me a little, that I may recover my
strength. I beg not to be forgiven, but to be
forborne my debt to nature. And I only crave
time for a while, till I am better fitted and
furnished to pay it.

XXIV.

IT seemed strange to me when I was told,
that aqua-vitæ, which restores life to others,
should itself be made of the droppings of dead
beer; and that strong waters should be extracted out of the dregs (almost) of small beer.
Surely many other excellent ingredients must
concur, and much art must be used in the
distillation. Despair not then, O my soul!
No extraction is impossible where the chemist
is infinite. He that is all in all can produce
anything out of anything; and he can make
my soul, which by nature is settled on her Zeph. i. 12.
lees, and dead in sin, to be quickened by the
infusion of his grace, and purified into a pious
disposition.

XXV.

HOW easy is pen and paper piety for one to write religiously! I will not say it costeth nothing, but it is far cheaper to work one's head than one's heart to goodness. Some, perchance, may guess me to be good by my writings, and so I shall deceive my reader. But if I do not desire to be good, I most of all deceive myself. I can make a hundred meditations sooner than subdue the least sin in my soul. Yea, I was once in the mind never to write more; for fear lest my writings at the last day prove records against me. And yet why should I not write? that by reading my own book, the disproportion betwixt my lines and my life may make me blush myself (if not into goodness) into less badness than I would do otherwise. That so my writings may condemn me, and make me to condemn myself, that so God may be moved to acquit me.

GOOD THOUGHTS IN
WORSE TIMES.

TO THE CHRISTIAN READER.

HEN I read the description of the tumult in Ephesus, Acts xix. 32, (wherein they would have their Diana to be *jure divino*, that it fell down from Jupiter,) it appears to me the too methodical character of our present confusions. Some therefore cried one thing, and some another, for the assembly was confused, and the more part knew not wherefore they were come together. O the distractions of our age! And how many thousands know as little why the sword was drawn, as when it will be sheathed. Indeed (thanks be to God!) we have no more house-burnings, but many heart-burnings; and though outward bleeding be stanched, it is to be feared that the broken vein bleeds inwards, which is more dangerous.

This being our sad condition, I perceive controversial writings (sounding somewhat of drums and trumpets) do but make the wound

6

2 Kings iii.
16. the wider. Meditations are like the minstrel the prophet called for, to pacify his mind discomposed with passion, which moved me to adventure on this treatise as the most innocent and inoffensive manner of writing.

I confess, a volume of another subject, and larger size, is expected from me. But in London I have learnt the difference betwixt downright breaking, and craving time of their creditors. Many sufficient merchants, though not solvable for the present, make use of the latter, whose example I follow. And though I cannot pay the principal, yet I desire such small treatises may be accepted from me, as interest, or consideration money, until I shall, God willing, be enabled to discharge the whole debt.

If any wonder that this treatise comes patronless into the world, let such know that dedications begin now-a-days to grow out of fashion. His policy was commended by many, (and proved profitable unto himself,) who, instead of select godfathers, made all the congregation witnesses to his child, as I invite the world to this my book, requesting each one would patronize therein such parts and passages thereof as please them, so hoping that by several persons the whole will be protected.

I have, Christian reader (so far I dare go, not inquiring into thy surname, of thy side, or sect), nothing more to burden thy patience with. Only I will add, that I find our Saviour in Tertullian, and ancient Latin Fathers, constantly styled a sequestrator,* in the proper notion of the word. For God and man being at odds, the difference was sequestered or referred into Christ's hand to end and umpire it. How it fareth with thy estate on earth I know not; but I earnestly desire, that in heaven both thou and I may ever be under sequestration in that Mediator for God's glory and our good, to whose protection thou art committed by

* Sequester.

Thy brother in all

Christian offices,

THOMAS FULLER.

GOOD THOUGHTS IN WORSE TIMES.

PERSONAL MEDITATIONS.

I. CURIOSITY CURBED.

FTEN have I thought with myself, what disease I would be best contented to die of. None please me. The stone, the colic, terrible as expected, intolerable when felt. The palsy is death before death. The consumption a flattering disease, cozening men into hope of long life at the last gasp. Some sicknesses besot, others enrage men, some are too swift, and others too slow.

If I could as easily decline diseases as I could dislike them, I should be immortal. But away with these thoughts. The mark must not choose what arrow shall be shot against it. What God sends I must receive. May I not be so curious to know what weapon shall wound me, as careful to provide the plaster of patience against it. Only thus much in general: commonly that sickness seizeth on men which they least suspect. He that expects to be drowned with a dropsy, may be burnt with a fever; and she that fears to be swoln with a tympany may be shrivelled with a consumption.

II. DECEIVED, NOT HURT.

HEARING a passing-bell, I prayed that the sick man might have, through Christ, a safe voyage to his long home. Afterwards I understood that the party was dead some hours before; and it seems in some places of London the tolling of the bell is but a preface of course to the ringing it out.

Bells better silent than thus telling lies. What is this but giving a false alarm to men's devotions, to make them to be ready armed with their prayers for the assistance of such who have already fought the good fight, yea, and gotten the conquest? Not to say that men's charity herein may be suspected of superstition in praying for the dead.

However, my heart thus poured out was not spilt on the ground. My prayers, too late to do him good, came soon enough to speak my good-will. What I freely tendered, God fairly took, according to the integrity of my intention. The party I hope is in Abraham's, and my prayers I am sure are returned into my own bosom.

III. NOR FULL, NOR FASTING.

L IVING in a country village, where a burial was a rarity, I never thought of death, it was so seldom presented unto me. Coming to London, where there is plenty of funerals, (so that coffins crowd one another, and corpses in the grave justle for elbow-room,) I slight and neglect death, because grown an object so constant and common.

How foul is my stomach to turn all food into bad humours? Funerals neither few nor frequent, work effectually upon me. London is a library of mortality. Volumes of all sorts and sizes, rich, poor, infants, children, youth, men, old men, daily die; I see there is more required to make a good scholar, than only the having of many books: Lord, be thou my schoolmaster, and teach me to number my days, that I may apply my heart unto wisdom.

IV. STRANGE AND TRUE.

Rev. xiii.
3.
I READ, in the Revelation, of a beast, one of whose heads was, as it were, wounded to death. I expected in the next verse that the beast should die, as the most probable consequence, considering : —

1. It was not a scratch, but a wound.

2. Not a wound in a fleshy part, or out-limbs of the body, but in the very head, the throne of reason.

3. No light wound, but in outward apparition, (having no other probe but St. John's eyes to search it,) it seemed deadly.

But mark what immediately follows : And his deadly wound was healed. Who would have suspected this inference from these premises. But is not this the lively emblem of my natural corruption? Sometimes I conceived that, by God's grace, I have conquered and killed, subdued and slain, maimed and mortified, the deeds of the flesh : never more shall I be molested or buffeted with such a bosom sin : when, alas! by the next return, the news is, it is revived and recovered. Thus tenches, though grievously gashed, presently plaster themselves whole by that slimy and unctuous humour they have in them; and thus the inherent balsam of badness quickly cures my corruption, not a scar to be seen. I perceive I shall never finally kill it, till first I be dead myself.

V. BLUSHING TO BE BLUSHED FOR.

A PERSON of great quality was pleased to lodge a night in my house. I durst not invite him to my family prayer; and therefore for that time omitted it: thereby making a breach in a good custom, and giving Satan advantage to assault it. Yea, the loosening of such a link might have endangered the scattering of the chain.

Bold bashfulness, which durst offend God whilst it did fear man. Especially considering, that, though my guest was never so high, yet by the laws of hospitality I was above him whilst he was under my roof. Hereafter, whosoever cometh within the doors shall be requested to come within the discipline of my house; if accepting my homely diet, he will not refuse my home devotion; and sitting at my table, will be entreated to kneel down by it.

VI. A LASH FOR LAZINESS.

SHAMEFUL my sloth, that have deferred my night prayer till I am in bed. This

7

lying along is an improper posture for piety. Indeed, there is no contrivance of our body, but some good man in Scripture hath hanselled it with prayer. The publican standing, Job sitting, Hezekiah lying on his bed, Elijah with his face between his legs. But of all gestures give me St. Paul's: For this cause I bow my knees to the Father of my Lord Jesus Christ. Knees, when they may, then they must be bended.

I have read a copy of a grant of liberty from Queen Mary to Henry Ratcliffe, Earl of Sussex, giving him leave to wear a nightcap or coif in her Majesty's presence, counted a great favour, because of his infirmity. I know, in case of necessity, God would graciously accept my devotion, bound down in a sick dressing; but now whilst I am in perfect health it is inexcusable. Christ commanded some to take up their bed, in token of their full recovery; my laziness may suspect, lest thus my bed taking me up prove a presage of my ensuing sickness. But may God pardon my idleness this once, I will not again offend in the same kind, by his grace hereafter.

Job ii. 8.
1 Kings xviii. 42.
Ephes. iii. 14.
Weever's Fun. Mon., p. 635.

VII. ROOT, BRANCH, AND FRUIT.

A POOR man of Seville in Spain, having a fair and fruitful pear-tree, one of the fathers of the Inquisition desired (such tyrants' requests are commands) some of the fruit thereof. The poor man, not out of gladness to gratify, but fear to offend, as if it were a sin for him to have better fruit than his betters, (suspecting on his denial the tree might be made his own rod, if not his gallows,) plucked up tree, roots and all, and gave it unto him.

Allured with love to God, and advised by my own advantage, what he was frighted to do, I will freely perform. God calleth on me to present him with fruits meet for repentance. ^{Matth. iii. 8.} Yea, let him take all, soul and body, powers and parts, faculties and members of both, I offer a sacrifice unto himself. Good reason; for indeed the tree was his before it was mine, and I give him of his own.

Besides, it was doubtful whether the poor man's material tree, being removed, would grow again. Some plants transplanted (especially when old) become sullen, and do not enjoy themselves in a soil wherewith they were unacquainted. But sure I am when I have given myself to God, the moving of my soul shall be the mending of it, he will so dress αἴρειν and ^{John xv. 2.} καθαίρειν, so prune and purge me, that I shall bring forth most fruit in my age.

VIII. GOD SPEED THE PLOUGH.

I SAW in seed-time a husbandman at plough in a very raining day; asking him the reason why he would not rather leave off than labour in such foul weather, his answer was returned me in their country rhyme:

> Sow beans in the mud,
> And they 'll come up like a wood.

This could not but mind me of David's expression, They that sow in tears shall reap in joy. He that goeth forth and weepeth, bearing precious seed, shall doubtless come again with rejoicing, bringing his sheaves with him.

Psalm cxxvi. 5, 6.

These last five years have been a wet and woful seed-time to me, and many of my afflicted brethren. Little hope have we, as yet, to come again to our own homes, and in a literal sense, now to bring our sheaves, which we see others daily carry away on their shoulders. But if we shall not share in the former or latter harvest here on earth, the third and last in heaven we hope undoubtedly to receive.

IX. CRAS, CRAS.

GREAT was the abundance and boldness of the frogs in Egypt, which went up Exod. viii. 3. and came into their bed-chambers, and beds, and kneading-troughs, and very ovens. Strange that those fen-dwellers should approach the fiery region; but stranger that Pharaoh should be so backward to have them removed; and being demanded of Moses when he would have them sent away, answered, To-morrow. He could Exod. viii. 10. be content with their company one night, at bed and at board, loath, belike, to acknowledge either God's justice in sending, or power in remanding them, but still hoping that they casually came, and might casually depart.

Leave I any longer to wonder at Pharaoh, and even admire at myself; what are my sins but so many toads, spitting of venom and spawning of poison; croaking in my judgment, creeping into my will, and crawling into my affections. This I see, and suffer, and say with Pharaoh, To-morrow, to-morrow I will amend. Thus, as the Hebrew tongue hath no proper present tense, but two future tenses, so all the performances of my reformation are only in promises for the time to come. Grant, Lord, that I may seasonably drown this Pharaoh-like procrastination in the sea of repentance, lest it drown me in the pit of perdition.

X. GREEN WHEN GRAY.

IN September I saw a tree bearing roses, whilst others of the same kind, round about it, were barren ; demanding the cause of the gardener, why that tree was an exception from the rule of the rest, this reason was rendered : because that alone being clipped close in May, was then hindered to spring and sprout, and therefore took this advantage by itself to bud in autumn.

Lord, if I were curbed and snipped in my younger years by fear of my parents, from those vicious excrescences to which that age was subject, give me to have a godly jealousy over my heart, suspecting an autumn-spring, lest corrupt nature (which without thy restraining grace will have a vent) break forth in my reduced years into youthful vanities.

XI. MISERERE.

De Tristibus, lib. ii. eleg. 10.

THERE goes a tradition of Ovid, that famous poet, (receiving some countenance from his own confession,) that when his father was about to beat him for following the pleasant but profitless study of poetry, he, under correction, promised his father never to make a verse, and made a verse in his very promise.

Probably the same in sense, but certainly more
elegant for composure, than this verse which
common credulity hath taken up :

Parce precor, genitor, posthac non versificabo.

Father, on me pity take,
Verses I no more will make.

When I so solemnly promise my Heavenly
Father to sin no more, I sin in my very promise ; my weak prayers made to procure my
pardon, increase my guiltiness. O the dulness
and deadness of my heart therein ! I say my
prayers as the Jews eat the passover, in haste. ^{Exod. xii.}
And whereas in bodily actions motion is the ^{11.}
cause of heat ; clean contrary, the more speed
I make in my prayers, the colder I am in my
devotion.

XII. MONARCHY AND MERCY.

IN reading the Roman (whilst under consuls)
and Belgic History of the United Provinces,
I remember not any capital offender, being condemned, ever forgiven, but always after sentence follows execution. It seems that the very
constitution of a multitude is not so inclinable
to save as to destroy. Such rulers in aristoc-
racies or popular states cannot so properly be
called gods, because, though having the great

attributes of a deity, power and justice, they want (or will not use) the most godly property of God's clemency, to forgive.

May I die in that government under which I was born, where a monarch doth command. Kings, where they see cause, have graciously granted pardons to men appointed to death; Dan. ix. 9. herein the lively image of God, to whom belongs mercies and forgivenesses. And although I will endeavour so to behave myself as not to need my sovereign's favour in this kind, yet, because none can warrant his innocency in all things, it is comfortable living in such a commonwealth, where pardons heretofore on occasion have been, and hereafter may be procured.

XIII. WHAT HELPS NOT HURTS.

A VAIN thought arose in my heart, instantly my corruption retains itself to be the advocate for it, pleading that the worst that could be said against it was this, that it was a vain thought.

And is not this the best that can be said for Luke xiii. it? Remember, O my soul, the fig-tree was 7. charged, not with bearing noxious, but no fruit. Yea, the barren fig-tree bare the fruit of annoyance, cut it down, why cumbereth it the ground? Vain thoughts do this ill in my heart, that they do no good.

Besides, the fig-tree pestereth but one part of the garden, good grapes might grow at the same time in other places of the vineyard. But seeing my soul is so intent on its object that it cannot attend two things at once, one tree for the time being is all my vineyard. A vain thought engrosseth all the ground of my heart; till that be rooted out, no good meditation can grow with it or by it.

XIV. ALWAYS SEEN, NEVER MINDED.

IN the most healthful times, two hundred and upwards was the constant weekly tribute paid to mortality in London. A large bill, but it must be discharged. Can one city spend according to this weekly rate, and not be bankrupt of people? At leastwise, must not my shot be called for to make up the reckoning?

When only seven young men, and those chosen by lot, were but yearly taken out of Athens to be devoured by the monster Minotaur, the whole·city was in a constant fright, children for themselves, and parents for their children. Yea, their escaping of the first was but an introduction to the next year's lottery.

Were the dwellers and lodgers in London

Plutarch's Lives, in Theseo.

weekly to cast lots who should make up this two hundred, how would every one be affrighted? Now none regard it. My security concludes the aforesaid number will amount of infants and old folk. Few men of middle age, and amongst them surely not myself. But oh! is not this putting the evil day far from me the ready way to bring it the nearest to me? The lot is weekly drawn (though not by me) for me, I am therefore concerned seriously to provide, lest that death's prize prove my blank.

XV. NOT WHENCE, BUT WHITHER.

FINDING a bad thought in my heart, I disputed in myself the cause thereof, whether it proceeded from the devil, or my own corruption, examining it by those signs divines in this case recommended.

1. Whether it came in incoherently, or by dependence on some object presented to my senses.

2. Whether the thought was at full age at the first instant, or, infant-like, grew greater by degrees.

3. Whether out or in the road of my natural inclination.

But hath not this inquiry more of curiosity than religion? Hereafter derive not the pedi-

gree, but make the mittimus of such malefactors. Suppose a confederacy betwixt thieves
without and false servants within, to assault
and wound the master of a family: thus wounded, would he discuss from which of them his
hurts proceeded? No, surely; but speedily
send for a surgeon before he bleed to death.
I will no more put it to the question, whence
my bad thoughts come, but whither I shall
send them, lest this curious controversy insensibly betray me into a consent unto them.

XVI. STORM, STEER ON.

THE mariners sailing with St. Paul bare
up bravely against the tempest whilst
either art or industry could befriend them.
Finding both to fail, and that they could not Acts xxvii.
any longer bear up into the wind, they even 15.
let their ship drive. I have endeavoured in
these distemperate times to hold up my spirits,
and to steer them steadily. A happy peace
here was the port whereat I desired to arrive.
Now, alas! the storm grows too sturdy for the
pilot. Hereafter all the skill I will use is no
skill at all, but even let my ship sail whither
the winds send it.

Noah's ark was bound for no other port, but
preservation for the present (that ship being all

the harbour), not intending to find land, but to float on water. May my soul (though not sailing to the desired haven) only be kept from sinking in sorrow.

This comforts me, that the most weather-beaten vessel cannot properly be seized on for a wreck which hath any quick cattle remaining therein. My spirits are not as yet forfeited to despair, having one lively spark of hope in my heart, because God is even where he was before.

XVII. WIT OUTWITTED.

JOAB chid the man (unknown in Scripture by his name, well known for his wisdom) for not killing Absalom, when he saw him hanged in the tree, promising him for his pains ten shekels and a girdle.

But the man, having the king's command to the contrary, refused his proffer. Well he knew that politic statesman would have dangerous designs fetched out of the fire, but with other men's fingers. His girdle promised might in payment prove a halter. Yea, he added moreover, that had he killed Absalom, Joab himself would have set himself against him.

Satan daily solicits me to sin (point blank against God's word), baiting me with proffers

2 Sam.
xviii. 13.

best pleasing my corruption. If I consent, he Rev. xii. 10.
who last tempted first accuseth me. The fawn-
ing spaniel turns a fierce lion, and roareth out
my faults in the ears of Heaven. Grant, Lord,
when Satan shall next serve me, as Joab did
this nameless Israelite, I may serve him as the
nameless Israelite did Joab, flatly refusing his
deceitful tenders.

XVIII. HEREAFTER.

DAVID fasted and prayed for his sick son,
that his life might be prolonged. But
when he was dead, this consideration comforted
him: I shall go to him, but he shall not return 2 Sam. xii. 23.
to me.

Peace did long lie languishing in this land.
No small contentment that to my poor power.
I have prayed and preached for the preservation
thereof. Seeing, since it is departed, this supports my soul, having little hope that peace here
should return to me, I have some assurance
that I shall go to peace hereafter.

XIX. BAD AT BEST.

LORD, how come wicked thoughts to perplex me in my prayers, when I desire
and endeavour only to attend thy service?

8

Now I perceive the cause thereof; at other
times I have willingly entertained them, and
now they entertain themselves against my will.
I acknowledge thy justice, that what formerly
I have invited, now I cannot expel. Give me
hereafter always to bolt out such ill guests.
The best way to be rid of such bad thoughts in
my prayers, is not to receive them out of my
prayers.

XX. COMPENDIUM DISPENDIUM.

POPE BONIFACE the Ninth, at the end
of each hundred years, appointed a jubi-
lee at Rome, wherein people, bringing themselves and money thither, had pardon for their
sins.

But centenary years returned but seldom;
popes were old before, and covetous when they
came to their place. Few had the happiness to
fill their coffers with jubilee-coin. Hereupon,
Examen
Con. Tri-
dent. p.
736, col. 2.
Clement the Sixth reduced it to every three
and thirtieth, Paul the Second and Sixtus the
Fourth to every twenty-fifth year.

Yea, an agitation is reported in the conclave,
to bring down jubilees to fifteen, twelve, or ten
years, had not some cardinals (whose policy
was above their covetousness) opposed it.

I serve my prayers as they their jubilees.

Perchance they may extend to a quarter of an hour, when poured out at large. But some days I begrudge this time as too much, and omit the preface of my prayer, with some passages conceived less material, and run two or three petitions into one, so contracting them to half a quarter of an hour.

Not long after, this also seems too long; I decontract and abridge the abridgment of
my prayers, yea (be it confessed to my
shame and sorrow, that hereafter I
may amend it) too often I shrink
my prayers to a minute,
to a moment, to a
Lord have mercy
upon me!

SCRIPTURE OBSERVATIONS.

I. PRAYER MAY PREACH.

FATHER, I thank thee, (said our Saviour, being ready to raise Lazarus,) that thou hast heard me. And I know that thou hearest me always, but because of the people that stand by, I said it, that they may believe that thou hast sent me. It is lawful for ministers in their public prayers to insert passages for the edifying of their auditors, at the same time petitioning God and informing their hearers. For our Saviour, glancing his eyes at the people's instruction, did no whit hinder the steadfastness of his looks, lifted up to his Father.

When, before sermon, I pray for my sovereign and master, king of great Britain, France, and Ireland, defender of the faith, in all causes, and over all persons, &c., some, who omit it themselves, may censure it in me for superfluous. But never more need to teach men the king's title, and their own duty, that the simple may be informed, the forgetful remembered thereof, and that the affectedly ignorant, who will not take advice, may have all excuse taken from them. Wherefore, in pouring forth my prayers to God, well may I therein sprinkle some by-drops for the instruction of the people.

II. THE VICIOUS MEAN.

Z OPHAR, the Naamathite, mentioneth a ^{Job xx. 12,} sort of men, in whose mouths wickedness is sweet, they hide it under their tongues, they spare it, and forsake it not, but keep it still in their mouths. This furnisheth me with a tri-. partite division of men in the world.

The first and best are those who spit sin out, loathing it in their judgments, and leaving it in their practice.

The second sort, notoriously wicked, who swallow sin down, actually and openly committing it.

The third, endeavouring an expedient betwixt heaven and hell, neither do nor deny their lusts; neither spitting them out nor swallowing them down, but rolling them under their tongues, epicurizing thereon, in their filthy fancies and obscene speculations.

9

If God at the last day of Judgment hath three hands, a right for the sheep, a left for the goats, the middle is most proper for these third sort of men. But both these latter kinds of sinners shall be confounded together. The rather because a sin thus rolled becomes so soft and supple, and the throat is so short and slippery a passage, that insensibly it may slide down from the mouth into the stomach ; and contemplative wantonness quickly turns into practical uncleanness.

III. STORE NO SORE.

JOB had a custom to offer burnt-offerings according to the number of his sons ; for he said, It may be that my sons in their feasting have sinned, and cursed God in their hearts. It may be, not it must be; he was not certain, but suspected it. But now, what if his sons had not sinned ? was Job's labour lost, and his sacrifice of none effect ? O no ! only their property was altered; in case his sons were found faulty, his sacrifices for them were propitiatory, and through Christ obtained their pardon ; in case they were innocent, his offerings were eucharistical, returning thanks to God's restraining grace, for keeping his sons from such sins, which otherwise they would have committed.

Job I. 5.

I see in all doubtful matters of devotion, it is wisest to be on the surest side; better both lock and bolt and bar it, than leave the least door of danger open. Hast thou done what is disputable whether it be well done? Is it a measuring cast whether it be lawful or no? So that thy conscience may seem in a manner to stand neuter, sue a conditional pardon out of the court of heaven, the rather because our self-love is more prone to flatter than our godly jealousy to suspect ourselves without a cause; with such humility Heaven is well pleased. For suppose thyself over cautious, needing no forgiveness in that particular, God will interpret the pardon thou prayest for to be the praises presented unto him.

IV.   LINE ON LINE.

MOSES, in God's name, did counsel Joshua, Deut. xxxi. 23: Be strong, and of a good courage, for thou shalt bring the children of Israel into the land which I sware unto them. God immediately did command him, Josh. i. 6: Be strong, and of a good courage; and again, ver. 7: Only be thou strong and very courageous; and again, ver. 9: Have not I commanded thee? be strong and of a good courage; be not afraid, neither be thou dismayed.   Lastly, the Reuben-

ites and Gadites heartily desired him, ver. 18:
Only be strong and of a good courage.

Was Joshua a dunce, or a coward? did his
wit or his valour want an edge, that the same
precept must so often be pressed upon him? No
doubt neither; but God saw it needful that
Joshua should have courage of proof, who was
to encounter both the froward Jew and the
fierce Canaanite.

Though metal on metal, colour on colour, be
false heraldry, line on line, precept on precept,
is true divinity.

Is. xxviii. 10.

Be not therefore offended, O my soul, if the
same doctrine be often delivered unto thee by
different preachers: if the same precept, like the
sword in Paradise, which turned every way,
doth hunt and haunt thee, tracing thee which
way soever thou turnest, rather conclude that
thou art deeply concerned in the practice thereof, which God hath thought fit should be so
frequently inculcated into thee.

Gen. iii. 24.

V. O! THE DEPTH.

HAD I beheld Sodom in the beauty thereof,
and had the angel told me that the same
should be suddenly destroyed by a merciless
element, I should certainly have concluded that
Sodom should have been drowned; led thereunto by these considerations: —

1. It was situated in the plain of Jordan, a flat, low, level country.

2. It was well watered everywhere; and where always there is water enough, there may sometimes be too much. Gen iii. 10.

3. Jordan had a quality in the first month to overflow all his banks. 1 Chron. xii. 15.

But no drop of moisture is spilt on Sodom, it is burnt to ashes. How wide are our conjectures, when they guess at God's judgments! How far are his ways above our apprehension! Especially when wicked men with the Sodomites wander in strange sins, out of the road of common corruption, God meets them with strange punishments, out of the reach of common conception, not coming within the compass of a rational suspicion.

VI. SELF, SELF-HURTER.

WHEN God, at the first day of judgment arraigned Eve, she transferred her fault on the serpent which beguiled her. This was one of the first-fruits of our depraved nature. But ever after regenerate men in Scripture, making the confession of their sins (whereof many precedents), cast all the fault on themselves alone: yea, David, when he numbered the people, though it be expressed that Satan Gen. iii. 13.

1 Chron. xxi. 1.

provoked him thereunto, and though David probably might be sensible of his temptation, yet he never accused the Devil, but derived all the guilt on himself: I it is that have sinned: good reason, for Satan hath no impulsive power; he may strike fire till he be weary (if his malice can be weary) ; except man's corruption brings the tinder, the match cannot be lighted. Away, then, with that plea of course: " The Devil owed me a shame." Owe thee he might, but pay thee he could not, unless thou wert as willing to take his black money as he is to tender it.

1 Chron.
xxi. 17.

VII. GAD, BEHOLD A TROOP COMETH.

2 Sam. i.

THE Amalekite who brought the tidings to David began with truth, rightly reporting the overthrow of the Israelites; cheaters must get some credit before they can cozen, and all falsehood, if not founded in some truth, would not be fixed in any belief.

But proceeding, he told six lies successively:—
1. That Saul called him.
2. That he came at his call.
3. That Saul demanded who he was.
4. That he returned his answer.
5. That Saul commanded him to kill him.
6. That he killed him accordingly.

A wilful falsehood told is a cripple not able to stand by itself, without some to support it; it is easy to tell a lie, hard to tell but a lie.

Lord, if I be so unhappy to relate a falsehood, give me to recall it, or repent of it. It is said of the pismires, that to prevent the growing (and so the corrupting) of that corn which they hoard up for their winter provision, they bite off both the ends thereof, wherein the generating power of the grain doth consist. When I have committed a sin, O let me so order it that I may destroy the procreation thereof, and, by a true sorrow, condemn it to a blessed barrenness.

VIII. OUT MEANS, IN MIRACLES.

WHEN the angel brought St. Peter out of prison, the iron gate opened of its own accord. But coming to the house of Mary the mother of John, mark, he was fain to stand before the door and knock. When iron gave obedience, how can wood make opposition?

The answer easy. There was no man to open the iron gate, but a portress was provided of course to unlock the door; God would not therefore show his finger, where men's hands were appointed to do the work. Heaven will not superinstitute a miracle, where ordinary means were formerly in peaceable possession. But if

they either depart or resign (ingenuously confessing their insufficiency) there miracles succeed in their vacancy.

Lord, if only wooden obstacles (such as can
be removed by might of man) hindered our hope
of peace, the arm of flesh might relieve us. But
alas! they are iron obstructions, as come not
within human power or policy to take away.
No proud flesh shall therefore presumptuously
pretend to any part of the praise, but ascribe
it solely to thyself, if now thou shouldst be
pleased, after seven years' hard apprenticeship
in civil wars, miraculously to burn our indentures, and restore us to our former liberty.

IX. MILITARY MOURNING.

SOME may wonder at the strange incohe-
rence in the words and actions, 2 Sam.
i. 17:

And David lamented with this lamentation
over Saul and over Jonathan his son: also he
bade them teach the children of Judah the use
of the bow.

But the connection is excellent. For that is
the most soldier-like sorrow, which in midst of
grief can give order for revenge on such as have
slain their friends.

Our general fast was first appointed to bemoan the massacre of our brethren in Ireland. But it is in vain to have a finger in the eye, if we have not also a sword in the other hand; such tame lamenting of lost friends is but lost lamentation. We must bend our bows in the camp, as our knees in the churches, and second our posture of piety with martial provisions.

X. NO STOOL OF WICKEDNESS.

SOMETIMES I have disputed with myself, which of the two was most guilty, David, who said in haste, All men are liars, or that [Psalm cxvi. 11.] wicked man who sat and spake against his [Psalm l. 20.] brother, and slandered his own mother's son.

David seems the greater offender; for mankind might have an action of defamation against him, yea, he might justly be challenged for giving all men the lie. But mark, David was in haste, he spake it *in transitu*, when he was passing, or rather posting by; or if you please, not David, but David's haste rashly vented the words. Whereas the other sat, a sad, solemn, serious, premeditate, deliberate posture, his malice had a full blow, with a steady hand, at the credit of his brother. Not to say that *sat* carries with it the countenance of a judicial proceeding, as if he made a session or bench-business thereof, as well condemning, as accusing unjustly.

Lord, pardon my cursory, and preserve me from sedentary sins. If in haste or heat of passion I wrong any, give me at leisure to ask thee and them forgiveness. But O let me not sit by it, studiously to plot or project mischief to any out of malice prepense. To shed blood in cool blood, is blood with a witness.

XI. BY DEGREES.

2 Kings xvi.

SEE by what stairs wicked Ahaz did climb up to the height of profaneness.

Ibld. ver. 10.

First, he saw an idolatrous altar at Damascus. Our eyes, when gazing on sinful objects, are out of their calling and God's keeping.

Secondly, he liked it. There is a secret fascination in superstition, and our souls are soon bewitched with the gaudiness of false service from the simplicity of God's worship.

Ibld. ver. 11.

Thirdly, he made the like to it. And herein Uriah the priest (patron and chaplain well met) was the midwife to deliver the mother altar of Damascus of a babe, like unto it, at Jerusalem.

Ibld. ver. 18.

Fourthly, he sacrificed on it. What else could be expected, but that, when he had tuned this new instrument of idolatry, he would play upon it.

Ibld. ver. 15.

Fifthly, he commanded the people to do the like. Not content to confine it to his personal impiety.

Lastly, he removed God's altar away. That venerable altar, by Divine appointment peaceably possessed of the place for two hundred years and upwards, must now be violently ejected by a usurping upstart.

No man can be stark naught at once. Let us stop the progress of sin in our soul at the first stage, for the farther it goes, the faster it will increase.

XII. THE BEST BED-MAKER.

WHEN a good man is ill at ease, God promiseth to make all his bed in his sickness. Pillow, bolster, head, feet, sides, all his bed. Surely that God who made him knows so well his measure and temper, as to make his bed to please him. Herein his art is excellent, not fitting the bed to the person, but the person to the bed, infusing patience into him. ^{Psalm xii. 3.}

But O, how shall God make my bed, who have no bed of mine own to make? Thou fool, he can make thy not having a bed to be a bed unto thee. When Jacob slept on the ground, who would not have had his hard lodging, therewithal to have his heavenly dream? Yea, the poor woman in Jersey, which, in the reign of Queen Mary, was delivered of a child as she ^{Gen. xxviii. 12.} ^{Fox's Martyrs, vol. 3.}

was to be burnt at the stake, may be said to be brought to bed in the fire. Why not? if God's justice threatened to cast Jezebel into a bed of fire, why might not his mercy make the very flames a soft bed to that his patient martyr?

Rev. ii. 22.

XIII. WHEN BEGUN, ENDED.

THE Scripture giveth us a very short account of some battles, as if they were flights without fights, and the armies parted as soon as met, as Gen. xiv. 10; 1 Sam. xxxi. 1; 2 Chron. xxv. 22.

Some will say the spirit gives in only the sum of the success, without any particular passages in achieving it. But there is more in it that so little is said of the fight. For some time the question of the victory is not disputed at all, but the bare propounding decides it. The stand of pikes, ofttimes no stand, and the footmen so fitly called as making more use of their feet than their hands. And when God sends a qualm of fear over the soldiers' hearts, it is not all the skill and valour of their commanders can give them a cordial.

Our late war hath given us some instances hereof. Yet let not men tax their armies for cowardice, it being probable that the badness of such as stayed at home of their respective sides

had such influence on those in field, that soldiers' hearts might be fear-broken by the score
of their sins who were no soldiers.

XIV. TOO LATE, TOO LATE.

THE elder brother laid a sharp and true ^{Luke xv.}
charge against his brother prodigal, for^{29.}
his riot and luxury. This nothing affected his
father; the mirth, meat, music at the feast, was,
notwithstanding, no whit abated. Why so?
Because the elder brother was the younger in
this respect, and came too late. The other had
got the speed of him, having first accused himself (nine verses before), and already obtained
his pardon.

Satan (to give him his due) is my brother,
and my elder by creation. Sure I am, he will
be my grievous accuser. I will endeavour to
prevent him, first condemning myself to God
my father. So shall I have an act of indemnity
before he can enter his action against me.

XV. LAWFUL STEALTH.

I FIND two (husband and wife) both stealing, and but one of them guilty of felony.
And Rachel had stolen the images that were ^{Gen. xxxi.}
her father's, and Jacob stole away unawares^{19.}

to Laban the Syrian. In the former a complication of theft, lying, sacrilege, and idolatry;
in the latter no sin at all. For what our conscience tells us is lawful, and our discretion
dangerous, it is both conscience and discretion
to do it with all possible secrecy. It was as
lawful for Jacob in that case privately to steal
away, as it is for that man who finds the sunshine too hot for him, to walk in the shade.

God keep us from the guilt of Rachel's
stealth. But for Jacob's stealing away, one
may confess the fact, but deny the fault therein.
Some are said to have gotten their life for a
prey, if any, in that sense, have preyed on
(or, if you will, plundered) their own liberty,
stealing away from the place where they conceived themselves in danger, none can justly
condemn them.

XVI. TEXT IMPROVED.

Numb.
xxii. 30.

I HEARD a preacher take for his text: Am
not I thine ass, upon which thou hast ridden
ever since I was thine unto this day? was I
ever wont to do so unto thee? I wondered
what he would make thereof, fearing he would
starve his auditors for want of matter. But
hence he observed : —

1. The silliest and simplest, being wronged,
may justly speak in their own defence.

2. Worst men have a good title to their own goods. Balaam a sorcerer; yet the ass confesseth twice he was his.

3. They who have done many good offices, and fail in one, are often not only unrewarded for former service, but punished for that one offence.

4. When the creatures, formerly officious to serve us, start from their wonted obedience, (as the earth to become barren, and air pestilential,) man ought to reflect on his own sin as the sole cause thereof.

How fruitful are the seeming barren places of Scripture. Bad ploughmen, which make balks of such ground. Wheresoever the surface of God's word doth not laugh and sing with corn, there the heart thereof within is merry with mines, affording, where not plain matter, hidden mysteries.

XVII. THE ROYAL BEARING.

GOD is said to have brought the Israelites out of Egypt on eagles' wings. Now eagles, when removing their young ones, have a different posture from other fowl, proper to themselves, (fit it is that there should be a distinction betwixt sovereign and subjects,) carrying their prey in their talons, but young ones

Exod. xix. 4.

on their backs, so interposing their whole bodies betwixt them and harm. The old eagle's body is the young eagle's shield, and must be shot through before her young ones can be hurt.

Thus God, in saving the Jews, put himself betwixt them and danger. Surely God, so loving under the Law, is no less gracious in the Gospel: our souls are better secured, not only above his wings, but in his body; your life is hid with Christ in God. No fear then of harm; God first must be pierced before we can be prejudiced.

Colos. iii. 8.

XVIII. NONE TO HIM.

Matth. iii. 12.

IT is said of our Saviour, his fan is in his hand. How well it fits him, and he it! Could Satan's clutches snatch the fan, what work would he make! He would fan as he doth winnow, in a tempest, yea, in a whirlwind, and blow the best away. Had man the fan in his hand, especially in these distracted times, out goes for chaff all opposite to the opinions of his party. Seeming sanctity will carry it away from such, who, with true but weak grace, have ill natures and eminent corruptions.

Luke xxii. 31.

There is a kind of darnel, called *lolium murinum*, because so counterfeiting corn, that even the mice themselves (experience should make them good tasters) are sometimes deceived therewith. Hypocrites in like manner so act holiness, that they pass for saints before men, whose censures often barn up the chaff, and burn up the grain.

Well then! Christ for my share. Good luck have he with his honour. The fan is in so good a hand it cannot be mended. Only his hand who knows hearts is proper for that employment.

XIX. HUMILITY.

IT is a strange passage, Rev. vii. 13, 14: And one of the elders answered, saying unto me, What are these who are arrayed in white robes? and whence came they? And I said unto him, Sir, thou knowest. And he said unto me, These are they who have come out of great tribulation, &c.

How comes the elder, when asking a question, to be said to answer? On good reason: for his query in effect was a resolution. He asked St. John, not because he thought he could, but knew he could not answer; that John's ingenuous confession of his ignorance might invite the elder to inform him.

As his question is called an answer, so God's

10

commands are grants. When he enjoins us,
Repent, believe, it is only to draw from us a
free acknowledgment of our impotency to perform his commands. This confession being made by us, what he enjoins he
will enable us to do. Man's own-
ing his weakness is the only
stock for God thereon
to graft the grace
of his assist-
ance.

MEDITATIONS ON THE TIMES.

I. NAME–GENERAL.

EBER had a son born in the days Gen. x. 25. when the earth was divided. Conceive we it just after the confusion of tongues, when mankind was parcelled out into several colonies. Wherefore Eber, to perpetuate the memory of so famous an accident happening at the birth of his son, called him Peleg, which in the Hebrew tongue signifieth partition, or division.

We live in a land and age of dissension. Counties, cities, towns, villages, families, all divided in opinions, in affections. Each man almost divided from himself, with fears and distractions. Of all the children born in England within these last five years, and brought to the font (or, if that displease, to the basin) to be baptized, every male may be called Peleg, and female Palgah, in the sad memorial of the time of their nativity.

II. WOFUL WEALTH.

BARBAROUS is the custom of some English people on the seaside to prey on the goods of poor shipwrecked merchants. But more devilish in their design, who make false fires to undirect seamen in a tempest, that thereby from the right road they may be misled into danger and destruction.

England hath been tossed with a hurricane of a civil war. Some men are said to have gotten great wealth thereby. But it is an ill leap when men grow rich *per saltum*, taking their rise from the miseries of a land, to which their own sins have contributed their share. Those are far worse (and may not such be found?) who, by cunning insinuations, and false glossings, have, in these dangerous days, trained and betrayed simple men into mischief.

Can their pelf prosper, not got by valour or industry, but deceit? surely it cannot be wholesome, when every morsel of their meat is mummy (good physic but bad food), made of the corses of men's estates. Nor will it prove happy, it being to be feared, that such who have been enriched with other men's ruins will be ruined by their own riches. The child of ten years is old enough to remember the beginning of such men's wealth, and the man of threescore and ten is young enough to see the ending thereof.

III. A NEW PLOT.

WHEN Herod had beheaded John the Baptist, some might expect that his disciples would have done some great matter in revenge of their master's death. But see how they behave themselves. And his disciples came and took up the body and buried it, and went and told Jesus. And was this all? and what was all this? Alas, poor men, it was some solace to their sorrowful souls that they might lament their loss to a fast friend, who, though for the present unable to help, was willing to pity them.

Hast thou thy body unjustly imprisoned, or thy goods violently detained, or thy credit causelessly defamed? I have a design whereby thou shalt revenge thyself, even go and tell Jesus. Make to him a plain and true report of the manner and measure of thy sufferings: especially there being a great difference betwixt Jesus then clouded in the flesh, and Jesus now shining in glory, having now as much pity and more power to redress thy grievances. I know it is counted but a cowardly trick for boys, when beaten but by their equals, to cry that

11

they will tell their father. But, during the present necessity, it is both the best wisdom and valour, even to complain to thy Father in heaven, who will take thy case into his serious consideration.

IV. PROVIDENCE.

MARVELLOUS is God's goodness in preserving the young ostriches. For the old one leaveth her eggs in the earth, and warmeth them in the dust, forgetting that the foot may crush them, or that the wild beast may break them. But Divine Providence so disposeth it, that the bare nest hatcheth the eggs, and the warmth of the sandy ground discloseth them.

Many parents, which otherwise would have been loving pelicans, are by these unnatural wars forced to be ostriches to their own children, leaving them to the narrow mercy of the wide world. I am confident that these orphans (so may I call them whilst their parents are alive) shall be comfortably provided for, when worthy master Samuel Hern, famous for his living, preaching, and writing, lay on his death-bed, (rich only in goodness and children,) his wife made much womanish lamentation, what should hereafter become of her little

Job xxxix. 14, 15.

ones: Peace, sweet heart, said he, that God who feedeth the ravens will not starve the Psalm cxlvii. 9. Herns. A speech censured as light by some, observed by others as prophetical, as, indeed, it came to pass that they were well disposed of. Despair not, therefore, O thou parent, of God's blessing, for having many of his blessings, a numerous offspring. But depend on his providence for their maintenance: find thou but faith to believe it, he will find means to effect it.

V. COALS FOR FAGOT. Prov. xxv. 22.

IN the days of King Edward the Sixth, when Fox's Martyrol. vol. iii. p. 432. Bonner was kept in prison, reverend Ridley having his bishopric of London, would never go to dinner at Fulham without the company of Bonner's mother and sister; the former always sitting in a chair at the upper end of the table ; these guests were as constant as bread and salt at the board, no meal could be made without them.

O the meekness and mildness of such men as must make martyrs! Active charity always goes along with passive obedience.

How many ministers' wives and children now-a-days are outed of house and home, ready to be starved! How few are invited to their tables who hold the sequestrations of their husbands' or fathers' benefices! Yea, many of them are so far from being bountiful, that they are not just, denying or detaining from those poor souls that pittance which the Parliament hath allotted for their maintenance.

VI. FUGITIVES OVERTAKEN.

THE city of Geneva is seated in the marches of several dominions, France, Savoy, Switzerland; now it is a fundamental law in that signiory, to give free access to all offenders, yet so as to punish their offence according to the custom of that place wherein the fault was committed. This necessary severity doth sweep their state from being the sink of sinners, the rendezvous of rogues, and headquarters of all malefactors, which otherwise would fly thither in hope of indemnity. Herein I highly approve the discipline of Geneva.

If we should live to see churches of several governments permitted in England, it is more than probable that many offenders, not out of conscience, but to escape censures, would fly 1 Sam. from one congregation to another. What Na- xxv. 10. bal said sullenly and spitefully, one may sadly foresee and foresay of this land, Many servants now-a-days will break every man from his master; many guilty persons, abandoning that discipline under which they were bred and brought up, will shift and shelter themselves under some new model of government. Well were it then if every man, before he be admitted a member of a new congregation, do therein first make satisfaction for such scandalous sins whereof he stands justly charged in that church which he deserted. This would conduce to the advancing of virtue and the retrenching of notorious licentiousness.

VII. BOTH AND NEITHER.

A CITY was built in Germany upon the river Weser, by Charles the Emperor and Vuidekind first Christian Duke of Saxony; and because both contributed to the structure thereof, it was called Mine-thine (at this day, by corrupt pronunciation, Minden), to show the joint interest both had in the place. _{Munster's Cosmog. lib. iii. cap. 450}

Send, Lord, in thy due time, such a peace in this land as prince and people may share therein; that the sovereign might have what he justly calls mine, his lawful prerogative: and leave to the subjects their propriety. Such may be truly termed an accommodation which is *ad commodum utriusque,* — for the benefit of both parties concerned therein.

VIII. FED WITH FASTING.

THE salmon may pass for the riddle of the river. The oldest fisherman never, as yet, met with any meat in the maw thereof, thereby to advantage his conjecture on what bill of fare that fish feedeth. It eats not flies with the perch, nor swallows worms with the roach, nor sucketh dew with oysters, nor devoureth his fellow fishes with the pike: what hath it in the water but the water? yet salmons grow great, and very fat in their season.

How do many (exiles in their own country) subsist now-a-days of nothing, and wandering in a wilderness of want (except they have manna miraculously from heaven) they have no meat on earth from their own means. At what ordinary, or rather extraordinary, do they diet, that for all this have cheerful faces, light hearts, and merry countenances? Surely some secret comfort supports their souls. Such never desire but to make one meal all the days of their lives on the continual feast of a good conscience. The fattest capons yield but sad merrythoughts to the greedy glutton in comparison of those delightful dainties which this dish daily affords such as feed upon it.

Prov. xv.
16.

IX. BARE IN FAT PASTURE.

FORESTERS have informed me, that out-lodging deer are seldom seen to be so fat as those which keep themselves within the park. Whereof they assign this reason: that those stragglers, though they have more ground to range over, more grass and grain to take their repast upon, yet they are in constant fear, as if conscious that they are trespassers, being out of the protection, because out of the pale of the park. This makes their eyes and ears always to stand sentinels for their mouths, lest the master of the ground pursue them for the damage done unto him.

Are there any which unjustly possess the houses of others? Surely such can never with quiet and comfort enjoy either their places or themselves. They always listen to the least noise of news, suspecting the right owner should be re-estated, whose restitution of necessity infers the other's ejection. Lord, grant that though my means be never so small, grant they may be my means, not wrongfully detained from others having a truer title unto them.

X. MUCH GOOD DO YOU.

Plutarch's
Morals.
ONE Nicias, a philosopher, having his shoes stolen from him, May they, said he, fit his feet that took them away. A wish at the first view very harmless, but there was that in it which poisoned his charity into a malicious revenge. For he himself had hurled or crooked feet, so that in effect he wished the thief to be lame.

Whosoever hath plundered me of my books and papers, I freely forgive him; and desire he may fully understand and make good use thereof, wishing him more joy of them than he hath right to them. Nor is there any snake under my herbs, nor have I (as Nicias) any reservation, or latent sense to myself, but from my heart do desire, that to all purposes and intents my books may be beneficial unto him. Only requesting him, that one passage in his (lately my) Bible [namely, Eph. iv. 28] may be taken into his serious consideration.

XI. THE USE OF THE ALPHABET.

THERE was, not long since, a devout but ignorant Papist dwelling in Spain. He perceived a necessity of his own private prayers to God, besides the Pater Nosters, Ave Marias,

&c., used of course in the Romish Church. But so simple was he, that how to pray he knew not. Only every morning, humbly bending his knees, and lifting up his eyes and hands to heaven, he would deliberately repeat the alphabet. And now, said he, O good God, put these letters together to spell syllables, to spell words, to make such sense as may be most to thy glory and my good.

In these distracted times I know what generals to pray for. God's glory, truth, and peace, his Majesty's honour, privileges of Parliament, liberty of subjects, &c. But when I descend to particulars, when, how, by whom I should desire these things to be effected, I may fall to that poor pious man's A, B, C, D, E, &c.

XII. THE GOOD EFFECT OF A BAD CAUSE.

GOD, in the Levitical law, gave reward to the woman causelessly suspected of her jealous husband, that the bitter water, which she was to drink in the priest's presence, should not only do her no harm, but also procure her children, if barren before; that water (drunk by her to quench the fire of her husband's jealousy) proved like the spa unto her, so

Numb. v. 28.

famous for causing fruitfulness. Thus her innocence was not only cleared but crowned.

His gracious Majesty hath been suspected to
be popishly inclined. A suspicion like those
Nat. Hist.
lib. xlx.
cap. 2. mushrooms which Pliny recounts amongst the
miracles in nature, because growing without
a root. Well, he hath past his purgation, a
bitter morning's draught hath he taken down
for many years together.

See the operation thereof; his constancy in
the Protestant religion hath not only been assured to such who unjustly were jealous of
him, but also, by God's blessing, he daily grows
greater in men's hearts, pregnant with the love
and affection of his subjects.

XIII.   THE CHILD–MAN.

In his Life,
Juxta
finem. JOHN GERSON, the pious and learned
Chancellor of Paris, beholding and be-
moaning the general corruption of his age,
in doctrine and manners, was wont to get a
choir of little children about him, and to en-
treat them to pray to God in his behalf. Supposing their prayers least defiled with sin, and
most acceptable to Heaven.

Men now-a-days are so infected with malice,
that little children are the best chaplains to
pray for their parents. But O, where shall

such be found, not resenting of the faults and factions of their fathers? Gerson's plot will not take effect, I will try another way.

I will make my address to the holy child Acts iv. 27. Jesus, so is he styled even when glorified in heaven; not because he is still under age (like Popish pictures, placing him in his mother's arms, and keeping him in his constant infancy), but because with the strength and perfection of a man he hath the innocency and humility of a child; him only will I employ to intercede for me.

XIV. WORSE BEFORE BETTER.

STRANGE was the behaviour of our Saviour toward his beloved Lazarus; informed by a messenger of his sickness, he abode two John xi. 6. days still in the place where he was. Why so slow? bad sending him on a dying man's errands. But the cause was, because Lazarus was not bad enough for Christ to cure, intending not to recover him from sickness, but revive him from death, to make the glory of the miracle greater.

England doth lie desperately sick of a violent disease in the bowels thereof. Many messengers we despatch (monthly fasts, weekly sermons, daily prayers) to inform God of our sad condition. He still stays in the same place, yea, which is worse, seems to go backward, for every day less likelihood, less hope of help. May not this be the reason, that our land must yet be reduced to more extremity, that God may have the higher honour of our deliverance?

XV. ALL SIN, ALL SUFFER.

THE mariners that guided the ship in the tempest, Acts xxvii. 30 – 32, had a design for their own safety with the ruin of the rest; intending (under pretence of casting out an anchor) to escape in a boat by themselves. But the soldiers prevented their purpose, and cut off the cord of the boat, and let it fall into the sea. One and all: all sink, or all save. Herein their martial law did a piece of exemplary justice.

Do any intend willingly (without special cause) to leave the land, so to avoid that misery which their sins, with others, have drawn upon it; might I advise them, better mourn in, than move out of sad Zion. Hang out the scarlet lace at the casement (eyes made red with sorrow for sin), but slide not down out of the window without better warrant. But if they be disposed to depart, and leave their native soil, let them take heed their fly-

Josh. chap.
ii.

boat meets not with such soldiers as will send them back, with shame and sorrow, into the ship again.

XVI. EAT WORTHILY.

SAUL, being in full pursuit of the flying Philistines, made a law that no Israelite should eat until evening. But it was the judgment of Jonathan, that the army, if permitted to eat, had done greater execution on their enemies. For time so lost was gained, being laid out in the necessary refection of their bodies.

1 Sam. xiv. 24.

Yea, mark the issue of their long fasting. The people at night, coming with ravenous appetites, did eat the flesh with the blood, to the provoking of God's anger.

Ibid. ver. 32.

Many English people, having conquered some fleshly lusts which fight against their souls, were still chasing them, in hope finally to subdue them. Was it a pious or a politic design to forbid such the receiving of the sacrament, their spiritual food?

I will not positively conclude that such, if suffered to strengthen themselves with that heavenly repast, had thereby been enabled more effectually to cut down their corruptions. Only two things I will desire.

First, that such Jonathans who, by breaking this custom, have found benefit to themselves, may not be condemned by others. Secondly, I shall pray that two hungry years make not the third a glutton. That communicants, two twelvemonths together forbidden the Lord's Supper, come not (when admitted thereunto) with better stomach than heart, more greediness than preparation.

XVII. DEVOTIONS DUPLICATE.

WHEN the Jewish Sabbath, in the primitive times, was newly changed into the Christian's Lord's day, many devout people twisted both together in their observation, abstaining from servile works, and keeping both Saturday and Sunday wholly for holy employments.

During these civil wars, Wednesday and Friday fasts have been appointed by different authorities. What harm had it been if they had been both generally observed.

But alas! when two messengers, being sent together on the same errand, fall out and fight by the way, will not the work be worse done than if none were employed? In such a pair of fasts it is to be feared that the divisions of our affections rather would increase than abate God's anger against us.

Two negatives make an affirmative. Days of humiliation are appointed for men to deny themselves and their sinful lusts. But do not our two fasts more peremptorily affirm and avouch our mutual malice and hatred? God forgive us, we have cause enough to keep ten, but not care enough to keep one monthly day of humiliation.

XVIII. LAW TO THEMSELVES.

SOME sixty years since, in the University of Cambridge, it was solemnly debated . betwixt the heads, to debar young scholars of that liberty allowed them in Christmas, as inconsistent with the discipline of students. But some grave governors maintained the good use thereof, because thereby in twelve days they may more discover the dispositions of scholars than in twelve months before. That is a vigilant virtue indeed, which would be early up at prayers and study, when all authority to punish lay asleep.

Vice, these late years, hath kept open house in England. Welcome all comers without any examination. No penance for the adulterer, stocks for the drunkard, whip for the petty larcener, brand for the felon, gallows for the murderer.

God all this time tries us as he did Heze-
2 Chron.
xxxii. 31. kiah, that he might know all that is in our
hearts. Such as now are chaste, sober, just,
true, show themselves acted with a higher prin-
ciple of piety than the bare avoiding of punishment.

XIX. A NEW DISEASE.

THERE is a disease of infants (and an
infant disease, having scarcely as yet
gotten a proper name in Latin) called the rick-
ets ; wherein the head waxeth too great, whilst
the legs and lower parts wain too little. A
woman in the west hath happily healed many,
by cauterizing the vein behind the ear. How
proper the remedy for the malady I engage
not, experience ofttimes outdoing art, whilst
we behold the cure easily effected, and the
natural cause thereof hardly assigned.

Have not many now-a-days the same sickness
in their souls? their heads swelling to a vast
proportion, and they wonderfully enabled with
knowledge to discourse? But, alas! how little
their legs, poor their practice, and lazy their
walking in a godly conversation! Shall I say
that such may be cured by searing the vein
in their head, not to hurt their hearing, but
hinder the itching of their ears.

Indeed, his tongue deserves to be burnt that talks of searing the ears of others; for faith cometh by hearing. But I would have men not to hear few sermons, but hear more in hearing fewer sermons. Less preaching better heard (reader, lay the emphasis not on the word *less*, but on the word *better*) would make a wiser and stronger Christian, digesting the word from his heart to practise it in his conversation.

. 12

MEDITATIONS ON ALL KIND OF PRAYERS.

I. NEWLY AWAKED.

Exod.
xxiv. 19.

Y the Levitical law, the firstling of every clean creature which opened the matrix was holy to God. By the moral analogy thereof, this first glance of mine eyes is due to him. By the custom of this kingdom there accrueth to the landlord a fine and heriot from his tenant taking a farther estate in his lease. I hold from God this clay cottage of my body (a homely tenement, but may I in some measure be assured of a better before outed of this). Now, being raised from last night's sleep, I may seem to renew a life. What shall I pay to my landlord? even the best quick creature which is to be found on my barren copyhold, namely, the calves of my lips, praising him for his protection over me. More he doth not ask, less I cannot give; yea, such is his goodness and my weakness, that before I can give him thanks he giveth me to be thankful.

II. FAMILY PRAYER.

L ONG have I searched the Scriptures to find a positive precept enjoining, or precedent observing, daily prayer in a family; yet hitherto have found none proper for my purpose. Indeed I read that there was a yearly ^{1 Sam. xx. 29.} sacrifice offered at Bethlehem for the family of Jesse; but if hence we should infer household holy duties, others would conclude they should only be annual. And whereas it is said, Pour out thine indignation on the heathen, and on the families which have not called on thy name; the word taken there in a large acceptation reproveth rather the want of national, than domestical service of God.

But let not profaneness improve itself, or censure family prayer for will-worship, as wanting a warrant in God's word. For where God enjoineth a general duty, as to serve and fear him, there all particular means (whereof prayer a principal) tending thereunto are commanded. And surely the pious households of ^{Gen. xviii. 19.} Abraham, Joshua, and Cornelius, had some ^{Josh. xxiv. 15.} holy exercises to themselves, as broader than ^{Acts x. 2.}

their personal devotion, so narrower than the public service, just adequate to their own private family.

III. SELF WITHOUT OTHER SELF.

SOME loving wife may perchance be (though not angry with) grieved at her husband for excluding her from his private prayers; thus thinking with herself, Must I be discommuned from my husband's devotion? what, several closet-chapels for those of the same bed and board? Are not our credits embarked in the same bottom, so that they swim or sink together? May I not be admitted an auditor at his petitions, were it only to say Amen thereunto?

But let such a one seriously consider what the prophet saith: The family of the house of David apart, and their wives apart; the family of the house of Nathan apart, and their wives apart. Personal private faults must be privately confessed. It is not meet she should know all the bosom sins of him in whose bosom she lieth. Perchance being now offended for not hearing her husband's prayers, she would be more offended if she heard them. Nor hath she just cause to complain, seeing herein Nathan's wife is equal with Nathan himself; what

Zech. xii. 12.

liberty she alloweth is allowed her, and may as well as her husband claim the privilege privately and apart to pour forth her soul unto God in her daily devotions.

Yet man and wife at other times ought to communicate in their prayers, all other excluded.

IV. GROANS.

HOW comes it to pass that groans made in men by God's spirit cannot be uttered? I find two reasons thereof. First, because those groans are so low and little, so faint, frail, and feeble, so next to nothing, these still-born babes only breathe without crying.

Secondly, because so much diversity, yea, contrariety of passion, is crowded within the compass of a groan, they are stayed from being expressive, and the groans become unutterable.

How happy is their condition who have God for their interpreter? who not only understands what they do, but what they would say. Daniel could tell the meaning of the dream which Nebuchadnezzar had forgotten. God knows the meaning of those groans which never as yet knew their own meaning, and understands the sense of those sighs which never understood themselves.

13

V. EJACULATIONS, THEIR USE.

EJACULATIONS are short prayers darted up to God on emergent occasions. If no other artillery had been used these last seven years in England, I will not affirm more souls had been in heaven, but fewer corses had been buried in earth. O that with David we might have said, My heart is fixed, being less busied about fixing of muskets.

Psalm lvii. 7.

The principal use of ejaculations is against the fiery darts of the Devil. Our adversary injects (how he doth it God knows, that he doth it we know) bad motions into our hearts, and that we may be as nimble with our antidotes as he with his poisons, such short prayers are proper and necessary. In barred havens, so choked up with the envious sands, that great ships, drawing many feet of water, cannot come near, lighter and lesser pinnaces may freely and safely arrive. When we are time-bound, place-bound, or person-bound, so that we cannot compose ourselves to make a large solemn prayer, this is the right instant for ejaculations, whether orally uttered, or only poured forth inwardly in the heart.

Ephes. vi. 16.

VI. THEIR PRIVILEGE.

EJACULATIONS take not up any room in the soul. They give liberty of callings, so that at the same instant one may follow his proper vocation. The husbandman may dart forth an ejaculation, and not make a balk the more. The seaman nevertheless steer his ship right in the darkest night. Yea, the soldier at the same time may shoot out his prayer to God, and aim his pistol at his enemy, the one better hitting the mark for the other.

The field wherein bees feed is no whit the barer for their biting; when they have taken their full repast on flowers or grass, the ox may feed, the sheep fat, on their reversions. The reason is because those little chemists distil only the refined part of the flower, leaving the grosser substance thereof. So ejaculations bind not men to any bodily observance, only busy the spiritual half, which maketh them consistent with the prosecution of any other employment.

VII. EXTEMPORARY PRAYERS.

IN extemporary prayer, what men most admire God least regardeth. Namely, the volubility of the tongue. Herein a Tertullus may equal, yea exceed, Saint Paul himself, whose

2 Cor. x. 10.

speech was but mean. O, it is the heart keeping time and tune with the voice which God listeneth unto. Otherwise the nimblest tongue tires, and loudest voice grows dumb, before it Heb. viii. 5 comes half-way to heaven. Make it, said God to Moses, in all things like the pattern in the mount. Only the conformity of the words with the mind, mounted up in heavenly thoughts, is acceptable to God. The gift of extemporary prayer, ready utterance, may be bestowed on a reprobate, but the grace thereof (religious affections) is only given to God's servants.

VIII. THEIR CAUSELESS SCANDAL.

SOME lay it to the charge of extemporary prayers, as if it were a diminution to God's majesty to offer them unto him, because (allud- 2 Sam. xxiv. 24. ing to David's expression to Ornan the Jebusite) they cost nothing, but come without any pains or industry to provide them. A most false aspersion.

Surely preparation of the heart (though not premeditation of every word) is required thereunto. And grant the party praying at that very instant fore-studieth not every expression, yet surely he hath formerly laboured with his heart and tongue too, before he attained that dexterity of utterance properly and readily to express himself. Many hours in night no doubt he is waking, and was by himself practising Scripture phrase, and the language of Canaan, whilst such as censure him for his laziness were fast asleep in their beds.

Suppose one should make an entertainment for strangers with flesh, fish, fowl, venison, fruit, all out of his own fold, field, ponds, park, orchard, will any say that this feast cost him nothing who made it? Surely, although all grew on the same, and for the present he bought nothing by the penny, yet he, or his ancestors for him, did at first dearly purchase these home accommodations, whence that this entertainment did arise.

So the party who hath attained the faculty and facility of extemporary prayer (the easy act of a laborious habit), though at the instant not appearing to take pains, hath been formerly industrious with himself, or his parents with him (in giving him pious education), or else he had never acquired so great perfection, seeing only long practice makes the pen of a ready writer.

IX. NIGHT PRAYER.

DEATH in Scripture is compared to sleep. Well then may my night prayer be resembled to making my will. I will be careful not to die intestate; as also not to defer my will-making till I am not *compos mentis*, till the lethargy of drowsiness seize upon me.

But, being in perfect memory, I bequeath my soul to God; the rather because I am sure the Devil will accuse me when sleeping. O the advantage of spirits above bodies! If our clay cottage be not cooled with rest, the roof falls afire. Satan hath no such need: the night is his fittest time. Thus man's vacation is the term for the beasts of the forest, they move most whilst he lies quiet in his bed.

Rev. xii. 10.

Lest, therefore, whilst sleeping I be outlawed for want of appearance to Satan's charge, I commit my cause to him who neither slumbers nor sleeps: Answer for me, O my God.

X. A NOCTURNAL.

Psalm viii. 3.

DAVID, surveying the firmament, brake forth into this consideration: When I consider the heavens, the work of thy fingers; the moon and the stars, which thou hast created; what is man, &c.

How cometh he to mention the moon and stars, and omit the sun? The other being but his pensioners, shining with that exhibition of light which the bounty of the sun allots them.

It is answered, This was David's night meditation, when the sun, departing to the other
world, left the lesser lights only visible in heav-
en; and as the sky is best beheld by day
in the glory thereof, so it is best surveyed
by night in the variety of the same.

Night was made for man to rest in. But
when I cannot sleep, may I with this psalm-
ist entertain my waking with good thoughts.
Not to use them as opium, to invite my corrupt nature to slumber, but to bolt out bad
thoughts, which otherwise would possess my
soul.

XI. SET PRAYERS.

SET prayers are prescript forms of our own
or other's composing; such are lawful
for any, and needful for some to use.

Lawful for any. Otherwise God would not
have appointed the priest (presumed of themselves best able to pray) a form of blessing
the people; nor would our Saviour have set
us his prayer, which (as the town-bushel is
the standard both to measure corn and other
bushels by) is both a prayer in itself, and a
pattern or platform of prayer. Such as accuse set forms to be pinioning the wings of
the dove, will by the next return affirm, that

girdles and garters, made to strengthen and adorn, are so many shackles and fetters, which hurt and hinder men's free motion.

Needful for some. Namely, for such who as yet have not attained (what all should endeavour) to pray extempore by the spirit. But as little children, to whom the plainest and evenest room at first is a labyrinth, are so ambitious of going alone, that they scorn to take the guidance of a form or bench to direct them, but will adventure by themselves, though often to the cost of a knock and a fall. So many confess their weakness in denying to confess it, who, refusing to be beholden to a set form of prayer, prefer to say nonsense rather than nothing in their extempore expressions. More modesty, and no less piety, it had been for such men to have prayed longer with set forms, that they might pray better without them.

XII. THE SAME AGAIN.

IT is no base and beggarly shift (arguing a narrow and necessitous heart), but a piece of holy and heavenly thrift, often to use the same prayer again. Christ's practice is my directory herein, who the third time said the same words.

Matth.
xxvi. 44.

A good prayer is not like a stratagem in war, to be used but once. No, the oftener the better. The clothes of the Israelites, whilst they wandered forty years in the wilderness, never waxed old, as if made of *perpetuano* indeed. So a good prayer, though often used, is still fresh and fair in the ears and eyes of Heaven.

Despair not then, thou simple soul, who hast no exchange of raiment, whose prayers cannot appear every day at Heaven's court in new clothes. Thou mayest be as good a subject, though not so great a gallant, coming always in the same suit. Yea, perchance the very same which was thy father's and grandfather's before thee, (a well-composed prayer is a good heir-loom in a family, and may hereditarily be descended to many generations,) but know thy comfort, thy prayer is well known to Heaven, to which it is a constant customer. Only add new, or new degrees of old affections thereunto, and it will be acceptable to God thus repaired, as if new erected.

XIII. MIXT PRAYERS.

MIXT prayers are a methodical composition (no casual confusion) of extem-

pore and premeditate prayers put together.
Wherein the standers still are the same, and
the essential parts (confession of sin, begging
of pardon, craving grace for the future, thank-
ing God for former favours, &c.), like the
bones of the prayer, remain always unaltered.
Whilst the movable petitions (like the flesh
and colour of thy prayers) are added, abridged,
or altered, as God's spirit adviseth and ena-
bleth us, according to the emergencies of present occasions.

In the midland sea, galleys are found to be
most useful, which partly run on the legs of
oars, and partly fly with the wings of sails,
whereby they become serviceable both in a
wind and in a calm. Such the conveniency
of mixt prayer, wherein infused and acquired
graces meet together, and men partly move
with the breath of the Holy Spirit, partly row
on by their own industry. Such medley prayers are most useful, as having the steadiness of
premeditate, and the activity of extemporary
prayer joined together.

XIV. TAKE YOUR COMPANY ALONG.

IT is no disgrace for such who have the
gift and grace of extemporary prayer sometimes to use a set form, for the benefit and

behoof of others. Jacob, though he could have marched on at a man's pace, yet was careful not to over-drive the children and ewes big ^Gen.xxxiii.^ ^13.^ with young. Let ministers remember to bring up the rear in their congregations, that the meanest may go along with them in their devotions.

God would have created the world extempore, in a moment, but was pleased (as I may say) to make it premeditately, in a set method of six days, not for his own ease, but our instruction, that our heads and hearts might the better keep pace with his hands, to behold and consider his workmanship.

Let no man disdain to set his own nimbleness backward, that others may go along with him. Such degrading one's self is the quickest proceeding in piety, when men prefer the edification of others before their own credit and esteem.

XV. PRAYER MUST BE QUOTIDIAN.

AMONGST other arguments enforcing the necessity of daily prayer, this not the least, that Christ enjoins us to petition for daily bread. New bread we know is best; and in a spiritual sense, our bread, though in itself as stale and mouldy as that of the Gibeonites, is every day new, because a new and hot blessing, as I might say, is daily begged, and bestowed of God upon it.

Manna must daily be gathered, and not provisionally be hoarded up. God expects that men every day address themselves unto him, by petitioning him for sustenance.

How contrary is this to the common practice of many. As camels in sandy countries are said to drink but once in seven days, and then *in præsens, præteritum, et futurum,* for time past, present, and to come, so many fumble this, last, and next week's devotion all in a prayer. Yea, some defer all their praying till the last day.

Constantine had a conceit, that because baptism washed away all sins, he would not be baptized till his death-bed, that so his soul might never lose the purity thereof, but immediately mount to heaven. But sudden death preventing him, he was not baptized at all, as some say, or only by an Arian bishop, as others affirm. If any erroneously, on the same supposition, put off their prayers to the last, let them take heed, lest long delayed, at last they prove either none at all or none in effect.

XVI. THE LORD'S PRAYER.

IN this age we begin to think meanly of the
Lord's prayer ; O how basely may the Lord
think of our prayers ! Some will not forgive
the Lord's prayer for that passage therein, as
we forgive them that trespass against us.

Others play the witches on this prayer.
Witches are reported (amongst many other
hellish observations, whereby they oblige themselves to Satan) to say the Lord's prayer back-
wards. Are there not many, who, though they
do not pronounce the syllables of the Lord's
prayer retrograde (their discretion will not suffer them to be betrayed to such a nonsense sin),
yet they transpose it in effect, desiring their
daily bread before God's kingdom come, preferring temporal benefits before heavenly blessings. O, if every one by this mark should be
tried for a witch, how hard would it go with all
of us ! *Lamiarum plena sunt omnia.*

XVII. ALL BEST.

AT the siege and taking of New Carthage in
Spain, there was a dissension betwixt the
soldiers, about the crown mural due to him who
first footed the walls of the city. Two pretended
to the crown : parts were taken, and the Roman

army, siding in factions, was likely to fall foul,
and mutually fight against itself. Scipio the
general prevented the danger by providing two
mural crowns, giving one to each who claimed
it, affirming that, on the examination of the
proofs, both did appear to him at the same
instant to climb the wall. O let us not set
several kinds of prayers at variance betwixt
themselves which of them should be most
useful, most honorable. All are most excellent at several times, crown-groans, crown-ejac-
ulations, crown-extemporary, crown-set, crown-
mixed prayer ; I dare boldly say, he that in
some measure loves not all kind of lawful prayers, loves no kind of lawful prayers. For if we
love God the Father, we can hate no ordinance,
his child, though perchance an occasion may
affect one above another.

Plutarch in
Scipio's
Life, p.
187.

XVIII. ALL MANNER OF PRAYER.

IT is an ancient stratagem of Satan, (yet still
he useth it, still men are cheated by it,) to set
God's ordinance at variance, as the disciples fell
out amongst themselves, which of them should be
the greatest. How hath the reader's pew been
clashed against the preacher's pulpit, to the
shaking almost of the whole church, whether
that the word preached or read be most effectual

to salvation. Also, whether the word preached
or catechised be most useful. But no ordinance so abused as prayer. Prayer hath been
set up against preaching, against catechising,
against itself. Whether public or private, church
or closet, set or extempore prayer be the best.
See how St. Paul determines the controversy,
πάσῃ προσευχῇ, with all manner of prayer (so Ephes. vi. 18.
the Geneva translation) and supplication in the
spirit. Preferring none, commending all lawful
prayer to our practice.

XIX. TO GOD ALONE.

AMONGST all manner of prayer to God, I
find in Scripture neither promise, precept,
nor precedent to warrant prayers to saints. And
were there no other reason, this would encour-
age me to pray to Christ alone, because

St. Paul struck Elimas blind; Christ made
blind Bartimeus see. St. Peter killed Ananias
and Sapphira with his word; Christ with his
word revived dead Lazarus. The disciples for-
bade the Syrophœnician woman to call after
Christ, Christ called unto her after they had
forbidden her. All my Saviour's works are
saving works, none extending to the death of
mankind.

Surely Christ, being now in heaven, hath not

less goodness because he hath more glory, his
bowels still yearn on us.   I will therefore rather
present my prayers to him who always did heal,
than to those who sometimes did hurt.
And though this be no convincing argument to Papists, it is a comfortable motive to Protestants.
A good third, where so
good firsts and sec-
onds have been
laid be-
fore.

OCCASIONAL MEDITATIONS.

I. LOVE AND ANGER.

I SAW two children fighting together in the street. The father of the one passing by, fetched his son away and corrected him; the other lad was left without any check, though both were equally faulty in the fray. I was half offended, that being guilty alike, they were not punished alike: but the parent would only meddle with him over whom he had an undoubted dominion, to whom he bare an unfeigned affection.

The wicked sin, the godly smart most in this world. God singleth out his own sons, and beateth them by themselves; whom he loveth Heb. xii. 6. he chasteneth. Whilst the ungodly, preserved from affliction, are reserved for destruction. It being needless that their hair should be shaved Is. vii. 20. with a hired razor, whose heads are intended for Matth. iii. 10. the axe of divine justice.

14

II. UPWARDS, UPWARDS.

HOW large houses do they build in London on little ground! Revenging themselves on the narrowness of their room with store of stories. Excellent arithmetic! from the root of one floor to multiply so many chambers. And though painful the climbing up, pleasant the staying there, the higher the healthfuller, with clearer light and sweeter air.

Small are my means on earth. May I mount my soul the higher in heavenly meditations, relying on Divine Providence; He that fed many Matth. xiv. thousands with five loaves, may feed me and 17. mine with the fifth part of that one loaf, that once all mine. Higher, my soul! higher! In bodily buildings, commonly the garrets are most empty, but my mind, the higher mounted, will be the better furnished. Let perseverance to death be my uppermost chamber, the roof of which grace is the pavement of glory.

III. BEWARE, WANTON WIT.

I SAW an indenture too fairly engrossed; for the writer (better scrivener than clerk) had so filled it with flourishes that it hindered my reading thereof; the wantonness of his pen made a new alphabet, and I was subject to mistake his dashes for real letters.

What damage hath unwary rhetoric done to religion! Many an innocent reader hath taken Damascene and Theophilact at their word, counting their eloquent hyperboles of Christ's presence in the sacrament, the exact standards of their judgment, whence after ages brought in transubstantiation. Yea, from the Father's elegant apostrophes to the dead (lively pictures by hasty eyes may be taken for living persons), prayers to saints took their original. I see that truth's secretary must use a set hand in writing important points of divinity. Ill dancing for nimble wits on the precipices of dangerous doctrines. For though they escape by their agility, others (encouraged by their examples) may be brought to destruction.

IV. ILL DONE, UNDONE.

I SAW one, whether out of haste or want of skill, put up his sword the wrong way; it cut even when it was sheathed, the edge being transposed where the back should have been; so that, perceiving his error, he was fain to draw it out, that he might put it up again.

" Wearied and wasted with civil war, we that formerly loathed the manna of peace, because common, could now be content to feed on it, though full of worms and putrefied: some so

desirous thereof, that they care not on what
terms the war be ended, so it be ended: but
such a peace would be but a truce, and the
conditions thereof would no longer be in force
than whilst they are in force. Let us pray that
the sword be sheathed the right way, with
God's glory; and without the dangerous dislo-
cation of prince and people's right: otherwise it
may justly be suspected, that the sword put up
will be drawn out again, and the articles of an
ill agreement, though engrossed in parchment,
not take effect so long as paper would continue.

V. APACE APACE.

ROWING on the Thames, the waterman
confirmed me in what formerly I had
learnt from the maps; how that river, west-
ward, runs so crooked, as likely to lose itself in
a labyrinth of its own making. From Reading
to London by land, thirty; by water a hundred
miles. So wantonly that stream disporteth
itself, as if as yet unresolved whether to advance
to the sea or retreat to its fountain.

But the same being past London, (as if sensible of its former laziness, and fearing to be
checked of the ocean, the mother of all rivers,
for so long loitering; or else, as if weary with
wandering, and loath to lose more way; or

lastly, as if conceiving such wildness inconsistent with the gravity of his channel, now grown old, and ready to be buried in the sea,) runs in so direct a line, that from London to Gravesend the number of the miles are equally twenty both by land and by water.

Alas! how much of my life is lavished away? O the intricacies, windings, wanderings, turnings, tergiversations, of my deceitful youth! I have lived in the midst of a crooked generation, Phil. ii. 15. and with them have turned aside unto crooked Psalm cxxv. 5. ways. High time it is now for me to make straight paths for my feet, and to redeem what Heb. xii. 13. is past by amending what is present and to come. Flux, flux (in the German tongue quick, quick) was a motto of Bishop Jewel's, pre- In his Life, saging the approach of his death. May I make p. 10. good use thereof; make haste, make haste, God knows how little time is left me, and may I be a good husband to improve the short remnant thereof.

VI. ALWAYS THE RISING SUN.

I HAVE wondered why the Romish Church do not pray to Saint Abraham, Saint David, Saint Hezekiah, &c., as well as to the apostles and their successors since Christ's time; for those ancient patriarchs, by the confession of

15

Papists, were long since relieved out of limbo (soon out who were never in), and admitted to the sight and presence of God. Especially Abraham, being father of the faithful, as well Gentile as Jew, would (according to their prin ciples) be a proper patron for their petitions.

But it seems that modern saints rob the old ones of their honour; a Garnet, or late Bernard of Paris, have severally more prayers made unto them than many old saints have together. New besoms sweep clean; new cisterns of fond men's own hewing most likely to hold water.

Protestants, in some kind, serve their living ministers as Papists their dead saints. For aged pastors, who have borne the heat of the day in our Church, are justled out of respect by young preachers, not having half their age, nor a quarter of their learning and religion. Yet let not the former be disheartened, for thus it ever was and will be: English Athenians, all for novelties, new sects, new schisms, new doctrines, new disciplines, new prayers, new preachers.

VII. CHARITY, CHARITY.

CHURCH story reports of Saint John, that being grown very aged (wellnigh a hundred years old), wanting strength and voice to make a long sermon, he was wont to go up into the pulpit, and often repeat these words : Babes, keep yourselves from idols ; brethren, love one another.

Our age may seem sufficiently to have provided against the growth of idolatry in England. O that some order were taken for the increase of charity! It were liberty enough, if for the next seven years all sermons were bound to keep residence on this text: Brethren, love one another.

But would not some fall out with themselves, if appointed to preach unity to others ? Vindictive spirits, if confined to this text, would confine the text to their passion ; by brethren understanding only such of their own party. But O ! seeing other monopolies are dissolved, let not this remain against the fundamental law of charity. Let all bend their heads, hearts, and hands, to make up the breaches in church and state. But too many now-a-days are like Pharaoh's magicians, who could conjure up with Exod. viii. 7. their charms more new frogs, but could not remove or drive away those multitudes of frogs which were there before. Unhappily happy in making more rents and dissensions, but unable or unwilling to compose our former differences.

VIII. THE SENSIBLE PLANT.

I HEARD much of a sensible plant, and counted it a senseless relation (a rational beast, carrying as little contradiction), until, beholding it, mine eyes ushered my judgment into a belief thereof. My comprehension thereof is this. God having made three great stairs (vegetable, sensible, and reasonable creatures), that men thereby might climb up into the knowledge of a Deity, hath placed some things of a middle nature as half paces betwixt the stairs, so to make the step less, and the ascent more easy for our meditations.

Thus this active plant, with visible motion, doth border and confine on sensible creatures. Thus in Afric, some most agile and intelligent marmasites may seem to shake (forefeet shall I say, or) hands with the rudest savages of that country, as not much more than one remove from them in knowledge and civility.

But by the same proportion may not man, by custom and improvement of piety, mount himself near to an angelical nature. Such was Enoch, who, whilst living on earth, walked with God. O may our conversation be in heaven. For shall a plant take a new degree and proceed sensible, and shall man have his grace stayed for want of sufficiency, and not whilst living here

Gen. v. 22.

Phil. iii. 20.

commence angel, in his holy and heavenly affections?

IX. CHRIST MY KING.

I READ how King Edward the First ingeniously surprised the Welsh into subjection, proffering them such a prince as should be,

1. The son of a king.
2. Born in their own country.
3. Whom none could tax for any fault.

The Welsh accepted the conditions, and the king tendered them his son Edward, an infant, newly born in the castle of Carnarvon.

Do not all these qualifications mystically centre themselves in my Saviour?

1. The King of heaven saith unto him, Thou Psalm ii. 7. art my son, this day have I begotten thee.

2. Our true countryman, real flesh, whereas he took not on him the nature of angels.

3. Without spot or blemish, like to us in all things, sin only excepted.

Away, then, with those wicked men who will Luke xix. not have this King to rule over them. May he 14. have dominion in and over me. Thy kingdom come. Heaven and earth cannot afford a more proper prince for the purpose, exactly accomplished with all these comfortable qualifications.

X. TRIBULATION.

I FIND two sad etymologies of tribulation. One from *tribulus*, a three-forked thorn, which intimates that such afflictions, which are as full of pain and anguish unto the soul as a thorn thrust into a tender part of the flesh is unto the body, may properly be termed tribulations.

The other from *tribulus*, the head of a flail, or flagel, knaggy and knotty, (made commonly, as I take it, of a thick black thorn,) and then it imports, that afflictions falling upon us as heavy as the flail threshing the corn are styled tribulations.

I am in a strait which deduction to embrace, from the sharp or from the heavy thorn. But, which is the worst, though I may choose whence to derive the word, I cannot choose so as to decline the thing; I must through much tribulation enter into the kingdom of God.

Acts xiv. 22.

Therefore I will labour, not to be like a young colt, first set to plough, which more tires himself out with his own untowardness (whipping himself with his misspent mettle) than with the weight of what he draws ; and will labour patiently to bear what is imposed upon me.

XI. BEWARE.

I SAW a cannon shot off. The men at whom it was levelled fell flat on the ground, and so escaped the bullet. Against such blows, falling is all the fencing, and prostration all the armour of proof.

But that which gave them notice to fall down, was their perceiving of the fire before the ordnance was discharged. O the mercy of that fire ! which, as it were, repenting of the mischief it had done, and the murder it might make, ran a race, and outstript the bullet, that men (at the sight thereof) might be provided, when they could not resist, to prevent it. Thus every murdering piece is also a warning piece against itself.

God, in like manner, warns before he wounds ; frights before he fights. Yet forty days and Nineveh shall be destroyed. O let us fall down before the Lord our maker ; then shall his anger be pleased to make in us a daily passover, and his bullets, levelled at us, shall fly above us.

XII. THE FIRST-FRUITS.

PAPISTS observe (such are curious priers into Protestants' carriage) that charity in England lay in a swoon from the dissolution of abbeys, in the reign of King Henry the Eighth, till about the tenth of Queen Elizabeth.

As if in that age of ruin none durst raise religious buildings, and as if the axe and hammer, so long taught to beat down, had forgot their former use to build up for pious intents.

At last comes William Lambert, Esquire, and first founds an hospital at Greenwich in Kent, calling that his society, (like politic Joab, after David's name,) the poor people of Queen Elizabeth. And after this worthy man followed many, that we may almost dazzle Papists' eyes with the light of Protestant good works. The same Papists, perchance, may now conceive charity so disheartened in our days by these civil wars and the consequences thereof, that no Protestants hereafter should be so desperate as to adventure upon a public good deed. O for a Lambert junior (and I hope some of his lineage are left heirs to his lands and virtues), who shall break through the ranks of all discouragements ; so that now English Protestants, being to begin a new score of good works, might from him date their epoch. Such a charity deserves to be knighted for the valour thereof.

(margin note:) See Camden's Brit. in Kent, p. 327.

2 Sam. xii. 28.

XIII. THE RECRUIT.

I READ how one main argument which the Apostle Paul enforceth on Timothy, to make full proof of his ministry, is this : For I am now 2 Tim. iv. 6. ready to be offered, and the time of my departure is at hand. Thus the dying saints, drawing near to heaven, their mark is the best spur for the surviving to make the more speed in their race.

How many excellent divines have these sad times hastened to their long home (so called in Eccles. xii. Scripture, not because long going thither, but 6. long [ever] tarrying there) ! How many have been sorrow-shot to their heart ! O that this would edge the endeavours of our generation, to succeed in the dead places of worthy men ! Shall the Papists curiously observe and suffi- ciently boast, that their Stapleton was born on Pitzeus in the same day on which Sir Thomas More was Vita Sta- pletoni. beheaded, (as if his cradle made of the other's coffin,) and shall not our nurseries of learning supply the void rooms of our worthies deceased ? No sin, I hope, to pray that our Timothies come not short of our Pauls ; as in time, so in learn- ing and religion.

XIV. THE MONGREL.

I FIND the natural philosopher, making a character of the lion's disposition, amongst other his qualities reporteth, that first the lion feedeth on men, and afterwards, if forced with extremity of hunger, on women.*

Satan is a roaring lion, seeking whom he may devour. Only he inverts the method, and in his bill of fare takes the second course first. Ever since he over-tempted our grandmother Eve, encouraged with success, he hath preyed first on the weaker sex. It seems he hath all the vices, not the virtues, of that king of beasts ; a wolf-lion, having his cruelty without his generosity.

XV. EDIFICATION.

I READ in a learned physician how our provident mother, Nature, foreseeing men (her wanton children) would be tampering with the edge-tools of minerals, hid them far from them, in the bowels of the earth ; whereas she exposed plants and herbs more obvious to their eye, as fitter for their use. But some bold empirics, neglecting the latter as too common,

* In viros priusquam in feminas sævit. Plin. Hist. Nat. lib. viii. cap. 10.

have adventured on those hidden minerals, oft-times (through want of skill) to the hurt of many, and hazard of more.

God, in the New Testament, hath placed all historical and practical matter (needful for Christians to know and believe) in the beginning of the Gospel. All such truths lie above ground, plainly visible in the literal sense. The prophetical and difficult part comes in the close. But though the Testament was written in Greek, too many read it like Hebrew, beginning at the end thereof. How many trouble themselves about the Revelation, who might be better busied in plain divinity! Safer prescribing to others, and practising in themselves, positive piety; leaving such mystical minerals to men of more judgment to prepare them.

XVI. MAD, NOT MAD.

I FIND St. Paul in the same chapter confess and deny madness in himself. Acts xxvi. 11: And being exceeding mad against them, I persecuted them even unto strange cities. Ver. 25: When Festus challenged him to be beside himself, I am not mad, most noble Festus. Whilst he was mad indeed, then none did suspect or accuse him to be distracted; but when converted, and in his right mind, then Festus taxeth him of madness.

Munst. Cosmog. There is a country in Africa, wherein all the natives have pendulous lips, hanging down like dog's ears, always raw and sore. Here only such as are handsome are pointed at for monsters in this age, wherein polluted and unclean lips are grown epidemical; if any refrain their tongues from common sins, they alone are gazed at as strange spectacles.

XVII. THE DEEPEST CUT.

I BEHELD a lapidary cutting a diamond with a diamond hammer and anvil, both of the same kind.

Mal. iii. 17. God in Scripture styled his servants his jewels. His diamonds they are; but alas! rude, rough, unpolished, without shape or fashion, as they arise naked out of the bed of the earth, before art hath dressed them. See how God, by rubbing one rough diamond against another, maketh both smooth. Bar- Acts xv. 39. nabas afflicts Paul, and Paul afflicts Barnabas, by their hot falling out; Jerome occasioneth trouble to Rufinus, and Rufinus to Jerome.

In our unnatural war, none I hope so weak and wilful as to deny many good men (though

misled) engaged on both sides. O how have
they scratched, and rased, and pierced, and
bruised, and broken one another! Behold Heav-
en's hand grating one diamond with another;
as for all those who uncharitably deny any
good on that party which they dislike,
such show themselves diamonds indeed in their hardness (cruel
censuring), but none
in any commenda-
ble quality in
their condi-
tions.

Mixt Contemplations
in Better Times.

LET YOUR MODERATION BE KNOWN TO ALL MEN.

THE LORD IS AT HAND.

To

The Truly Honourable and Most Virtuous Lady,

THE LADY MONCK.

MADAM, —

I HAD the happiness, some sixteen years since, to be minister of that parish wherein your Ladyship had your nativity, and this I humbly conceive doth afford me some title to dedicate my weak endeavours to your Honour.

It is notoriously known in our English Chronicles, that there was an ill May-day, Anno Dom. 1517, in the ninth year of King Henry the Eighth, wherein much mischief was done in London, the lives of many lost, and estates of more confounded.

This last good May-day hath made plentiful amends for that evil one, and hath laid a foundation for the happiness of an almost ruined church and state ; which as under God it was effected by the prudence and valour of your noble and most renowned husband, so you are eminently known to have had a finger, yea, a hand, yea, an arm happily instrumental therein. God reward you with honour here, and glory hereafter, which is the desire of millions in the three nations, and amongst them of

Your Honour's most humble Servant,

THOMAS FULLER.

Zion College, May 2, 1660.

16

TO THE COURTEOUS READER.

JUSTLY presume thee too much Christian and gentleman to trample on him who prostrates himself. I confess myself subject to just censure, that I have not severally sorted these contemplations, setting such which are, 1. Of Scripture; 2. Historical; 3. Occasional; 4. Personal; distinctly by themselves, which now are confusedly heaped, or rather huddled, together.

This I confess was caused by my haste, the press hourly craving, with the daughter of the horseleech, Give, give.

However, such a confused medley may pass for the lively emblem of these times, the subject of this our book. And when these times shall be reduced into better order, my book, at the next impression, may be digested into better method. Meantime I remain

Thy Servant in Christ Jesus,

THOMAS FULLER.

MIXT CONTEMPLATIONS ON THESE TIMES.

I. PLAY AN AFTER-GAME.

WE read how at the rebuilding of the walls of Jerusalem, Neh. iii. 12: Next unto him repaired Shallum, the son of Halohesh, he and his daughters. Was it woman's work to handle a trowel? Did it consist with the modesty of that sex to clamber scaffolds?

Surely those females did only repair by the proxy of their purses, in which sense Solomon is said to have built the temple.

Our weaker sex hath been overstrong · in making and widening the breaches in our English Zion, both by their purses and persuasions. To redeem their credit, let them hereafter be as active in building as heretofore they were in breaking down.

Such wives, who not only lie in the bosoms, but lodge in the affections, of loving husbands,

who are empowered with places of command,
joining IMPORTUNITY to their OPPORTUNITY, may
be marvellously instrumental to the happiness
of our nation.

We read of Ahab, 1 Kings xxi. 25, that
none was like him, who sold himself to work
wickedness in the sight of the Lord, whom
Jezebel his wife stirred up. By the same proportion that person will prove peerless in piety,
who hath a godly consort in his bosom, seasonably to incite him, who is so forward in himself
to all honorable actions.

II. MIRACULOUS CURE.

WE read, Luke xiii. 11, of a woman
who had a spirit of infirmity eighteen
years, and was bowed together, and could in
no wise lift up herself. This woman may pass
for the lively emblem of the English nation;
from the year of our Lord 1642 (when our
wars first began) unto this present 1660, are
eighteen years in my arithmetic; all which time
our land hath been bowed together, past possibility of standing upright.

Some will say that the weight of heavy taxes
have caused this crookedness. But alas! this
is the least and lightest of all things I reflect at
in this allusion. It is chiefly the weight of our

sins, Heb. xii. 1, which doth so easily beset us. Our mutual malice and animosities which have caused this incurvation.

A pitiful posture wherein the face is made to touch the feet, and the back is set above the head. God in due time set us right, and keep us right, that the head may be in its proper place. Next the neck of the nobility, then the breast of the gentry, the loins of the merchants and citizens, the thighs of the yeomanry, the legs and feet of artificers and day-laborers. As for the clergy (here by me purposely omitted) what place soever shall be assigned them; if low, God grant patience; if high, give humility unto them.

When thus our land in God's leisure shall be restored to its former rectitude, and set upright again, then I hope she may leave off her steel bodies, which have galled her with wearing them so long, and return again to her peaceable condition.

III. HAND ON MOUTH.

IT is said, Gen. vi. 11, how before the flood the earth was filled with violence. Some will say, with Nicodemus, How can these things be? violence being relative, and requiring a counterpart. Though such tyrants were hammers, others must be patient anvils for them to smite upon. Such persons, purely passive in oppression, were to be pitied, not punished ; to be delivered, not drowned in the flood.

But the answer is easy, seeing we read in the same chapter, ver. 5, that God saw that the imagination of the thoughts of man was only evil continually. God plainly perceived that the sufferers of violence would have been offerers of it, if empowered with might equal to their malice. Their cursedness was as sharp, though their horns were not so long ; and what they lacked in deed and actions, they made up in desires and endeavours. So that in sending a general deluge over all, God was clearly just, and men justly miserable.

Let such Englishmen who have been of the depressed party during our civil wars, enter into a scrutiny and serious search of their own souls, whether or no (if armed with power) they would not have laid as great load on others as themselves underwent. Yea, let them out of a godly jealousy suspect more cruelty in themselves than they can conceive. Then will they find just cause to take the blame and shame on themselves, and give God the glory that he hath not drowned all in a general deluge of destruction.

IV. AT LAST.

A LADY of quality, formerly forward to promote our civil wars, and whose well-intending zeal had sent in all her plate to Guild-hall, was earnestly discoursing with a divine concerning these times, a little before dinner ; her face respecting the cupboard in the room, which was furnished with plenty of pure Venice glasses : " Now," said she, " I plainly perceive, that I and many of my judgment have been abused with the specious pretences of liberty and religion, till in the indiscreet pursuance thereof we are almost fallen into slavery and atheism."

To whom the other, betwixt jest and earnest, replied : " Madam, it is no wonder that now your eyes are opened ; for so long as this cupboard was full of thick and massy plate, you could perceive nothing through them ; but now so many clear and transparent glasses are sub-stituted in their room, all things are become obvious to your intuition."

The possessing of superfluous wealth some-times doth hinder our clear apprehensions of matters ; like a pearl in the eye of the soul, prejudicing the sight thereof ; whilst poverty may prove a good collyrium, or eye-salve unto us, to make a true discovery of those things we knew not before.

17

V. MISTAKEN.

I BEHELD honour as of a mounting and aspiring nature, and therefore I expected, rationally enough as I conceive, to have found it ascending to the clouds.

I looked upon wealth as what was massy, ponderous, and by consequence probable to settle and be firmly fixed on the earth.

But oh! how much is my expectation frustrated and defeated! For David, Psalm vii. 5, maketh mention of honour lying in the dust; and Solomon his son, Prov. xxiii. 5, informeth me, how riches certainly make themselves wings, and flee away as an eagle toward heaven: what I looked for below is towered aloft, and what I expected above is fallen below.

Our age hath afforded plentiful experiments of both: honour was near the dust, when a new nobility of a later stamp were in a fair likelihood to have outshined those of a purer standard. The wealth of the land doth begin (to use the falconer's phrase), to fly to lessen. And if these taxes continue, will soon fly out of sight. So uncertain and unsafe it is for men to bottom their happiness on any earthly perfection.

VI. TRUTH.

I SAW a traveller in a terrible tempest take his seasonable shelter under a fair and thick tree : it afforded him protection for a good time, and secured him from the rain.

But, after that it held up, and was fair round about, he unhappily continued under the tree so long, till the droppings thereof made him soundly wet, and he found more to condemn his weakness than pity his wetting.

A Parliament is known to be the best refuge and sanctuary to shelter us from the tempest of violence and oppression. It is sometimes the sole, and always the surest, remedy in that kind. But alas! the late Parliament lasted so long, that it began to be the grievance of the nation, after that the most and best members thereof were violently excluded.

The remedy turned the malady of the land, and we were in fear to be drowned by the droppings of that tree, if God of his gracious goodness had not put an unexpected period to their power.

VII. AFTER-BORN.

A LADY big with child was condemned to perpetual imprisonment, and in the dun-

geon was delivered of a son, who continued with
her till a boy of some bigness. It happened
that one time he heard his mother (for see
neither of them could, as to discern in so dark a
place) bemoan her condition.

Why, mother, (said the child,) do you complain, seeing you want nothing you can wish,
having clothes, meat, and drink sufficient? Alas!
child, (returned the mother,) I lack liberty, con-
verse with Christians, the light of the sun, and
many things more, which thou, being prison-
born, neither art nor can be sensible of in thy
condition.

The *post-nati*, understand thereby such strip-
lings born in England since the death of monarchy therein, conceive this land, their mother,
to be in a good estate. For one fruitful harvest
followeth another, commodities are sold at reasonable rates, abundance of brave clothes are
worn in the city, though not by such persons
whose birth doth best become, but whose purses
can best bestow them.

But their mother, England, doth justly bemoan
the sad difference betwixt her present and former condition, when she enjoyed full and free
trade without payment of taxes, save so small
they seemed rather an acknowledgment of their
allegiance than a burden to their estate; when
she had the court of a king, the House of Lords,

yea, and the Lord's house, decently kept, constantly frequented, without falsehood in doctrine, or faction in discipline. God of his goodness restore unto us so much of these things as may consist with his glory and our good.

VIII. A HEAP OF PEARLS.

I SAW a servant maid, at the command of her mistress, make, kindle, and blow a fire. Which done, she was posted away about other business, whilst her mistress enjoyed the benefit of the fire. Yet I observed that this servant, whilst industriously employed in the kindling thereof, got a more general, kindly, and continuing heat than her mistress herself. Her heat was only by her, and not in her, staying with her no longer than she stayed by the chimney; whilst the warmth of the maid was inlaid, and equally diffused through the whole body.

An estate suddenly gotten is not so lasting to the owner thereof, as what is duly got by industry. The substance of the diligent, saith Solomon, Prov. xii. 27, is precious. He cannot be counted poor that hath so many pearls, precious brown bread, precious small beer, precious plain clothes, &c. A comfortable consideration in this our age, wherein many hands have learned their lesson of labour, who were neither born nor bred unto it.

IX. SILENT SADNESS.

TWO captains on the same side in our civil wars, discoursing together, one of them (with small cause and without any measure) did intolerably boast of his personal performances, as if he had been of the quorum in all considerable actions ; at last, not ashamed of, but weaned with his own loquacity, he desired the other captain to relate what service he had done in these wars ; to whom he returned, " Other men can tell you of that."

We meet with many, living at the sign of the Royalist, who much brag of their passive services (I mean their sufferings) in the late war. But that spoke in the wheel which creaketh most doth not bear the greatest burden in the cart. The loudest criers are not always the largest losers.

How much hath Sir John Stowel lost ? How many new gentlemen have started up out of the estate of that ancient knight ? What hath the Lord Craven lost ? Whether more, or more unjustly, hard to decide ? Others can tell of their and many other men's sufferings, whilst they themselves hold their peace.

Here we dare not speak of him who, though the greatest loser of all, speaketh nothing of himself ; and therefore his silence putteth a greater obligation on us, both to pity him here on earth, and pray for him to Heaven.

X. LOST AND KEPT.

THIS seeming paradox will, on examination, prove a real truth, viz. that though Job lost his seven thousand sheep consumed by fire of God, Job i. 16, (understand it, by his permission, and Satan's immission,) yet he still kept the wool of many of them.

For Job, in the vindication of his integrity, (not to praise but purge himself,) doth relate, how the loins of the poor blessed him, being warmed with the fleece of his sheep (Job xxxi. 20). So much of his wool (in the cloth made thereof) he secured in a safe hand, lending it to God (in poor people), Prov. xix. 17, as the best of debtors, being most able and willing to repay it.

Such as have been plundered of their estates in these wars may content and comfort themselves with this consideration, that so long as they enjoyed plenty they freely parted with a proportion thereof to the relief of the poor: what they gave, that they have; it still remaineth theirs, and is safely laid up for them in a place where rust and moth do not corrupt, nor thieves break through and steal.

XI. ALL.

THE Magdeburgenses, out of a spirit of opposition to the Papists, over-prizing the person and actions of St. Peter, do, in my mind, on the other side too much decry him, causelessly cavilling at his words to our Saviour (Mark x. 28): *Ecce reliquimus omnia*, Behold, we have left all and followed thee.

What, say they, had he left? He maketh as if he had left great matters, and a mighty estate; whereas this his all was not more than an old ship, some few rotten nets, and suchlike inconsiderable accommodations.

But Bellarmine (always ingenuous, sometimes satirical) payeth them home for their causeless exception against that Apostle: What! saith he, would they have him have left more than he had? All was all, how little soever it was.

Different, I confess, is the standard and measure of men's losses in this time. Some, in preserving of their consciences, have lost manners; others farms, others cottages. Some have had a *hin*, others a *homer*, others an *ephah* of afflictions. However, those men must on all hands be allowed the greatest losers who have lost all (how small soever that their all was), and who, with the widow (Mark xii. 44), have parted with ὅλον τὸν βίον αὐτῶν, all their livelihood.

XII. GOOD ACCOUNTANT.

I WAS present in the West country some twenty-five years since, when a bishop made a partage of money collected by a brief amongst such who in a village had been sufferers by a casual fire; one of whom brought in the inventory of his losses far above all belief.

Being demanded how he could make out his losses to so improbable a proportion, he alleged the burning of a pear-tree growing hard by his house, valuing the same at twenty years' purchase, and the pears at twenty shillings per annum, presuming every one would be a bearing year; and by such windy particulars did blow up his losses to the sum by him nominated.

Some pretend in these wars to have lost more thousands than ever they were possessed of hundreds. These reckon in, not only what they had, but what they might, yea, would have had. They compute not only their possessions, but reversions, yea, their probabilities, possibilities, and impossibilities also, which they might desire, but could never hope to obtain.

The worst is, I might term many of these men anti-Mephibosheths, who, out of his loyalty to David, 2 Sam. xix. 30, Let them take all, said he, forasmuch as my lord the king is come home again in peace unto his own house. But these, except they may have all, and more than all, they ever possessed, care not a whit whether or no the king ever return; so unconcerned are they in his condition.

XIII. NO TITTLE OF TITLE.

TWO young gentlemen were comparing their revenues together, vying which of them were the best. My demesnes, saith the one, is worth two, but mine, saith the other, is worth four hundred pounds a year.

My farms, saith the one, are worth four, but mine, saith the other, are worth eight hundred pounds a year.

My estate, saith the one, is my own, to which the other returned no answer, as conscious to himself that he kept what lawfully belonged to another.

I care not how small my means be, so they be my means: I mean my own without any injury to others. What is truly gotten may be comfortably kept. What is otherwise may be possessed, but not enjoyed.

Upon the question, What is the worst bread which is eaten? One answered, in respect of the coarseness thereof, Bread made of beans.

Another said, Bread made of acorns. But the third hit the truth, who said, Bread taken out of other men's mouths, who are the true proprietaries thereof. Such bread may be sweet in the mouth to taste, but is not wholesome in the stomach to digest.

XIV. FREELY, FREELY.

A GRAVE divine in the West country, (familiarly known unto me,) conceiving himself over-taxed, repaired to one of the governors of the king's garrisons for to move for some mitigation.

The governor perceiving the satin cap of this divine to be torn, Fie, fie, said he, that a man of your quality should wear such a cap; the rats have gnawed it. O no, sir, answered he, the rates have gnawed it.

The print or impression of the teeth of taxes is visible in the clothes of many men, yea, it hath corroded holes in many men's estates. Yea, as Hatto, Archbishop of Mentz, is reported Munster's to have been eaten up by rats, so the vermin Cosmog. in of taxes, if continuing, is likely to devour our German. nation.

However, let us not in the least degree now grudge the payment thereof. Let us now pay taxes that we may never pay taxes; for, as

matters now stand, our freeness at the present
may cause our freedom at the future, if once
the arrears of the army and navy were discharged.

I care not how much I am let blood, so it be
not by the adventure of an empiric, but advice
of a physician, who I am sure will take no more
ounces from me than may consist with my
safety, and need doth require.   Such the piety
and policy of the present Parliament, they will
impose no more payments than the necessity of
the estate doth extort.   The rather because
they are persons (blessed be God) of the primest
quality in the nation, and let us blood through
their own veins, the greatest part of the payments they impose lighting first on their own
estates.

XV. CRY WITHOUT CAUSE, AND BE WHIPT.

I HAVE known the city of London almost
forty years, their shops did ever sing the
same tune, that trading was dead.   Even in the
reign of King James (when they wanted nothing but thankfulness) this was their complaint.

. It is just with God, that they who complained without cause should have just cause to
complain.   Trading, which then was quick, and

in health, hath since been sick, yea, in a swoon, yea, dead, yea, buried. There is a vacation in the shops in the midst of high term; and if shops be in a consumption, ships will not be long in good health.

Yet I know not whether to call this decay of trade in London a mishap or a happy miss. Probably the city, if not pinched with poverty, had never regained her wealth.

XVI. SPRING BEGAN.

I MEET with two etymologies of bonfires. Some deduce it from fires made of bones, relating it to the burning of martyrs, first fashionable in England in the reign of King Henry the Fourth. But others derive the word (more truly in my mind) from boon, that is, good, and fires; whether good be taken here for great, or for merry and cheerful, such fires being always made on welcome occasions.

Such an occasion happened at London last February, 1659. I confess the 11th of March is generally beheld as the first day of the spring, but hereafter London (and in it all England) may date its vernal heat (after a long winter of woes and war) from the 11th of February.

On which day so many boon-fires (the best new lights I ever saw in that city) were made;

although I believe the fagots themselves knew as much as some who laid them on for what purpose those fires were made.

The best is, such fires were rather prophetical than historical, not so much telling as foretelling the condition of that city and our nation, which, by God's gracious goodness, is daily bettered and improved.

But O the excellent boon-fire which the converted Ephesians made, Acts xix. 19: Many also of them which used curious arts brought their books together, and burned them before all men: and they counted the price of them, and found it fifty thousand pieces of silver.

What was a pint of ashes worth, according to that proportion. But oh! in the imitation of the Ephesians, let us Englishmen labor to find out our bosom sin, and burn it (how dear soever unto us) in the flames of holy anger and indignation. Such boon-fires would be most profitable to us, and acceptable to God, inviting him to perfect and complete the good which he had begun to our nation.

XVII. THE HAND IS ALL.

A GENTLEWOMAN some sixty years since came to Winchester school, where she had a son, and where Dr. Love (one emi nent in his profession) was then schoolmaster. This tender mother, seeing the terrible rods (the properties of that school), began with tears to bemoan the condition of her son, subject to so cruel correction. To whom the schoolmaster replied: Mistress, content yourself, it matters not how big the rod be, so it be in the hand of Love to manage it.

Alas! he was only Love in his surname; but what saith the Apostle, 1 John iv. 16: God is love, even in his own essence and nature.

What then, though the wicked be not only a rod in the hand of God, but what is worse, a sword, Psalm xvii. 13, the wicked which is thy sword, they shall do no hurt as long as God hath the ordering of them.

A pregnant experiment hereof we have in (the, call it, *rod* or *sword* of) our late civil war, which lasted so long in our land, yet left so little signs behind it. Such who consider how much was destroyed in the war may justly wonder that any provision was left, whilst such who behold the plenty we have left will more admire that any was ever destroyed.

XVIII. ALL TONGUE AND EARS.

WE read, Acts xvii. 21, All the Athenians, and strangers which were there, spent their time in nothing else but either to tell or to hear some new thing.

How cometh this transposition? tell and hear; it should be hear and tell; they must hear it before they could tell it; and in the very method of nature, those that are deaf are dumb.

But know, it is more than probable that many Athenians told what they never heard, being themselves the first finders, founders, and forgers of false reports, therewith merely to entertain the itching curiosity of others.

England aboundeth with many such Athenians; it is hard to say whether more false coin or false news be minted in our days. One side is not more pleased with their own factions than the other is with their own fictions.

Some pretend to intelligence without understanding, whose relations are their own confutations. I know some who repair to such novelants on purpose to know what news is false by their reporting thereof.

XIX. GIVE AND TAKE.

THE Archbishop of Spalatro, when Dean of Windsor, very affectionately moved the prebendaries thereof to contribute bountifully towards the relieving of a distressed for-

eigner, reporting him a person of much worth
and want; to whom one of the company replied: *Qui suadet sua det*, Let him who per-
suadeth others, give something of his own.
But the Archbishop, who was as covetous as
ambitious, and whose charity had a tongue
without hands, would not part with a penny.

The Episcopal party doth desire and expect
that the Presbyterian should remit of his rigid-
ness in order to an expedient betwixt them.
The Presbyterians require that the Episcopal
side abate of their austerity to advance an
accommodation.

But some on both sides are so wedded to
their wilfulness, stand so stiff in their judgments, are so high and hot in their passions,
they will not part with the least punctilio in
their opinions and practices.

Such men's judgments cannot pretend to the
exactness of the Gibeonites, Judges xx. 16,
that they hit the mark of the truth at a hair's
breadth, and fail not, yet will they not abate a
hair's breadth in order to unity; they will take
all, but tender nothing; make motions with
their mouths, but none with their feet, for
peace, not stirring a step towards it.

O that we could see some proffers and performances of condescension on either side, and
then let others who remain obstinate, and will

18

embrace no peace, be branded with Pharez, Gen. xxxviii. 29, the breach be upon them.

XX. CHARITY, CHARITY.

IN my father's time, there was a fellow of Trinity College, Cambridge, a native of Carlton, in Leicestershire, where the people (through some occult cause) are troubled with a wharling in their throats, so that they cannot plainly pronounce the letter R. This scholar, being conscious of his infirmity, made a Latin oration of the usual expected length, without an R therein ; and yet did he not only select words fit for his mouth, easy for pronunciation, but also as pure and expressive for signification, to show that men might speak without being beholden to the dog's letter.

Camd.
Brit. in
Leicester-
shire.

Our English pulpits, for these last eighteen years, have had in them too much caninal anger, vented by snapping and snarling spirits on both sides. But if you bite and devour one another, (saith the Apostle, Gal. v. 15,) take heed ye be not devoured one of another.

Think not that our sermons must be silent if not satirical, as if divinity did not afford smooth subjects enough to be seasonably insisted on in this juncture of time ; let us try our skill 'whether we cannot preach without any dog letter or biting word: the art is half learned by intending, and wholly by serious endeavouring it.

I am sure that such soft sermons will be more easy for the tongue of the preacher in pronouncing them, less grating to the ears of pious people that hear them, and more edifying to the heart of both speaker and hearers of them.

XXI. BUT ONE FAVOURITE.

WE read how Abraham (Gen. xxv. 5) gave all he had unto Isaac. As for his six sons, Zimran, Jokshan, Medan, Midian, Ishback, and Shuah, which he had by Keturah his concubine, he only gave them gifts, and sent them away into the east country.

England hath but one Isaac, or legitimate religion of the Church, namely, the Protestant, as the doctrine thereof is established in the Thirty-nine Articles. But how many spurious ones she hath (whether six, sixty, or six score) I neither do know nor will inquire, nor will I load my book and trouble the reader with their new, numerous, and hard names.

O may the state be pleased so far to reflect on this Isaac, as to settle the solid inheritance upon him! Let the Protestant religion only be countenanced by the law, be owned and acknowledged for the received religion of the nation.

As for other sects (the sons of Keturah), we grudge not that gifts be bestowed upon them. Let them have a toleration (and that I assure you is a great gift indeed) and be permitted peaceably and privately to enjoy their consciences both in opinions and practices. Such favour may safely (not to say ought justly to) be afforded unto them so long as they continue peaceably in our Israel, and disturb not the estate.

This gift granted unto them, they need not to be sent away into the east or any other country. If they dislike their condition, they will either leave the land, and go over seas of their own accord, or else (which is rather to be desired and hoped for) they will blush themselves out of their former follies, and by degrees cordially reconcile themselves to the Church of England.

XXII. CALMLY, CALMLY.

WE read, (Gen. iii. 8,) that when God solemnly proceeded in the sentencing of our first parents, he was heard walking in the garden in the cool of the day; to teach men, when they go about matters of moment, (wherein not only the present age, but posterity, is also concerned,) to becalm their souls of all passion. But alas! much reformation made (rather under than) by King Charles, was done in the heat of the day, in the dog-days of our civil discords, and midsummer moon of our military distractions. So that possibly, when that which was done in the heat of the day shall be reviewed, even by the self-same persons, in the cool of the day, they will perceive something by them so reformed, now to need a new reformation.

But this motion (and all that follow) I humbly lay down at their feet who have power and place to reform, who may either trample upon it or take it up, as their wisdoms shall see just occasion.

XXIII. TRY AND TRUST.

IT was wisely requested by the children of the captivity, Dan. i., and warily granted by the king's chamberlain unto them, that, by way of trial, they should feed on pulse for ten days, and then an inspection to be made on their countenances, whether the lilies therein did look as white and roses as red as before, that so their bill of fare might be either changed or continued as they saw just occasion.

Let such new practices as are to be brought into our Church be for a time candidates and probationers on their good behaviour, to see how the temper of the people will fit them, and they fadge with it, before they be publicly enjoined.

Let them be like St. Paul's deacons, 1 Tim. iii. 10, first be proved, then be used if found blameless. I cannot, therefore, but commend the discretion of such statesmen, who, knowing the Directory to be but a stranger, and considering the great inclination the generality of our nation had to the Common Prayer, made their temporary act to stand in force but for three years.

XXIV. ALIKE, BUT CONTRARY.

I OBSERVE in Scripture, that power to do some deeds is a sufficient authority to do them. Thus Samson's power to pluck down the two fundamental pillars of the Dagon's temple, was authority enough for him to do it.

Elijah's power to make fire to come at his call on the two captains was authority enough to do it, because such deeds were above the strength, stature, and standard of human proportion.

However, hence it doth not follow that it is lawful for a private man with axes and hammers to beat down a Christian church, because Samson plucked down Dagon's temple; nor doth it follow that men may burn their brethren with fagot and fire, because Elijah called for fire from heaven; these being acts not miraculous but mischievous, and no might from heaven, but mere malice from hell, required for the achieving thereof.

Here it is hard to say which of these two things have done most mischief in England; public persons having private souls and narrow hearts consulting their own ease and advantage, or private persons having vast designs to invade public employments. This is most sure, that betwixt them both they have almost undone the most flourishing church and state in the Christian world.

XXV. CHASMA, PHASMA.

HOW bluntly and abruptly doth the seventy-third Psalm begin! Truly God is good to Israel, even to such as are of a clean heart.

Truly is a term of continuation, not inception of a speech. The head or top of this psalm seems lost or cut off, and the neck only remaining in the room thereof.

But know that this psalm hath two moieties; one unwritten, made only in the trying-house of David's heart: the other written, visible on the theatre, beginning as is aforesaid.

Thomas Aquinas, sitting silent in a musing posture, at the table of the king of France, at last brake forth in these words: *Conclusum est contra Manichæos*, It is concluded against the

Manichæans ; which speech, though nonsense to the persons in the place, at the best independent, without any connection to the discourse at table, had its necessary coherence in the mind of that great schoolman.

David, newly awaking in this psalm out of the sweet slumber of his meditation, openeth his eyes with the good handsel of these words : Truly God is good to Israel, even to such as are of a clean heart.   A maxim of undoubted truth, and a firm anchor to those who have been tossed in the tempest of these times.

XXVI.   SHARE AND SHARE-LIKE.

CHESHIRE hath formerly been called chief of men.   Indeed, no county in England of the same greatness, or (if you will rather) of the same littleness, can produce so many families of ancient gentry.

Now let it break the stomachs, but not the hearts, abate the pride, not destroy the courage, of the inhabitants of this shire, that they miscarried in their late undertakings, not so much by any defect in them as default in others.

If ten men together be to lift a log, all must jointly συναντιλαμβάνειν, that is, heave up their parts (or rather their counterparts) together.

But if nine of them fail, it is not only uncivil, but unjust that one man should be expected to be a giant to do ten men's work.

Cheshire is Cheshire (and so I hope will ever be), but it is not all England ; and valour itself may be pressed down to death under the weight of multitude.

The Lord Bacon would have rewards given to those men who, in the quest of natural exper-iments, make probable mistakes, both because they are industrious therein, and because their aberrations may prove instructions to others after them ; and to speak plainly, an ingenious miss is of more credit than a bungling casual hit. *In his Advancement of Learning.*

On the same account let Cheshire have a reward of honour, the whole kingdom faring the better for this county's faring the worse.

XXVII. NATALE SOLUM DULCEDINE, ETC.

I MUST confess myself born in Northamptonshire, and if that worthy county esteem me no disgrace to it, I esteem it an honour to me. The English of the common people therein (lying in the very heart of the land) is generally very good.

And yet they have an odd phrase not so usual in other places.

They used to say, when at cudgel plays (such

tame were far better than our wild battles) one gave his adversary such a sound blow as that he knew not whether to stand or to fall, that he settled him at a blow.

The relics and stump (my pen dares write no worse) of the Long Parliament pretended they would settle the church and state ; but surely had they continued, it had been done in the dialect of Northamptonshire ; they would so have settled us, we should neither have known how to have stood, or on which side to have fallen.

XXVIII. SEASONABLE PREVENTION.

WHEN the famine in Egypt had lasted so long, the estates of the people were so exhausted by buying corn of the king, that, their money failing, they were forced to sell their cattle unto Joseph, Gen. xlvii. 17 ; and this maintained them with bread for one year more.

But the famine lasting longer, and their stock of cattle being wholly spent, they then sold all their lands, and after that their persons, to Joseph, as agent for Pharaoh, so that the king of Egypt became proprietary of the bodies of all the people in his land, Gen. xlvii. 23 : Then Joseph said unto the people, Behold, I have bought you this day, and your land, for Pharaoh.

If our taxes had continued longer, they could not have continued longer. I mean, the nation was so impoverished, that the money (so much was hoarded up, or transported by military grandees) could not have been paid in specie.

Indeed, we began the war with brazen trumpets and silver money, and then came unto silver trumpets and brazen money, especially in our Parliament half-crowns.

We must afterwards have sold our stocks of cattle, and then our lands, to have been able to perform payments. This done, it is too, too suspicious; they would have seized on our persons too, and have envassalled us forever unto them.

But, blessed be God, they are stricken upon the cheek-bone, Psalm iii. 7, whereby their teeth are knocked out. Our fathers were not more indebted to God's goodness for delivering them from the Spanish Armada, than we are from our own English army.

XXIX. WOLF IN A LAMB'S SKIN.

BUT where is the Papist all this while? One may make hue and cry after him. He can as soon not be, as not be active. Alas! with the maid in the Gospel, he is not dead, but sleepeth; or rather, he sleepeth not, but only shutteth his eyes in dog-sleep, and doth awake when he seeth his advantage, and snappeth up many a lamb out of our flocks.

Where is the Papist? do any say? Yea, where is he not? They multiply as maggots in May, and act in and under the fanatics. What is faced with faction is lined with Popery; Faux's dark lantern, by a strange inversion, is under our new lights.

Quakers of themselves are a company of dull, blunt, silly souls. But they go down to the Romish Philistines, and from them they whet all the edge-tools of their arguments: a formal syllogism in the mouth of an Anabaptist is plain . jesuitical equivocation.

Meantime we Protestant ministers fish all night and catch nothing; yea, lose many, who in these times fall from our Church as leaves in autumn. God in his due time send us a seasonable spring, that we may repair our losses again.

XXX. VARIOUS FANCIES.

I KNOW not what Fifth-Monarchy men would have, and wish that they knew themselves.

I dare not flatly condemn them, lest I come within the Apostle's reproof, 2 Peter ii. 12: Speaking evil of things they understand not.

If by Christ's reigning they only intend his powerful and effectual ruling by his grace in the hearts of his servants; we all will, not turn, but continue, Fifth-Monarchy men, having always been of this judgment since we were of any judgment; had we as many arms as fingers, we would use them all herein to embrace their persons and opinions.

But some go farther, to expect an actual and personal reign of Christ on earth a thousand years, though not agreeing.

For herein since some make him but about to set forth, others to be well onwards of his way, others to be alighting in the court, others to stand before the door, others that he is entering the palace, according to the slowness or swiftness of their several fancies herein.

However, if this be but a bare speculation, and advanceth not any farther, let them peaceably enjoy it. But if it hath a dangerous influence on men's practices to unhinge their allegiance, and if the pretence to wait for Christ in his person be an intent to slight him in his proxy (the magistrate), we do condemn their opinion as false, and detest it as damnable, leaving their persons to be ordered by the wisdoms of those in authority.

XXXI. MADE LOYAL.

WHEN King Edward the First marched into Scotland, the men of the bishopric of Durham refused to follow his standard, pleading for themselves, that they were holy-work folk, only to wait on the shrine of St. Cuthbert, and not to go out of their own country. But that wise and valiant prince cancelled their pretended privileges.

He levelled them with the rest of his subjects for civil and military as well as holy-work folk, and made them to march with his army against his enemies.

If Fifth-Monarchy (alias first-anarchy) men challenge to themselves, that (by virtue of their opinion they hold) they must be exempted from their obedience to the government, because they, forsooth, (as the lifeguard to his person,) must attend the coming of Christ to reign on earth: such is the wisdom of the state, it will make them know they must share in subjection with the rest of our nation.

But charity doth command me to believe that, in stating their opinions, Fifth-Monarchy men's expressions are more offensive than their intentions, mouths worse than their minds, whose brains want strength to manage their own wild notions: and God grant their arms

may never have power to produce them into
action.

XXXII. ATTEND, ATTEND.

SOME of those whom they call Quakers
are, to give them their due, very good
moral men, and exactly just in their civil trans-
actions. In proof whereof let me mention this
passage, though chiefly I confess for the application thereof, which having done me (I praise
God) some good, I am confident will do no
hurt to any other.

A gentleman had two tenants, whereof one,
being a Quaker, repaired to his landlord on the
quarter-day: Here, thou, said he, tell out and
take thy rent, without stirring his cap, or show-
ing the least sign of respect.

The other came cringing and congéing: If it
please your worship, said he, the times are very
hard, and trading is dead, I have brought to
your worship five pounds (the whole due being
twenty) and shall procure the rest for your
worship with all possible speed.

Both these tenants put together would make
a perfect one, the rent-completing of the one,
and tongue-compliments of the other. But
seeing they were divided, I am persuaded that
of the two the landlord was less offended with

the former, imputing his ill manners to his folly, but ascribing his good dealing to his honesty.

God expecteth and requireth both good works and good words. We cannot make our addresses and applications unto him in our prayers with too much awe and reverence.

However, such who court God with luscious language, give him all his attributes, and (as King James said of a divine, who shall be nameless) compliment with God in the pulpit, will be no whit acceptable unto him, if they do not also endeavour to keep his commandments.

It is the due paying of God's quit-rents which he expecteth; I mean, the realizing of our gratitude unto him for his many mercies, in leading the remainder of our lives according to his will and his word.

XXXIII. NO REMEDY BUT PATIENCE.

ONCE a gaoler demanded of a prisoner newly committed unto him, whether or no he were a Roman Catholic. No, answered he. What then, said he, are you an Anabaptist? Neither, replied the prisoner. What, said the other, are you a Brownist, or a Quaker? Nor so, said the man, I am a Protestant, without wealth or gard, or any addition, equally opposite to all heretics and sectaries. Then, said the gaoler, get you unto the dungeon; I will afford no favour to you, who shall get no advantage by you. Had you been of any of the other religions, some hope I had to gain by the visits of such as are of your own persuasion, whereas now you will prove to me but an unprofitable prisoner.

This is the misery of moderation; I recall my word (seeing misery properly must have sin in it). This is an affliction attending moderate men, that they have not an active party to side with them and favour them.

Men of great stature will quickly be made porters to a king, and those diminutively little, dwarfs to a queen, whilst such who are of a middle height may get themselves masters where they can. The moderate man, eminent for no excess or extravagancy in his judgment, will have few patrons to protect, or persons to adhere unto him. But what saith St. Paul, 1 Cor. xv. 19: If in this life only we have hope in Christ, we are of all men the most miserable.

XXXIV. POTTAGE FOR MILK.

IN these licentious times, wherein religion lay in a swoon, and many pretended ministers (minions of the times) committed or omitted in

19

divine service what they pleased; some, not only in Wales, but in England, and in London itself, on the Lord's day (sometimes with, sometimes without a psalm) presently popped up into the pulpit, before any portion of Scripture, either in the Old or New Testament, was read to the people.

Hereupon one in jest-earnest said, that formerly they put down bishops and deans, and now they had put down chapters too. It is high time that this fault be reformed for the future, that God's word, which is all gold, be not justled out to make room for men's sermons, which are but parcel-gilt at the best.

XXXV. MODERATE MAY MEET.

WHEN St. Paul was at Athens, Acts xvii. 18, then certain philosophers of the Epicureans and of the Stoics encountered him, &c. ·

Some will say, Why was there no mention here of the Peripatetics and Academics, both notable sects of philosophers, and then numerous in the city of Athens?

The answer is this: These being persons acted with more moderate principles, were contented to be silent, though not concurring in their judgments; whilst the Epicureans and

Stoics were violent in the extremes, the first for the anarchy of Fortune, the other for the tyranny of Fate.

Peace in our land, like St. Paul, is now likely to be encountered with two opposite parties, such as are for the liberty of a commonwealth, and such as are for an absolute monarchy in the full height thereof; but I hope neither of both are so considerable in their number, parts, and influence on the people, but that the moderate party, advocates for peace, will prevail for the settling thereof.

XXXVI. WHAT, NEVER WISE!

IN the year of our Lord 1606, there happened a sad overflowing of the Severn Sea, on both sides thereof, which some still alive do (one I hope thankfully) remember.

An account hereof was written to John Stow, the industrious chronicler, from Dr. Still, then Bishop of Bath and Wells, and three other gentlemen of credit, to insert it in his story; one passage wherein I cannot omit: —

Stow's Chronicle, p. 889. " Among other things of note, it happened that, upon the tops of some hills, divers beasts of contrary nature had got up for their safety, as dogs, cats, foxes, hares, conies, moles, mice, and rats, who remained together very peaceably, without any manner or sign of fear of violence one towards another."

How much of man was there then in brute creatures? How much of brutishness is there now in men? Is this a time for those who are sinking for the same cause to quarrel and fall out? I dare add no more but the words of the Apostle, 2 Tim. ii. 7: Consider what I say; and the Lord give you understanding in all things.

XXXVII. RECEDE A TITTLE.

I SAW two ride a race for a silver cup; he who won it outran the post many paces: indeed, he could not stop his horse in his full career, and therefore was fain to run beyond the post, or else he had never come soon enough unto it.

But presently after when he had won the wager, he reined his horse back again, and softly returned to the post, where from the judges of the match he received the cup, the reward of his victory.

Surely many moderate men designed a good mark to themselves, and propounded pious ends and aims in their intentions. But query whether, in pursuance thereof, in our late civil destruction, they were not violented to outrun the mark, (so impossible it is to stop a soul in the full speed thereof,) and whether they did not in some things overdo and exceed what they intended.

If so, it is neither sin nor shame, but honourable and profitable, for such persons (sensible of their over-activity) even fairly to go back to the post which they have outrun, and now calmly to demonstrate to the whole world that this only is the true and full measure of their judgments, whilst the rest was but the superfluity of their passions.

XXXVIII. BEAT THYSELF.

I SAW a mother threatening to beat her little child for not rightly pronouncing that petition in the Lord's prayer : And forgive us our trespasses, as we forgive them that trespass against us. The child essayed and offered as well as it could to utter it, adventuring at te-passes, trepasses, but could not pronounce the word aright. Alas ! it is a shibboleth to a child's tongue, wherein there is a confluence of hard consonants together ; and therefore if the mother had beaten defect in the infant for default, she deserved to have been beaten herself.

The rather because what the child could not pronounce the parents do not practise. O how lispingly and imperfectly do we perform the close of this petition: As we forgive them that trespass against us.   It is well if with the child we endeavour our best, though falling short in the exact observance thereof.

XXXIX. WITHOUT BLOOD.

IT passeth for a general report of what was customary in former times, that the sheriff of the county used to present the judge with a pair of white gloves at those which we call maiden assizes, viz. when no malefactor is put to death therein ; a great rarity (though usual in small) in large and populous countries.

England, a spacious country, is full of numerous factions in these distracted times.   It is above belief, and will hardly find credit with posterity, that a general peace can be settled in our nation without effusion of blood.

But if we should be blessed with a dry peace, without one drop of blood therein, O let the white gloves of honour and glory be in the first place presented to the God of heaven, the principal giver ; and a second white pair of gratitude be given to our general, the instrumental procurer thereof.

XL. AGAINST THE HAIR AND THE FLESH.

ALL devils are not equally easy to be ejected out of possessed people ; some are of a more sullen, sturdy, stubborn nature, good (or rather bad) at holdfast, and hard to be cast out.

In like manner all bosom sins are not conquered with facility alike, and these three are of the greatest difficulty : —

1. Constitutionary sins, riveted in our tempers and complexions.

2. Customary sins, habited in us by practice and presumption.

3. Such sins to the repentance whereof restitution is required.

Oh! when a man hath not only devoured widows' houses, Matt. xxiii. 14, but also they have passed the first and second concoction in his stomach ; yea, when they are become blood in the veins, yea, sinews in the flesh of his estate, O then to refund, to mangle and disinter one's demesnes, this goeth shrewdly against flesh and blood indeed ! But what saith the Apostle, Flesh and blood shall not inherit the kingdom of God.

Yet even this devil may be cast out with fasting and prayer, Matt. xvii. 21. This sin, notwithstanding it holdeth violent possession, may by those good means, and God's blessing thereon, have a firm ejection.

XLI. A FREE–WILL OFFERING.

WHEN Job began to set up the second time, he built his recruited estate upon three bottoms : —

1. God's blessing.
2. His own industry.
3. His friends' charity.

Job xlii. 11 : Every man also gave him a piece of money, and every one also an ear-ring of gold. Many drops meeting together filled the vessel.

When our patient Job, plundered of all he had, shall return again, certainly his loyal subjects will offer presents unto him (though they, alas ! who love him best can give him least). Surely all is not given away in making the golden calf, but that there is some left for the business of the tabernacle.

But surely those have cause to be most bountiful, who may truly say to him what David said humbly to the God of heaven, 1 Chron. xxix. 14 : Of thine own have I given unto thee.

XLII. A GOOD ANCHOR.

ISAAC, ignorantly going along to be offered, propounded to his father a very hard question, Gen. xxii. 7: Behold the fire and wood, but where is the lamb for a burnt-offering?

Abraham returned, God will provide himself a lamb for a burnt-offering.

But was not this *gratis dictum* of Abraham? Did not he herein speak without book? Where and when did God give him a promise to provide him a lamb?

Indeed, he had no particular promise as to this present point, but he had a general one, Gen. xv. 1: Fear not, Abraham, I am thy shield, and thy exceeding great reward. Here was not only a lamb, but a flock of sheep, yea, a herd of all cattle promised unto him.

It hath kept many an honest soul in these sad times from sinking into despair, that though they had no express in Scripture that they should be freed from the particular miseries relating to this war, yet they had God's grand charter for it, Rom. viii. 28: And we know that all things work together for good to them that love God, to them who are the called according to his purpose.

XLIII. EYES BAD, NOT OBJECT.

I LOOKED upon the wrong or back side of a piece of arras: it seemed to me as a continued nonsense, there was neither head nor foot therein; confusion itself had as much method in it: a company of thrums and threads, with many pieces and patches of several sorts, sizes, and colours, all which signified nothing to my understanding.

But then looking on the reverse or right side thereof, all put together did spell excellent proportions and figures of men and cities. So that indeed it was a history, not wrote with a pen, but wrought with a needle.

If men look upon our late times with a mere eye of reason, they will hardly find any sense therein, such their huddle and disorder. But, alas! the wrong side is objected to our eyes, whilst the right side is presented to the high God of heaven, who knoweth that an admirable order doth result out of this confusion, and what is presented to him at present may hereafter be so showed to us as to convince our judgments in the truth thereof.

XLIV. EVER, NEVER.

WE read, Psalm lv. 19: Because they have no changes, therefore they [the wicked] fear not God.

Profaneness is a strange logician, which can collect and infer the same conclusion from contrary premises. Libertines here in England, because they have had so many changes, therefore they fear not God.

Jacob taxed Laban, Gen. xxxi. 41: Thou hast changed my wages ten times. I have neither list nor leisure to inquire how far our alterations of government, within these few years, fall short of that number.

But it is a sad truth, that as King Mithridates is said to have fed on poison so long, that at last it became ordinary food to his body; so the multitude of changes have proved no change in many men's apprehensions, being so common and ordinary it hath made no effectual impression on their spirits. Yea, which is worse, they (as if all things came by casualty) fear God the less for these alterations.

XLV. HEAR ME OUT.

I MUST confess myself to be (what I ever was) for a commonwealth: but give me leave to state the meaning of the word, seeing so much mischief hath taken covert under the homonymy thereof.

A commonwealth and a king are no more contrary than the trunk or body of a tree and the top branch thereof; there is a republic included in every monarchy.

The Apostle speaketh of some Ephesians, in the ii. and 12, aliens from the commonwealth of Israel: that the commonwealth is neither aristocratical nor democratical, but hath one sole and single person, Jesus Christ, the supreme head thereof.

May I live (if it may stand with God's good will and pleasure) to see England a commonwealth in such a posture, and it will be a joyful object to all who are peaceable in our nation.

XLVI. MONS MOBILIS.

I OBSERVE that the mountains now extant do fall under a double consideration.

Those by creation, and those by inundation.

The former were of God's making, primitive mountains; when at the first his wisdom did here sink a vale, there swell a hill, so to render the prospect of the earth the more grateful by the alternate variety thereof.

The second by inundation were such as owe

their birth and being to Noah's flood : when the water lying long in a place, (especially when driven on with the fury of the wind,) corroded a hollow, and so by consequence cast up a hill on both sides.

For such mountains of God's making, who either by their birth succeed to estates, or have acquired them by God's blessing on their lawful industry, good success may they have with their wealth and honour. And yet let not them be too proud, and think, with David, that God hath made their mountain so strong it cannot be moved ; but know themselves subject to the earthquakes of mutability as well as others.

As for the many mountains of our age, grandized by the unlawful ruin of others, swoln to a tympany by the consumption of their betters ; I wish them just as much joy with their greatness as they have right unto it.

XLVII. NOT INVISIBLE.

A WAGGISH scholar (to say no worse), standing behind the back of his tutor, conceived himself secured from his sight, and on this confidence he presumed to make antic mocks and mouths at him. Meantime his tutor had a looking-glass (unknown to the scholar) before his face, wherein he saw all which his pupil did, and the pupil soon after felt something from his tutor.

Many things have been done in huggermugger in our age, profane persons conceited that their privacy protected them from Divine inspection. Some say with the wicked in the psalm, Tush, shall the Lord see?

But know that, Rev. iv. 6, before the throne there was a sea of glass, like unto crystal. This is God's omnisciency. Sea, there is the largeness; crystal, there is the pureness thereof. In this glass all persons and practices are plainly represented to God's sight, so that such who sin in secret shall suffer openly.

XLVIII. BEST RACE.

GOD hath two grand attributes, first, *optimus*, that he is the best of beings. Secondly, *maximus*, that he is the greatest of essences. It may justly seem strange that all men naturally are ambitious, with the Apostles, Luke xxii. 24, to contest and contend for the latter, who shall be accounted for the greatest. Outward greatness having no reality in itself, but founded merely in outward account and reputation of others.

But as for his goodness, they give it a goby, no whit endeavouring the imitation thereof;

whereas, indeed, greatness without goodness is not only useless, but also dangerous and destructive, both to him that hath it and those who are about him.

This is a fruit of Adam's fall, and floweth from original corruption. Oh! for the future let us change this our ambition into holy emulation, and fairly run a race of grace, who shall outstrip others in goodness.

In which race strive lawfully to gain the victory, supplant not those that run before thee, justle not those who are even with thee, hinder not those who come behind thee.

XLIX. FEED THE LAMBS.

WHAT may be the cause why so much cloth so soon changeth colour? It is because it was never wet wadded, which giveth the fixation to a colour, and setteth it in the cloth.

What may be the reason why so many now-a-days are carried about with every wind of doctrine, even to scour every point in the compass round about? Surely it is because they were never well catechised in the principles of religion.

O for the ancient and primitive ordinance of catechising! every youth can preach, but he must be a man indeed who can profitably catechise.

Indeed, sermons are like whole joints for men to manage, but catechising is mincemeat, shred into questions and answers, (fit for children to eat, and easy for them to digest,) whilst the minister may also, for the edification of those of riper years, enlarge and dilate himself on both as he seeth just occasion.

L. NAME AND THING.

THERE is a new word coined, within few months, called fanatics, which, by the close stickling thereof, seemeth well cut out and proportioned to signify what is meant thereby, even the sectaries of our age.

פנה vidit. Some (most forcedly) will have it Hebrew, derived from the word to see or face one, importing such whose piety consisteth chiefly in visage, looks, and outward shows; others will have it Greek, from φάνομαι, to show and appear; their meteor piety consisting only in short blazing, the forerunner of their extinction. But most certainly the word is Latin, from *fanum*, a temple; and *fanatici* were such who, living in or attending thereabouts, were frighted with *spectra*, or apparitions, which they either saw or fancied themselves to have seen. These people, in their fits and wild raptures, pretended to strange predictions:

> "Ut fanaticus œstro
> Percussus, Bellona tuo, divinat et ingens
> Omen habes, inquit, magni clarique triumphi."
> Juv. Sat. 4.

> "Ut mala quem scabies et morbus regius urget,
> Aut fanaticus error."
> Hor. in Poet.

It will be said we have already (more than a good) many nicknames of parties, which doth but inflame the difference, and make the breach the wider betwixt us. It is confessed; but withal it is promised, that when they withdraw the thing we will subtract the name.

Let them leave off their wild fancies,
inconsistent with Scripture, antiqui-
ty, and reason itself, and then
we will endeavour to bury
the fanatic, and all
other names, in
perpetual ob-
livion.

20

MIXT CONTEMPLATIONS ON THESE TIMES.

I. ALL AFORE.

DEAR friend of mine (now I hope with God) was much troubled with an impertinent and importunate fellow, desirous to tell him his fortune. For things to come, said my friend, I desire not to know them, but am contented to attend Divine Providence ; tell me, if you can, some remarkable passages of my life past. But the cunning man was nothing for the preter tense (where. his falsehood might be discovered), but all for the future, counting himself therein without the reach of confutation.

There are in our age a generation of people, who are the best of prophets and worst of historians ; Daniel and the Revelation are as easy to them as the ten commandments and the Lord's prayer : they pretend exactly to know the time of Christ's actual reign on earth, of the ruin of the Romish Antichrist, yea, of the day of judgment itself.

But these oracles are struck quite dumb, if demanded anything concerning the time past; about the coming of the children of Israel out of Egypt and Babylon, the original increase and ruin of the four monarchies; of these and the like they can give no more account than the child in the cradle. They are all for things to come, but have gotten (through a great cold of ignorance) such a crick in their neck, they cannot look backward on what was behind them.

II. TRUE TEXT. FALSE GLOSS.

A HUSBANDMAN, anabaptistically inclined, in a pleasant humour came to his minister, and told him, with much cheerfulness, that this very seeds-time the words of the Apostle, 1 Cor. ix. 10, were fulfilled : That he that plougheth may plough in hope.

Being desired farther to explain himself; I mean, said he, we husbandmen now plough in hope that at harvest we shall never pay tithes, but be eased from that Antichristian yoke for the time to come. It seemeth he had received such intelligence from some of his own party, who reported what they desired.

He might plough in hope to reach his nine parts, but in despair to have the tenth ; especially since God hath blessed us with so wise a Parliament, consisting not only of men chosen, but of persons truly the choice of the nation, who will be as, if not more, tender of the Church's right than their own interest. They have read how Pharaoh, king of Egypt, Gen. xlvii. 22, would in no case alienate the lands of the priests. The very Gypsies, who generally have no good name, (condemned for crafty cheaters and cozeners,) were conscientiously precise in this particular, and they would not take away what.was given to their God in his ministers.

III. FOUL MOUTH STOPT.

A MBITIOUS Absalom endeavoured to bring a scandal on his father's government, complaining, the petitioners who repaired to his court for justice were slighted and neglected. 2 Sam. xv. 3: See, thy matters are good and right, but there is no man deputed of the king to hear thee.

But we know the English proverb, Ill-will never speaketh well. Let us do that justice to David, yea, to our own judgments, not to believe a graceless son and subject, against a gracious father and sovereign.

Some malecontents (Ishmaels, whose swords are against every one) seek to bring a false report on the Parliament, as if the clergy must expect no favour, not to say justice, from them, because there are none in the house elected and deputed either to speak for them or hear them speak for themselves.

Time was, say they, when the clergy was represented in the House of Lords by two arch-bishops and four-and-twenty bishops. Time was, when the clergy had their own convocation, granting subsidies for them, so that their purses were only opened by the hands of their own proxies ; but now, though our matters be good and right, there is no man deputed to hear us.

I am, and ever will be, deaf to such false and scandalous suggestions ; if there be four hundred and odd (because variously reckoned up) in the House of Parliament, I am confident we clergy-men have four hundred and odd advocates for us therein. What civil Christian would not plead for a dumb man? Seeing the clergy hath lately lost their voice they so long had in Parliaments ; honour and honesty will engage those pious persons therein to plead for our just concern-ments.

21

IV. ATOMS AT LAST.

I MEET not, either in sacred or profane writ, with so terrible a rout as Saul gave unto the host of the Ammonites, under Nahash their king, 1 Sam. xi. 11 : And it came to pass, that they which remained were scattered, so that two of them were not left together. And yet we have daily experience of greater scatterings and dissipations of men in their opinions.

Suppose ten men, out of pretended purity, but real pride and peevishness, make a wilful separation from the Church of England, possibly they may continue some competent time in tolerable unity together.

Afterwards, upon a new discovery of a higher and holier way of divine service, these ten will split asunder into five and five, and the purer moiety divide from the other, as more drossy and feculent.

Then the five in process of time, upon the like occasion of clearer illumination, will cleave themselves into three and two.

Some short time after, the three will crumble into two and one, and the two part into one and one, till they come into the condition of the Ammonites, so scattered that two of them were not left together.

I am sad, that I may add with too much

truth, that one man will at last be divided in himself, distracted often in his judgment betwixt many opinions; that, what is reported of Tostatus, lying on his death-bed, *in multitudine controversiarum non habuit, quod crederet;* amongst the multitude of persuasions through which he had passed, he knoweth not where to cast anchor and fix himself at the last.

V. AN ILL MATCH.

DIVINE Providence is remarkable in ordering, that a fog and a tempest never did, nor can, meet together in nature. For as soon as a fog is fixed, the tempest is allayed; and as soon as a tempest doth arise, the fog is dispersed. This is a great mercy; for otherwise such small vessels as boats and barges, which want the conduct of the card and compass, would irrecoverably be lost.

How sad, then, is the condition of many sectaries in our age; which in the same instant have a fog of ignorance in their judgments, and a tempest of violence in their affections, being too blind to go right, and yet too active to stand still.

VI. DOWN, YET UP.

HYPOCRITE, in the native etymology of the word, as it is used by ancient Greek authors, signifieth such a one, *qui alienæ personæ in comœdia aut tragœdia est effector et repræsentator*, who in comedy or tragedy doth feign and represent the person of another; in plain English, hypocrite is neither more nor less than a stage-player.

We all know that stage-players some years since were put down by public authority; and though something may be said for them, more may be brought against them, who are rather in an employment than a vocation.

But let me safely utter my too just fears; I suspect the fire was quenched in the chimney, and in another respect scattered about the house. Never more strange stage-players than now, who wear the vizards of piety and holiness, that under that covert they may more securely commit sacrilege, oppression, and what not.

In the days of Queen Elizabeth, a person of honour or worship would as patiently have digested the lie as to have been told that they did wear false pendants, or any counterfeit pearl or jewels about them, so usual in our age; yet would it were the worst piece of hypocrisy in fashion. O, let us all labour for integrity of heart, and either appear what we are, or be what we appear!

VII. CALEB, ALL HEART.

I WAS lately satisfied in what I heard of before, by the confession of an excellent artist, (the most skilful in any kind are most willing to acknowledge their ignorance,) that the mystery of annealing of glass, that is, baking it so that the colour may go clean through it, is now by some casualty quite lost in England, if not in Europe.

Break a piece of red glass, painted some four hundred years since, and it will be found as red in the middle as in the outsides; the colour is not only on it, but in it and through it.

Whereas, now all art can perform is only to fix the red on one side of the glass, and that ofttime so faint and fading, that within few years it falleth off, and looketh piebald to the eye.

I suspect a more important mystery is much lost in our age, viz. the transmitting of piety clean through the heart, that a man become inside and outside alike. O the sincerity of the ancient patriarchs, inspired prophets, holy apostles, patient martyrs, and pious fathers of the primitive Church, whereas only outside sanctity is too usual in our age. Happy the man on whose monument that character of Asa (1 Kings xv. 14) may be truly inscribed for his epitaph: Here lieth the man whose heart was perfect with the Lord all his days. Heart perfect, O the finest of wares! All his days, O the largest of measures!

VIII. FIE, FOR SHAME.

CONSIDERING with myself the causes of the growth and increase of impiety and profaneness in our land, amongst others this seemeth to me not the least, viz. the late many false and erroneous impressions of the Bible. Now know, what is but carelessness in other books is impiety in setting forth of the Bible.

As Noah in all unclean creatures preserved but two of a kind, so among some hundreds in several editions we will insist only on two instances.

In the Bible printed at London, 1653, we read, 1 Cor. vi. 9: Know ye not that the unrighteous shall inherit the kingdom of God? for *not* inherit.

Now, when a reverend doctor in divinity did mildly reprove some libertines for their licentious life, they did produce this text, from the authority of this corrupt edition, in justification of their vicious and inordinate conversations.

The next instance shall be in the Bible printed at London in quarto (forbearing the name of the printer, because not done wilfully by him) in the singing Psalms, Ps. lxvii. 2:

> That all the earth may know
> The way to *worldly* wealth,

for *godly* wealth.

It is too probable that too many have perused and practised this erroneous impression, namely, such who by plundering, oppression, cozening, force, and fraud, have in our age suddenly advanced vast estates.

IX. LITTLE LOUD LIARS.

I REMEMBER one in the University gave for his question, *Artis compendium artis dispendium,* The contracting of arts is the corrupting of them. Sure I am, the truth hereof appeareth too plainly in the pearl Bible printed at London, 1653, in the volume of twenty-four; for therein all the dedications and titles of David's Psalms are wholly left out, being part of the original text in Hebrew, and intimating the cause and the occasion of the writing and composing those Psalms, whereby the matter may be better illustrated.

The design may be good to reduce the Bible to so small a volume, partly to make it the more portable in men's pockets, partly to bring down the price of them, that the poor people may the better compass them.   But know that *vilis*, in the Latin tongue, in the first sense signifieth what is cheap, in the second sense what is base. The small price of the Bible hath caused the small prizing of the Bible, especially since so many damnable and pernicious mistakes have escaped therein.

I cannot omit another edition in a large 12mo. making the Book of Truth to begin with a loud lie, pretending this title:

Imprinted at London by Robert Barker, etc., Anno 1638.

whereas, indeed, they were imported from Holland, 1656, and that contrary to our statutes. What can be expected from so lying a frontispiece but suitable falsehoods, wherewith it aboundeth?

O that men in power and place would take these things into their serious considerations! a caution too late to amend what is past, but early enough for the future to prevent the importing of foreign, and misprinting of home-made Bibles.

X. NAME GENERAL.

W E read of Joseph (when advanced in the court of Pharaoh), that he called his eldest son, Gen. xli. 51, Manasseh; for God, said he, hath made me forget all my toil, and my father's house.

Forget his father's house! the more unnatural and undutiful son he (may some say) for his ungodly oblivion.

O no! Joseph never historically forgot his father's house, nor lost the affection he bare thereunto, only he forgot it both to the sad and to the vindictive part of his memory; he kept no grudge against his brethren for their cruel usage of him.

If God should be pleased to settle a general peace betwixt all parties in our land, let us all name our next-born child (it will fit both sexes) Manasseh. That is, forgetting; let us forget all our plunderings, sequestrations, injuries offered unto us, or suffered by us; the best oil is said to have no taste, that is, no tang. Though we carry a simple and single remembrance of our losses unto the grave, it being impossible to do otherwise, (except we rase the faculty of memory, root and branch, out of our mind,) yet let us not keep any record of them with the least reflection of revenge.

XI. APT SCHOLARS.

MOTHERS generally teach their children three sins before they be full two years old.

First, pride: Point, child, where are you fine? Where are you fine?

Secondly, lying: It was not A that cried, it was B that cried.

Thirdly, revenge: Give me a blow, and I will beat him. Give me a blow, and I will beat him.

Surely children would not be so bad, nor so soon bad, but partly for bad precedents set before them, partly for bad precepts taught unto them.

As all three lessons have taken too deep impressions in our hearts, so chiefly the last of revenge. How many blows have been given on that account within our remembrance, and yet I can make it good, that we in our age are more bound to pardon our enemies than our fathers and grandfathers in their generation.

For charity consisteth in two main parts; *in donando et condonando*, in giving and forgiving. Give we cannot so much as those before us, our estates being so much impaired and impoverished with taxes unknown to former ages.

Seeing, therefore, one channel of charity must be the less, the stream thereof ought to run broader and deeper in the other. The less we can give, the more we should forgive : but alas ! this is the worst of all, that giving goeth not so much against our covetousness, but forgiving goeth more against our pride and ambition.

XII. ALL WELL WEARIED.

TWO gentlemen, father and son, both of great quality, lived together ; the son on a time, Father, said he, I would fain be satisfied how it cometh to pass, that of such agreements which I make betwixt neighbours fallen out, not one of twenty doth last and continue. Whereas not one of twenty fails wherein you are made arbitrator.

The reason, answered the other, is plain. No sooner do two friends fall out, but presently you offer yourself to compromise the difference, wherein I more commend your charity than your discretion. Whereas I always stay till the parties send or come to me, after both sides, being well wearied by spending much money in law, are mutually desirous of an agreement.

Had any endeavoured, some sixteen years since, to have advanced a firm peace betwixt the two opposite parties in our land, their success would not have answered their intentions, men's veins were then so full of blood, and purses of money.

But since there hath been so large an evacuation of both, and men begin soberly to consider that either side may (by woful experience) make other miserable, but it is only our union can make both happy, some hope there is, that a peace, if now made, may probably last and continue, which God in his mercy make us worthy of, that we may in due time receive it.

XIII. O, INCONSTANCY!

In his Brit.
p. 82. LEARNED Master Camden, treating in an astrological way under what planet Britain is seated, allegeth but one author, viz. Johannes de Muris, who placeth our island under Saturn, whilst he produceth three, viz. the friar Perscrutator, Esquidius, and Henry Silen, which place Britain under the moon.

It will add much (in the general apprehension of people) to the judgment of the latter, that so many changes and vicissitudes in so short a time have befell our nation; we have been in twelve years a kingdom, commonwealth, protectordom, afterwards under an army, Parliament, &c. Such inconstancy doth speak us under the moon indeed; but the best is, if we be under the moon, the moon is under God, and nothing shall happen unto us but what shall be for his glory, and, we hope, for our good; and that we may in due time be under the sun again.

XIV. RECOVERED.

TYRANNUS was a good word at first, importing no more than a king; the pride and cruelty of some made the word to bear ill, as it doth in the modern acceptation thereof.

Providence, as good a word as any in divinity, hath suffered so much in the modern abusing thereof, that conscientious people begin to loathe and hate it. For God's providence hath been alleged against God's precepts. King's bare word was never in our land produced against his broad seal. Yet success (an argument borrowed from the Turks) hath been pleaded as the voice of God's approbation against his positive and express will in his word.

But God hath been pleased to vindicate his own honour, and to assert the credit of providence, which is now become a good word again. If impulsive providence (a new-coined phrase) hath given the late army their greatness, expulsive providence (a newer phrase) hath given them their smallness: being now set by, laid aside as useless; and not set by, so far from terrifying of any, by few they are regarded.

XV. GRATITUDE.

NEWCASTLE on Tyne is, without corri-
val, the richest town in England, which
Camden's Brit. in Northumb. before the Conquest was usually known by the
name of *Monk-Chester*.

Exeter must be allowed of all, one of the
neatest and sweetest cities of England, which
Idem in Devon. anciently by the Saxons was called *Monk-Town*,
both which names are now utterly out of use,
and known only to antiquaries.

God hath done great things already, whereof
we rejoice, by the hand of our great general, in
order to the settlement of our nation. When
the same (as we hope in due time) shall be completed, not only Newcastle and Exeter shall
have just cause, with comfort, to remember their
old names, but every county, city, market-town,
parish, and village in England may have the
name of Monk put upon them. But oh, the
modesty of this worthy person is as much as
his merit, who hath learned from valiant, wise,
2 Sam. xii. 28. and loyal Joab to do nothing prejudicial to David, and delighteth not so much in having a
great name, as in deserving it.

XVI. THE HEIR.

I EVER beheld Somersetshire, in one respect,
as the most ancient and honourable shire in
England. For Glastonbury in that county was
the British Antioch, where the Britons were
first called Christians, by the preaching of Joseph of Arimathea, though the truth of the
story be much swoln by the leaven of legen-
dary fictions.

But hereafter Somersetshire, in another respect, must be allowed the eldest county in
England; as Christianity first grew there, so
charity first sprang thence, in that their sober,
serious, and seasonable declaration, wherein they
renounce all future animosities in relation to
their former sufferings.

Now, as the zeal of Achaia provoked very 2 Cor. ix. 2.
many, so the example of Somersetshire hath been
precedential to other counties to follow it. Kent
and Essex since have done, and other shires are
daily doing the same; yea, and I hope that
those counties which lag the last in writing, will
be as forward as the first in performing their
solemn promises therein.

XVII. SAD TRANSPOSITION.

IT seemeth marvellous to me that many me-
chanics, (few able to read, and fewer to write
their names,) turning soldiers and captains in
our wars, should be so soon and so much improved. They seemed to me to have commenced
per saltum in their understandings. I profess,
without flouting or flattering, I have much admired with what facility and fluentness, how
pertinently and properly, they have expressed
themselves, in language which they were never
born nor bred to, but have industriously acquired
by conversing with their betters.

What a shame would it be, if such who have
been of genteel extraction, and have had liberal
education, should (as if it were by exchange of
souls) relapse into ignorance and barbarism!

What an ignominy would it be for them to
be buried in idleness, and in the immoderate
pursuit of pleasures and vicious courses, till
they besot their understandings, when they see
soldiers arrived at such an improvement, who
were bred tailors, shoemakers, cobblers, &c.

Not that I write this (God knoweth my
heart) in disgrace of them, because they were
bred in so mean callings, which are both honest
in themselves and useful in the commonwealth;
yea, I am so far from thinking ill of them for

being bred in so poor trades, that I should think better of them for returning unto them again.

XVIII. BIRD IN THE BREAST.

I SAW two men fighting together, till a third, casually passing by, interposed himself to part them; the blows of the one fell on his face, of the other on his back, of both on his body, being the screen betwixt the fiery anger of the two fighters. Some of the beholders laughed at him, as well enough served for meddling with matters which belonged not to him.

Others pitied him, conceiving every man concerned to prevent bloodshed betwixt neighbours, and Christianity itself was commission enough to interest him therein.

However, this is the sad fate which attended all moderate persons, which will mediate betwixt opposite parties. They may complain with David, They have rewarded me evil for good, and hatred for my good-will. Yet let not such hereby be disheartened, but know that (besides the reward in heaven) the very work of moderation is the wages of moderation. For it carrieth with it a marvellous contentment in his conscience who hath endeavoured his utmost

22

in order to unity, though unhappy in his success.

XIX. FAIR HOPES.

A TRAVELLER who had been newly robbed inquired of the first gentleman he met, who also was in a melancholy humour, (a cause having lately gone against him,) where he might find a justice of peace, to whom the gentleman replied: You ask for two things together, which singly and severally are not to be had.   I neither know where justice is, nor yet where peace is to be found.

Let us not make the condition of our land worse than it was; Westminster Hall was ever open, though the proceedings of justice therein were much interrupted and obstructed with military impressions. Peace, we confess, hath been a stranger unto us a long time, heart-burnings remaining when house-burnings are quenched; but now, blessed be God, we are in a fair probability of recovering both, if our sins and ingratitude blast not our most hopeful expectations.

XX. RIDDLE UNRIDDLED.

WE read, (1 Sam. xv. 11,) that when Absalom aspired to his father's kingdom, with him went two hundred men out of Jerusalem, that were called, and they went in their simplicity, and they knew not anything. If any have so little charity as to call these persons traitors, I will have so much confidence as to term them loyal traitors, and (God willing) justify the seeming contradiction.

For they lodged not in their hearts the least disloyal thought against the person and power of King David. But alas! when these two hundred were mixed among two thousand, ten thousand, twenty thousand of active and designing traitors, these poor men might in the violent multitude be hurried on, not only beyond their intentions, but even against their resolutions.

Such as are sensible with sorrow that their well-intending simplicity hath been imposed on, abused, and deluded by the subtlety of others, may comfort and content themselves in the sincerity of their own souls; God, no doubt, hath already forgiven them, and therefore men ought to revoke their uncharitable censures of them. And yet Divine justice will have its full tale of intended stripes, taking so many off from the back of the deceived, and laying them on the shoulders of the deceivers.

XXI. NO RECORD TO REMAIN.

I NEVER did read, nor can learn from any, that ever Queen Elizabeth had any ship-royal, which in the name thereof carried the memorial of any particular conquest . she got either by land or by water. Yet was she as victorious as any prince in her age, and (which is mainly material) her conquests were mostly achieved against foreign enemies.

The ships of her navy had only honest and wholesome names, the Endeavour, the Bona-venture, the Return, the Unity, &c.

Some of our modern ships carry a very great burden in their names; I mean the memorial of some fatal fights in the civil wars in our own nation, and the conquerors ought not to take much joy, as the conquered must take grief in the remembrance thereof.

I am utterly against the rebaptizing of Christians, but I am for the redipping of ships, that not only some inoffensive, but ingratiating names may be put upon them; the Unity, the Reconciliation, the Agreement, the Concord, and healing titles, (I speak more like a book-man than a seaman,) and others to that purpose.

XXII. ALL FOR THE PRESENT.

THERE is a pernicious humour, of a catching nature, wherewith the mouths of many, and hearts of more, are infected. Some there are that are so covetous to see the settlement of church and state according to their own desires, that if it be not done in our days, say they, we care not whether it be done at all or no.

Such men's souls live in a lane, having weak heads and narrow hearts, their faith being little, and charity less, being all for themselves and nothing for posterity. These men, living in India, would prove ill commonwealth's-men, and would lay no foundation for porcelain or china dishes, because despairing to reap benefit thereby, as not ripened to perfection in a hundred years.

Oh! give me that good man's gracious temper, who earnestly desired the prosperity of the Church, whatsoever became of himself, whose verses I will offer to translate:

Seu me terra tegit, seu vastum contegit æquor ;
Exoptata piis sæcula fausta precor.

Buried in earth, or drowned in the main,
   Eat up by worms or fishes;
I pray the pious may obtain
   For happy times their wishes.

2 Sam. xix.
32.

And if we ourselves, with aged Barzillai, be superannuated to behold the happy establish-

Heb. xi. 13.

ment of church and state, may we, dying in faith, though not having received the promises, bequeath the certain reversions of our Chimhams, I mean the next generation which shall rise up after us.

XXIII. COURTESY GAINETH.

I HAVE heard the royal party (would I could say without any cause) complained of, that they have not charity enough for converts, who came off unto them from the opposite side; who, though they express a sense of and sorrow for their mistakes, and have given testimony, though perchance not so plain and public as others expected, of their sincerity, yet still they are suspected as unsound; and such as frown not on, look but asquint at them.

This hath done much mischief, and retarded the return of many to their side; for had these their van-couriers been but kindly entertained, possibly ere now their whole army had come over unto us; which now are disheartened by the cold welcome of these converts.

Let this fault be mended for the future, that such proselytes may meet with nothing to discourage, all things to comfort and content them.

Let us give them not only the right hand of fellowship, but even the upper hand of superiority. One asked a mother who had brought up many children to a marriageable age, what art she used to breed up so numerous an issue; "None other," said she, " save only, I always made the most of the youngest." Let the Benjamins ever be darlings, and the last born, whose eyes were newest opened with the sight of their errors, be treated with the greatest affection.

XXIV. MODERATION.

ARTHUR PLANTAGENET Viscount Lisle, natural son to King Edward the Fourth, and (which is the greatest honour to his memory) direct ancestor, in the fifth degree, to the right honourable and most renowned lord general George Monk, was, for a fault of his servants, (intending to betray Calais to the king of France,) committed to the Tower by King Henry the Eighth, where, well knowing the fury and fierceness of that king, he daily expected death.

But the innocence of this lord appearing after much search, the king sent him a rich ring off his own finger, with so comfortable words that, at the hearing thereof, a sudden joy over- Speed. charged his heart, whereof he died that night; Chron. p. 692.

so fatal was not only the anger, but the love, of that king.

England for these many years hath been in a languishing condition, whose case hath been so much the sadder than this lord's was, because conscious of a great guilt, whereby she hath justly incurred God's displeasure. If God of his goodness should be pleased to restore her to his favour, may he also give her moderation safely to digest and concoct her own happiness, that she may not run from one extreme to another, and excessive joy prove more destructive unto her than grief hath been hitherto.

XXV. PREPARATIVE.

TWILIGHT is a great blessing of God to mankind: for, should our eyes be instantly posted out of darkness into light, out of midnight into morning, so sudden a surprisal would blind us. God, therefore, of his goodness, hath made the intermediate twilight to prepare our eyes for the reception of the light.

Such is his dealing with our English nation. We were lately in the midnight of misery. It was questionable whether the law should first draw up the will and testament of dying divinity, or divinity first make a funeral sermon for expiring law. Violence stood ready to invade our property, heresies and schisms to oppress religion.

Blessed be God, we are now brought into a better condition, yea, we are past the equilibrium; the beam beginning to break on the better side, and our hopes to have the mastery of our despairs. God grant this twilight may prove *crepusculum matutinum*, forerunning the rising of the sun, and increase of our happiness.

XXVI. REVENGE WITH A WITNESS.

FREDERIC the Second, Emperor of Germany, being at Pisa, in Italy, and distressed for want of money to pay his army, sent for Petrus de Vineis, an able man, who formerly had been his secretary, but whose eyes he had caused to be bored out for some misdemeanour.

Swinger's Theat. vol. vii. lib. 5, p. 1959, sub titulo Ultionis.

Being demanded of the Emperor which way he might most speedily and safely (as to outward danger) recruit his treasury, his secretary gave him counsel to seize on the plate of all the churches and monasteries of that city, which he did accordingly, and amongst the rest he took *zonam auream*, or the golden girdle, out of one church, of inestimable value.

This blind secretary, returning home to his wife, told her, " Now I am even with the Emperor for putting out my eyes, having put him on such a project which I hope he will pursue to his own destruction. He hath made me a spectacle to men, but I have made him a monster unto God."

Let such who are concerned herein see what success the Emperor had in this his expedition, founded on sacrilege; and the longer they look thereon, the worse I am sure they will like it, to bar further application.

XXVII. A GNAT, NO GNAT.

ONE, needlessly precise, took causeless exception at a gentleman for using the word "in troth" in his discourse, as if it had been a kind of an oath. The gentleman pleaded for himself, that " in truth " was a word inoffensive, even in his judgment who accused him.

Secondly, that he was born far north, where their broad and Doric dialect pronounced truth, troth, and he did humbly conceive the tone of the tongue was no fault of the heart.

Lastly, he alleged the twenty-fifth Psalm as it is translated in metre:

> To them that keep his testament,
> The witness of his troth.

And thus at last, with much ado, his seeming fault was remitted.

I am afraid if one should declare for troth and peace, and not for truth and peace, it would occasion some offence; however, rather than it should make any difference, the former will be as acceptable to the north of Trent, as the latter will please all good people south thereof.

XXVIII. SILENCE AWHILE.

HAD not mine eyes, as any other man's may, read it in the printed proclamations of King Edward the Sixth, (when the pulpits, generally Popish, sounded the alarm to Kett's rebellion, and the Devonshire commotion,) I would not have believed what followeth: —

2 *Edw. VI. Sept.* 13.

" *By these presents, Wee inhibite generally all manner of Preachers whatsoever they be, to preach in this meane space,* to the intent that the whole Clergy might apply themselves in prayer to Almightie God, for the better atchieving of the same most Godlie intent, and purpose of Reformation.*"

What hurt were it if in this juncture of time all our preaching were turned into praying for one month together, that God would settle a happy peace in this nation?

* This lasted in full force but for some few weeks.

However, if this be offensive to any, and giveth cause of distaste, the second motion may be embraced : that for a year, at least, all pulpits may be silent as to any part of differences relating to our times, and only deliver what belongeth to faith and good works.

XXIX. SEND HUMILITY.

I DO not remember that the word Infinite is in Scripture attributed to any creature save to the city of Nineveh, Nahum iii. 9 : Ethiopia and Egypt were her strength, and it was infinite.

But what is now become of Nineveh ? It is even buried in its own ruins, and may have this epitaph upon it :

HIC JACET FINIS INFINITI.

Here lieth the end of what was endless.

He who beheld the multitude of actors and beholders at the mustering in Hyde Park on the twenty-fourth of April last, will say that there was an infinite number of people therein. Some would hardly believe that the whole nation could afford so many as the city of London alone did then produce.

My prayer shall ever be, that this great city may be kept either in the wholesome ignorance or humble knowledge of its own strength, lest the people numberless prove masterless therein. And let them remember (God forefend the parallel) what is become of great Nineveh at this day, annihilated for the pride thereof!

XXX. RATHER FOLD OVER THAN FALL SHORT.

SOLOMON'S temple was seven years in building, 1 Kings vi. 38. And such who seriously consider the magnificence thereof, will more wonder that it was done so soon, than doing so long.

Now had Solomon at the beginning of this building abolished the tabernacle made by Moses, because too mean and little for so mighty and so numerous a nation, God had been seven years without any place of public service.

But that wise prince continued the tabernacle to all uses and purposes until the temple was finished, and then, 1 Kings viii. 4, They brought up the ark of the Lord, and the tabernacle of the congregation, and all the holy vessels that were in the tabernacle, even those did the priests and the Levites bring up. And as it followeth afterwards, ver. 6: They brought in the ark of the covenant of the Lord unto his place, into the oracle of the house. And certainly all the rest of the tabernacle, consisting of such materials as might be taken down and kept in chests and coffers, were deposited in the temple, though it may be no use was made thereof.

It had been well if, before the old government of the Church was taken down, a new one had first been settled. Yea, rather let God have two houses together, than none at all; lest piety be starved to death with cold, by lying out of doors in the interval betwixt the demolishing of an old, and the erecting of a new church discipline.

XXXI. NO MAN'S WORK.

CHRIST when on earth cured many a spot, especially of leprosy, but never smoothed any wrinkle; never made any old man young again.

But in heaven he will do both, Eph. v. 27: When he shall present it to himself a glorious church, not having spot, or wrinkle, or any such thing; but that it should be holy and without blemish.

Triumphant perfection is not to be hoped for in the militant church; there will be in it many spots and wrinkles as long as it consist-

eth of sinful mortal men, the members thereof:
it is Christ's work, not man's work, to make
a perfect reformation.

Such, therefore, are no good politicians who
will make a sore to mend a spot, cause a wound
to plain a wrinkle, do a great and certain mischief, when a small and uncertain benefit will
thereby redound.

XXXII. THREE MAKE UP ONE.

YOUNG King Jehoash had only a lease of
piety, and not for his own but his uncle's
life, 2 Kings xii. 2 : He did that which was right
in the sight of the Lord all his days, wherein
Jehoiada the priest instructed him.

Jehu was good in the midst of his life and a
zealous reformer to the utter abolishing of Baal
out of Israel, but in his old age, 2 Kings x. 31,
he returned to the politic sins of Jeroboam,
worshipping the calves in Dan and Bethel.

Manasseh was bad in the beginning and middle of his life, filling Jerusalem with idolatry ;
only towards the end thereof, when carried into 2 Chron.
a strange land, he came home to himself, and xxxiii. 15.
destroyed the profane altars he had erected.

These three put together make one perfect
servant of God. Take the morning and rise
with Jehoash, the noon and shine with Jehu,

the night and set with Manasseh. Begin with
youth-Jehoash, continue with man-Jehu, conclude with old-man-Manasseh, and all put together will spell one good Christian, yea, one
good perfect performer.

XXXIII. SERO, SED SERIO.

NEBUCHADNEZZAR observed three gra-
dations in plundering the temple; first,
he mannerly sipped and took but a taste of the
wealth thereof, 2 Chron. xxxvi. 7 : He carried
of the vessels of the house of the Lord to Babylon.

Next, he mended his draught, and drank very
deep, ver. 10 : When the year was expired, Nebuchadnezzar sent and brought Jehoiachin to
Babylon, with the goodly vessels of the house
of the Lord.

Lastly, he emptied the cup, not leaving one
drop behind, ver. 18 : And all the vessels of
the house of the Lord, great and small, brought
he to Babylon.

It was the mercy of God to allow his people
space to repent : had they made their seasonable
composition with God after the first inroad,
they had prevented the second; if after the
second, they had prevented the last and final
destruction.

God hath suffered our civil wars some sixteen years since, first to taste of the wealth of our nation; and we met not God with suitable humiliation. His justice then went farther, and the sword took the goodly vessels, the gallantry and gayety of England from us; 1. Our massy plate; 2. Pleasant pictures; 3. Precious jewels; 4. Rare libraries; and 5. Magnificent palaces [Holdenby, Theobalds, Richmond]; carrying majesty in their structure; 1. Melted down; 2. Sold; 3. Lost, or drowned; 4. Transported; 5. Levelled to the ground.

God grant that we may sue out our pardon by serious repentance, before all the vessels, great and small, be taken away in a renewed war, that the remnant of wealth which is left in the land may be continued therein.

XXXIV. BY DEGREES.

WE read that the nails in the holy of holies, 2 Chron. iii. 8 and 9, were of fine gold. Hence ariseth a question, how such nails could be useful? pure gold being so flexible that a nail made thereof will bow, and not drive.

Now, I was present at the debate hereof, betwixt the best working-goldsmiths in London, where, among many other ingenious answers,

23

this carried away the credit for the greatest probability thereof, viz. that they were screw-nails, which had holes prepared for their reception, and so were wound in by degrees.

God's work must not be done lazily, but leisurely: haste maketh waste in this kind. In reformations of great importance, the violent driving in of the nail will either break the head, or bow the point thereof, or rive and split that which should be fastened therewith.

That may insensibly be screwed which cannot suddenly be knocked into people. Fair and softly goeth far; but, alas! we have too many fiery spirits, who, with Jehu, drive on so furiously they will overturn all in church and state, if their fierceness be not seasonably retrenched.

XXXV. GOOD AUGURY.

I WAS much affected with reading that distich in Ovid, as having somewhat extraordinary therein :

> *Tarpeia quondam prædixit ab ilice cornix,*
> *Est, bene non potuit dicere, dixit, erit.*

> The crow sometimes did sit and spell *
>   On top of Tarpie-Hall;
> She could not say, All 's well, all 's well,
>   But said, It shall, it shall.

* To foretell; hence Spelman.

But what, do I listen to the language of the crow, whose black colour hath a cast of hell therein, in superstitious soothsaying? Let us hearken to what the dove of the Holy Spirit saith, promising God's servants, though the present times be bad, the future will be better, Psalm xxxvii. 11: The meek shall inherit the earth, and shall delight themselves in the abundance of peace.

XXXVI. SUBTRACT NOT, BUT ADD.

A COVETOUS courtier complained to King Edward the Sixth, of Christ's College in Cambridge, that it was a superstitious foundation, consisting of a master and twelve fellows, in imitation of Christ and his twelve apostles. He advised the king, also, to take away one or two fellowships, so to discompose that superstitious number.

O no, said the king, I have a better way than that to mar their conceit, I will add a thirteenth fellowship unto them; which he did accordingly, and so it remaineth to this day.

Well fare their hearts who will not only wear out their shoes, but also their feet, in God's service, and yet gain not a shoe-latchet thereby.

When our Saviour drove the sheep and oxen

out of the temple, he did not drive them into his own pasture, nor swept the coin into his own pockets when he overturned the tables of the money-changers. But we have in our days many who are forward to offer to God such zeal which not only cost them nothing, but wherewith they have gained great estates.

XXXVII. SEND SUCH MUSIC.

WE read, 1 Kings viii. 55, that Solomon, when he had ended his excellent prayer, he blessed the people. But was not this invading the sacerdotal function ? seeing it was not crown work, but mitre work to do it.

Numb. vi. 23.

No, surely, Solomon's act therein was lawful and laudable, there being a threefold blessing.

1. Imperative ; so God only blessed his people, who commandeth deliverances for Israel.

2. Indicative ; solemnly to declare God's blessing to, and put his name upon, the people, and this was the priest's work.

3. Optative ; wishing and desiring God's blessing on the people, and this was done by Solomon.

Yea, it is remarkable that, in the same chapter, ver. 66, the people blessed the king. O happy reciprocation betwixt them ! when the king blesseth his people, if his words be rightly understood, all may be well. But when a people blesseth their king, all is well.

XXXVIII. BY HOOK AND BY CROOK.

MARVELLOUS was the confidence of those merchants, James iv. 13: Go to now, ye that say, To-day or to-morrow we will go into such a city, and continue there a year, and buy, and sell, and get gain.

What false heraldry have we here, presumption on presumption! What insurance office had they been at to secure their lives for a twelvemonth!

But, this being granted, how could they certainly promise themselves that they this year should get gain, except they had surely known what would have been dear the next year? Merchandising is a ticklish matter, seeing many buy and sell, and live by the loss.

Either, then, trading in those times was quicker and better than in ours, or (which is most probable) they were all resolved on the point, to cheat, cozen, lie, swear, and forswear, and to gain by what means soever.

Our age and land affordeth many of their temper, and of such St. Paul speaketh, 1 Tim. vi. 9: They will be rich. Will, whether God will or will not; will, though it cost them the forfeiture of their conscience to compass their designs.

XXXIX. WITHOUT CARE NO CURE.

A WOMAN, when newly delivered of a child, her pain is ended, her peril is but new begun; a little distemper in diet, or a small cold taken, may inflame her into a fever, and endanger her life. Wherefore, when the welfare of such a person is inquired after, this answer-general is returned. She is well for one in her condition; the third, fifth, and ninth days (all critical) must be expected, till which time *bene-male* is all the health which the Latin tongue will allow her.

England is this green woman, lately brought to bed of a long-expected child, Liberty. Many wise men suspected that she would have died in travail, and both child and mother miscarry. But God be thanked for a good midwife, who would not prevent, but attend the date of nature.

However, all, yea, most of the danger is not yet past. Numerous is the multitude of malecontents, and many difficulties must be encountered before our peace can be settled.

God grant the woman be not wilful in fits of her distemper, to be ordered by the discretion of her nurses, which now in Parliament most carefully attend her recovery.

XL. KEEP YOUR CASTLE.

SOON after the king's death I preached in a church near London, and a person then in great power, now levelled with his fellows, was present at my sermon. Now, I had this passage in my prayer: God in his due time settle our nation on the true foundation thereof.

The [then] great man demanded of me, what I meant by true foundation. I answered, That I was no lawyer, nor statesman, and therefore skill in such matters was not to be expected from me.

He pressed me farther to express myself, whether thereby I did not intend the king, lords, and commons.

I returned that it was a part of my prayer to God, who had more knowledge than I had ignorance in all things, that he knew what was the true foundation, and I remitted all to his wisdom and goodness.

When men come with nets in their ears, it is good for the preacher to have neither fish nor fowl in his tongue. But, blessed be God, now we need not lie at so close a guard. Let the

gentleman now know, that what he suspected
I then intended in my words; and let him make
what improvement he pleaseth thereof.

XLI. TOO MUCH BENEATH.

KING Henry the Seventh was much troubled (as he was wont to say) with idols,
scenecal royaletts, poor, petty, pitiful persons,
who pretended themselves princes.

One of these was called Lambert Simnel,
whom the king at last, with much care and cost,
some expense of blood, but more of money,
reduced into his power and got his person into
his possession. Then, instead of other punishment, he made him a turn-broach, and afterwards (on his peaceable behaviour) he was
preferred one of the king's under-falconers, and,
as one tartly said, a fit place for the buzzard, to
keep hawks, who would have been an eagle.

*Lord Ba-
con, in the
Life of King
Henry VII.*

The king perceived that this Lambert was
no daring, dangerous, and designing person,
and therefore he would not make him, who
was contemptible in himself, considerable for
any noble punishment imposed upon him.

Royal revenge will not stoop to a low object; some malefactors are too mean to be
made public examples. Let them live, that the
pointing of people's fingers may be so many

arrows to pierce them. See, there goes ingratitude to his master; there walks, &c.

Such a life will smart as death; and such a death may be sanctified for life unto them: I mean, may occasion their serious sorrow, and cordial repentance, whereby God's pardon and their eternal salvation may be obtained; which ought to be the desire of all good Christians, as well for others as themselves.

XLII. PATIENCE AWHILE.

THE soldiers asked of John Baptist, Luke iii. 14, &c.: And what shall we do? Every man ought (not curiously to inquire into the duty of others, but) to attend his own concernments. The Baptist returned: Do violence to no man, neither accuse any falsely; and be content with your wages.

Good counsel to the soldiers of this age. Do violence to no man, plunder no man, accuse no man falsely.

Make no men malignants by wrongful information, and be content with your wages.

But I have heard some of the most moderate of the soldiers, not without cause, to complain: " He is a mutineer indeed who will not be content with his wages; but alas! we must be content without our wages, having so much of our arrears due unto us: this is a hard chapter indeed. And John Baptist himself, though feeding hardly on locusts and wild honey, could not live without any food."

Indeed, their case is to be pitied, and yet such as are ingenuous amongst them will be persuaded to have patience but awhile, the nation being now in fermentation, and tending to a consistency. The wisdom of the Parliament is such, they will find out the most speedy and easy means to pay them; and such their justice, no intent is there to defraud them of a farthing, whatsoever ill-affected malecontents may suggest to the contrary.

XLIII. IN THE MIDDLE.

GOD in his providence fixed my nativity in a remarkable place.

I was born at Aldwinkle, in Northamptonshire, where my father was the painful preacher of St. Peter's. This village was distanced one good mile west from Achurch, where Mr. Brown, founder of the Brownists, did dwell, whom, out of curiosity, when a youth, I often visited.

It was likewise a mile and a half distant east from Lavenden, where Francis Tresham, Esquire, so active in the Gunpowder Treason, had a large demesne and ancient habitation.

My nativity may mind me of moderation, whose cradle was rocked betwixt two rocks. Now, seeing I was never such a churl as to desire to eat my morsel alone, let such who like my prayer join with me therein.

God grant we may hit the golden mean, and endeavour to avoid all extremes; the fanatic Anabaptist on the one side, and the fiery zeal of the Jesuit on the other, that so we may be true Protestants, or, which is a far better name, real Christians indeed.

XLIV. AMENDING.

ALL generally hate a sluttish house, wherein nastiness hath not only taken livery and seizin, but also hath been a long time in the peaceable possession thereof.

However, reasonable men will be contented with a house belittered with straw, and will dispense with dust itself, whilst the house is sweeping, because it hath uncleanness, in order to cleanness.

Many things in England are out of joint for the present, and a strange confusion there is in church and state; but let this comfort us, we trust it is confusion in tendency to order. And, therefore, let us for a time more patiently comport therewith.

XLV. TOO MUCH TRUTH.

SOME, perchance, will smile, though I am sure all should sigh, at the following story.

A minister of these times sharply chid one of his parish for having a base child, and told him, he must take order for the keeping thereof.

" Why, sir," answered the man, " I conceive it more reasonable that you should maintain it. For I am not book-learned, and ken not a letter in the Bible ; yea, I have been your parishioner this seven years, present every Lord's day at the church, yet did I never there hear you read the ten commandments; I never heard that precept read, Thou shalt not commit adultery. Probably, had you told me my duty, I had not committed this folly."

It is an abominable shame, and a crying sin of this land, that poor people hear not in their churches the sum of what they should pray for, believe, and practise ; many mock-ministers having banished out of divine service the use of the Lord's prayer, creed, and ten commandments.

XLVI. AS IT WAS.

SOME alive will be deposed for the truth of this strange accident, though I forbear the naming of place or persons.

A careless maid, which attended a gentleman's child, fell asleep whilst the rest of the family were at church ; an ape, taking the child out of the cradle, carried it to the roof of the house, and there (according to his rude manner) fell a dancing and dandling thereof, down head, up heels, as it happened.

The father of the child, returning with his family from the church, commented with his own eyes on his child's sad condition. Bemoan he might, help it he could not. Dangerous to shoot the ape where the bullet might hit the babe ; all fall to their prayers as their last and best refuge, that the innocent child (whose precipice they suspected) might be preserved.

But when the ape was well wearied with its own activity, he fairly went down, and formally laid the child where he found it, in the cradle.

Fanatics have pleased their fancies these late years with turning and tossing and tumbling of religion, upward and downward, and backward and forward ; they have cast and contrived it into a hundred antic postures of their own imagining. However, it is now to be hoped, that, after they have tired themselves out with doing of nothing, but only trying and tampering this and that way to no purpose, they may at last return, and leave religion in the same condition wherein they found it.

XLVII. NOT SO, LONG.

SOLOMON was the riddle of the world, being the richest and poorest of princes.

Richest, for once in three years the land of Ophir sailed to Jerusalem, and caused such plenty of gold therein.

Poorest, as appeareth by his imposing so intolerable taxes on his subjects, the refusal of the mitigation whereof caused the defection of the ten tribes from the house of David.

But how came Solomon to be so much behindhand? Some, I know, score it on the account of his building of the temple, as if so magnificent a structure had impaired and exhausted his estate.

But in very deed, it was his keeping of seven hundred wives and three hundred concubines, and his concubines in all probability more expensive than his wives (as the thief in the candle wasteth more wax than the wick thereof). All these had their several courts, which must needs amount to a vast expense.

How cometh the great treasure of our land to be low, and the debts thereof so high? Surely it is not by building of churches; all the world will be her compurgators therein. It is rather because we maintain (and must for a time for our safety) such a numerous army of soldiers.

Well it had been both for the profit, credit, and conscience of Solomon, to have reduced his wives to a smaller number, as we hope in due time our standing army shall be epitomized to a more moderate proportion.

XLVIII. THANK GOD.

A NUNCIO of the Pope's was treated at Sienna, by a prime person, with a great feast. It happened there was present thereat a syndic of the city (being a magistrate, parallel in his place to one of our aldermen), who, as full of words as empty of wit, engrossed all the discourse at the table to himself, who might with as good manners have eaten all the meat at the supper.

The entertainer, sorry to see him discover so much weakness to the disgrace of himself, endeavoured to stop the superfluity of his talk. All in vain : the leaks in a rotten ship might sooner be stanched. At last, to excuse the matter (as well as he might) he told the nuncio privately, You, I am sure, have some weak men at Rome, as well as we have at Sienna. We have so, said the nuncio, but we make them no syndics.

It cannot be otherwise but that, in so spacious a land, so numerous a people as England is, we must have many weak men, and some of them of great wealth and estates. Yea, such who are not only guilty of plain and simple ignorance, but of ignorance guarded and embroidered with their own conceitedness. But, blessed be God, they are not chosen Parliament men ; the diffusive nation was never more careful in their elections of their representatives.

God grant, that, as the several day's works in the creation were singly by God pronounced good, but the last day's work (being the collection and complication of them all) very good, so these persons, good as single instruments, may be best in a concert as met together.

Gen. 1. 31.

XLIX. CAN GOOD COME FROM IGNORANCE?

KING James was no less dexterous at, than desirous of, the discovery of such who belied the father of lies, and falsely pretended themselves possesssed with a devil.

Now a maid dissembled such a possession, and for the better colour thereof, when the first verses of the Gospel of St. John were read in her hearing, she would fall into strange fits of fuming and foaming, to the amazement of the beholders.

But when the king caused one of his chaplains to read the same in the original, the same maid (possessed it seems with an English devil, who understood not a word of Greek) was tame and quiet, without any impression upon her.

I know a factious parish, wherein, if the minister in his pulpit had but named the word kingdom, the people would have been ready to have petitioned against him for a malignant. But as for realm, the same in French, he might safely use it in his sermons as oft as he pleased. Ignorance, which generally inflameth, sometimes, by good hap, abateth men's malice.

The best is, that now one may, without danger, use either word, seeing England was a kingdom a thousand years ago, and may be one (if the world last so long) a thousand years hereafter.

L. TRUSTING MAKETH ONE TRUSTY.

CHARLES the Second,* King of the Scots, when a child, was much troubled with a weakness in his legs, and was appointed to wear steel boots for the strengthening of them.

The weight of these so clogged the child, that he enjoyed not himself in any degree, but

---

* From the mouth of my worthy friend, now gone to God, D. Clare, chaplain then to his Highness.

moaned himself, fasting at feasts, yea, his very play being work unto him, he may be said to be a prisoner in his own palace.

It happened that an aged rocker, which waited on him, took the steel boots from his legs, and cast them in a place where it was hard to find them there, and impossible to fetch them thence, promising the Countess of Dorset (governess of the prince) that, if any anger arised thereof, she would take all the blame on herself.

Not long after, the king, coming into the nursery, and beholding the boots taken from his legs, was offended thereat, demanding, in some anger, who had done it.

"It was I, sir," said the rocker, "who had the honour, some thirty years since, to attend on your Highness in your infancy, when you had the same infirmity wherewith now the prince, your very own son, is troubled. And then the Lady Cary (afterwards Countess of Monmouth) commanded your steel boots to be taken off, who, blessed be God, since have gathered strength and arrived at a good stature."

The nation is too noble, when his Majesty (who hitherto hath had a short course, but a long pilgrimage) shall return from foreign parts, to impose any other steel boots upon him than the observing the laws of the land, (which are his own stockings,) that so with joy and comfort he may enter on what was his own inheritance.

But I remember, when Luther began first to mislike some errors in the Romish Church, and complained thereof to Staupitius, his confessor, he used to say unto him, *Abi in cellam et ora,* Get you gone into your cell and pray. So will I do, (who have now done,) and leave the managing of the rest to those to whom it is most proper to advance God's glory and their country's good. Amen.

THE

CAUSE AND CURE

OF A

WOUNDED CONSCIENCE.

THE SPIRIT OF A MAN WILL SUSTAIN HIS INFIRMITY ; BUT A
WOUNDED SPIRIT WHO CAN BEAR? PROV. xviii. 14.

25

To

The Right Honourable and Virtuous Lady,

F R A N C E S   M A N N E R S,

Countess of Rutland.

MADAM, —

BY the judicial law of the Jews, if a servant had children Exodus by a wife which was given him by his master, though xxi. 4. he himself went forth free in the seventh year, yet his children did remain with his master, as the proper goods of his possession. I ever have been and shall be a servant to that noble family, whence your Honour is extracted. And of late in that house I have been wedded to the pleasant embraces of a private life, the fittest wife and meetest helper that can be provided for a student in troublesome times : and the same hath been bestowed upon me by the bounty of your noble brother, Edward Lord Montague. Wherefore, what issue soever shall result from my mind, by his means most happily married to a retired life, must of due redound to his Honour, as the sole proprietary of my pains during my present condition. Now, this book is my eldest offspring, which, had it been a son, (I mean, had it been a work of masculine beauty and bigness,) it should have waited as a page in dedication to his Honour. But finding it to be of the weaker sex, little in strength, and low in stature, may it be admitted (madam) to attend on your Ladyship, his Honour's sister.

I need not mind your Ladyship how God hath measured outward happiness unto you by the cubit of the sanctuary, or the largest size, so that one would be perplexed to wish more than what your Ladyship doth enjoy. My prayer to God shall be, that, shining as a pearl of grace here, you may shine as a star in glory hereafter. So resteth,

Your Honour's,

In all Christian offices,

THOMAS FULLER.

Boughton, January 25, 1646.

TO THE CHRISTIAN READER.

S one was not anciently to want a wedding-garment at a marriage feast, so now-a-days wilfully to wear gaudy clothes at a funeral is justly censurable as unsuiting with the occasion. Wherefore, in this sad subject, I have endeavoured to decline all light and luxurious expressions: and if I be found faulty therein, I cry and crave God and the reader pardon. Thus desiring that my pains may prove to the glory of God, thine, and my own edification, I rest,

Thine in Christ Jesus,

THOMAS FULLER.

THE CAUSE AND CURE OF A WOUNDED CONSCIENCE.

DIALOGUE I.

What a wounded Conscience is, wherewith the Godly and Reprobate may be tortured.

TIMOTHEUS.

SEEING the best way never to know a wounded conscience by woful experience, is speedily to know it by a sanctified consideration thereof: give me, I pray you, the description of a wounded conscience, in the highest degree thereof.

PHILOLOGUS. It is a conscience frightened at the sight of sin, and weight of God's wrath, even unto the despair of all pardon during the present agony. ^{Psalm xxxviii. 3.}

TIM. Is there any difference betwixt a broken spirit and a wounded conscience, in this your acception? ^{Psalm li. 17.}

PHIL. Exceeding much: for a broken spirit is to be prayed and laboured for, as the most healthful and happy temper of the soul, letting in as much comfort as it leaks out sorrow for sin: whereas, a wounded conscience is a miserable malady of the mind, filling it for the present with despair.

TIM. In this your sense, is not the conscience wounded every time that the soul is smitten with guiltiness for any sin committed?

PHIL. God forbid: otherwise his servants would be in a sad condition, as in the case of David, smitten by his own heart, for being, as he thought, overbold with God's anointed, in cutting off the skirt of Saul's garment; such hurts are presently healed by a plaster of Christ's blood, applied by faith, and never come to that height to be counted and called wounded consciences.

1 Sam. xxiv. 6.

TIM. Are the godly, as well as the wicked, subject to this malady?

PHIL. Yes, verily; vessels of honour, as well as vessels of wrath in this world, are subject to the knocks and bruises of a wounded conscience. A patient Job, pious David, faithful Paul, may be vexed therewith, no less than a cursed Cain, perfidious Achitophel, or treacherous Judas.

TIM. What is the difference betwixt a wounded conscience in the godly, and in the reprobate?

PHIL. None at all, ofttimes, in the parties' apprehensions; both, for the time being, conceiving their estates equally desperate: little, if any, in the wideness and anguish of the wound itself, which for the time may be as tedious and torturing in the godly, as in the wicked.

TIM. How then do they differ?

PHIL. Exceeding much in God's intention: gashing the wicked, as malefactors, out of justice; but lancing the godly, out of love, as a surgeon his patients. Likewise they differ in the issue and event of the wound, which ends in the eternal confusion of the one, but in the correction and amendment of the other.

TIM. Some have said, that, in the midst of their pain, by this mark they may be distinguished, because the godly, when wounded, complain most of their sins, and the wicked of their sufferings.

PHIL. I have heard as much; but dare not lay too much stress on this slender sign, (to make it generally true,) for fear of failing. For sorrow for sin and sorrow for suffering are ofttimes so twisted and interwoven in the same person, yea, in the same sigh and groan, that sometimes it is impossible for the party himself so to separate and divide them in his own sense and feeling, as to know which pro-

26

ceeds from the one and which from the other. Only the all-seeing eye of an infinite God is able to discern and distinguish them.

Tim. Inform me concerning the nature of wounded consciences in the wicked.

Phil. Excuse me herein: I remember a passage in St. Augustine,* who inquired what might be the cause that the fall of the angels is not plainly set down in the Old Testament, with the manner and circumstances thereof, resolves it thus: God, like a wise surgeon, would not open that wound which he never intended to cure. Of whose words thus far I make use, that, as it was not according to God's pleasure to restore the devils, so, it being above man's power to cure a wounded conscience in the wicked, I will not meddle with that which I cannot mend: only will insist on a wounded conscience in God's children, where, by God's blessing, one may be the instrument to give some ease and remedy unto their disease.

---

* " Angelicum vulnus verus medicus qualiter factum sit indicare noluit, dum illud postea curare non destinavit." De Mirab. Scrip. lib. 1, c. 2.

DIALOGUE II.

What use they are to make thereof, who neither hitherto were, nor haply hereafter shall be, visited with a wounded Conscience.

TIMOTHEUS.

A RE all God's children, either in their life or at their death, visited with a wounded conscience?

PHIL. O no: God invites many with his golden sceptre, whom he never bruises with his rod of iron. Many, neither in their conversion, nor in the sequel of their lives, have ever felt that pain in such a manner and measure as amounts to a wounded conscience.

TIM. Must not the pangs in their travel of the new birth be painful unto them?

PHIL. Painful, but in different degrees. The Blessed Virgin Mary (most hold) was delivered without any pain; as well may that child be born without sorrow, which is conceived without sin. The women of Israel were spright- Exod. 1. 19. ful and lively, unlike the Egyptians. The former favour none can have in their spiritual travel; the latter some receive, who, though other whiles tasting of legal frights and fears, yet God so preventeth them with his blessings Psalm xxi. 3. of goodness, that they smart not so deeply therein as other men.

Tim. Who are those which commonly have such gentle usage in their conversion?

Phil. Generally such who never were notoriously profane, and have had the benefit of godly education from pious parents. In some corporations, the sons of freemen, bred under their fathers in their profession, may set up and exercise their father's trade, without ever being bound apprentices thereunto. Such children whose parents have been citizens of new Jerusalem, and have been bred in the mystery of godliness, oftentimes are entered into religion without any spirit of bondage seizing upon them, a great benefit and rare blessing where God in his goodness is pleased to bestow it.

Gal. iv. 26.
Eph. ii. 19.
Heb. xii. 22.

Tim. What may be the reason of God's dealing so differently with his own servants, that some of them are so deeply, and others not at all, afflicted with a wounded conscience?

Phil. Even so, Father, because it pleaseth thee. Yet in humility these reasons may be assigned, — 1. To show himself a free agent, not confined to follow the same precedent, and to deal with all as he doth with some. 2. To render the prospect of his proceedings the more pleasant to their sight who judiciously survey it, when they meet with so much diversity and variety therein. 3. That men, being both ignorant when, and uncertain whether or not God will visit them with wounded consciences, may wait on him with humble hearts in the work of their salvation, looking as the eyes of the servants to receive orders from the hand of their master; but what, when, and how, they know not, which quickens their daily expectations and diligent dependence on his pleasure.

Psalm cxxiii. 2.

TIM. I am one of those whom God hitherto hath not humbled with a wounded conscience: give me some instruction for my behaviour.

PHIL. First, be heartily thankful to God's infinite goodness, who hath not dealt thus with every one. Now because repentance hath two parts, mourning and mending, or humiliation and reformation, the more God hath abated thee in the former, out of his gentleness, the more must thou increase in the latter, out of thy gratitude. What thy humiliation hath wanted of other men, in the depth thereof, let thy reformation make up in the breadth thereof, spreading into an universal obedience unto all God's commandments. Well may he expect more work to be done by thy hands, who hath laid less weight to be borne on thy shoulders.

TIM. What other use must I make of God's kindness unto me?

PHIL. You are bound the more patiently to bear all God's rods, poverty, sickness, disgrace, captivity, &c., seeing God hath freed thee from the stinging scorpion of a wounded conscience.

Tim. How shall I demean myself for the time to come?

Phil. Be not high-minded, but fear; for thou canst not infallibly infer, that, because thou hast not hitherto, hereafter thou shalt not taste of a wounded conscience.

Tim. I will, therefore, for the future, with continual fear, wait for the coming thereof.

Phil. Wait not for it with servile fear, but watch against it with constant carefulness. There is a slavish fear to be visited with a wounded conscience, which fear is to be avoided, for it is opposite to the free spirit of grace, derogatory to the goodness of God in his Gospel, destructive to spiritual joy, which we ought always to have, and dangerous to the soul, racking it with anxieties and unworthy suspicions. Thus to fear a wounded conscience, is in part to feel it antedating one's misery, and tormenting himself before the time, seeking for that he would be loath to find : like the wicked in the Gospel, of whom it is said, Men's hearts failing them for fear, and looking for those things which are coming. Far be such a fear from thee, and all good Christians.

Luke xxi. 26.

Tim. What fear, then, is it, that you so lately recommended unto me?

PHIL. One, consisting in the cautious avoiding of all causes and occasions of a wounded conscience, conjoined with a confidence in God's goodness, that he will either preserve us from, or protect us in the torture thereof; and if he ever sends it, will sanctify it in us, to his glory and our good. May I, you, and all God's servants ever have this noble fear (as I may term it) in our hearts.

DIALOGUE III.

Three solemn Seasons when Men are surprised with wounded Consciences.

TIMOTHEUS.

WHAT are those times wherein men most commonly are assaulted with wounded consciences?

PHIL. So bad a guest may visit a man at any hour of his life; for no season is unseasonable for God to be just, Satan to be mischievous, and sinful man to be miserable; yet it happens especially at three principal times.

TIM. Of these, which is the first?

PHIL. In the twilight of a man's conversion, in the very conflict and combat betwixt nature and initial grace. For then he that formerly slept in carnal security is awakened with his fearful condition : God, as he saith, Psalm l. 21, setteth his sins in order before his eyes. Imprimis, the sin of his conception. Item, the sins of his childhood. Item, of his youth. Item, of his man's estate, &c. Or, Imprimis, sins against the first table. Item, sins against the second ; so many of ignorance, so many of knowledge, so many of presumption, severally sorted by themselves. He committed sins confusedly, huddling them up in heaps ; but God sets them in order, and methodizes them to his hand.

TIM. Sins thus set in order must needs be a terrible sight.

PHIL. Yes, surely, the rather because the metaphor may seem taken from setting an army in battle array. At this conflict, in his first conversion, behold a troop of sins cometh, and when God himself shall marshal them in rank and file, what guilty conscience is able to endure the furious charge of so great and well-ordered an army?

TIM. Suppose the party dies before he be completely converted in this twilight condition, as you term it, what then becomes of his soul, which may seem too good to dwell in outer darkness with devils, and too bad to go to the God of light?,

PHIL. Your supposition is impossible. Remember our discourse only concerns the godly. Now God never is father to abortive children, but to such who, according to his appointment, shall come to perfection.

TIM. Can they not therefore die in this interim, before the work of grace be wrought in them?

PHIL. No, verily. Christ's bones were in themselves breakable, but could not actually be broken by all the violence in the world, because God hath fore-decreed, A bone of him shall not be broken. So we confess God's children mortal; but all the power of Devil or man may not, must not, shall not, cannot, kill them before their conversion, according to God's election of them to life, which must be fully accomplished.

TIM. What is the second solemn time wherein wounded consciences assault men?

PHIL. After their conversion completed, and this either upon the committing of a conscience-wasting sin, such as Tertullian calls *peccatum devoratorium salutis*, or upon the undergoing of some heavy affliction of a bigger standard and proportion, blacker hue and complexion, than what befalls ordinary men, as in the case of Job.

TIM. Which is the third and last time when wounded consciences commonly walk abroad?

PHIL. When men lie on their death-beds, Satan must now roar, or else forever hold his peace; roar he may afterwards with very anger to vex himself, not with any hope to hurt us. There is mention in Scripture of an evil day, which is most applicable to the time of our death. We read also of an hour of temptation; and the prophet tells us there is a moment, wherein God may seem to forsake us. Now Satan being no less cunning to find out, than careful to make use of, his time of advantage, in that moment of that hour of that day, will put hard for our souls, and we must expect a shrewd parting blow from him.

Rev. iii. 10.

Isa. liv. 7.

TIM. Your doleful prediction disheartens me, for fear I may be foiled in my last encounter.

PHIL. Be of good comfort: through Christ we shall be victorious, both in dying and in death itself. Remember God's former favours bestowed upon thee. Indeed, wicked men, from the premises of God's power, collect a conclusion of his weakness, Psalm lxxviii. 20: Behold he smote the rock, that the waters gushed out, and the streams overflowed: can he give bread also? can he provide flesh for his people? But God's children, by better logic, from the prepositions of God's former preservations, infer his power and pleasure to protect them for the future. Be assured, that God,

1 Sam.
xvii. 36.
2 Cor. i. 10.

which hath been the God of the mountains,
and made our mountains strong in time of our
prosperity, will also be the God of the valleys,
and lead us safe through the valley of the _{Psalm}
shadow of death.

Psalm
xxiii. 4.

DIALOGUE IV.

*The great Torment of a wounded Conscience, proved
by Reasons and Examples.*

TIMOTHEUS.

IS the pain of a wounded conscience so great
as is pretended?

PHIL. God saith it, we have seen it, and
others have felt it, whose complaints savour as
little of dissimulation, as their cries in a fit of
the colic do of counterfeiting.

Prov.
xviii. 14.

TIM. Whence comes this wound to be so
great and grievous?

PHIL. Six reasons may be assigned thereof.
The first drawn from the heaviness of the hand
which makes the wound; namely, God himself,
conceived under the notion of an infinite angry
judge. In all other afflictions, man encounters
only with man, and in the worst temptations,
only with Satan; but in a wounded conscience,
he enters the lists immediately with God himself.

TIM. Whence is the second reason brought?

Heb. iv. 12. PHIL. From the sharpness of the sword wherewith the wound is made, being the word of God, and the keen threatenings of the law therein contained. There is mention, Gen. iii. 24, of a sword turning every way: parallel whereto is the word of God in a wounded conscience. Man's heart is full of windings, turnings, and doublings, to shift and shun the stroke thereof if possible; but this sword meets them wheresoever they move, — it fetches and finds them out, — it haunts and hunts them, forbidding them, during their agony, any entrance into the paradise of one comfortable thought?

TIM. Whence is the third reason derived?

PHIL. From the tenderness of the part itself which is wounded; the conscience being one of the eyes of the soul, sensible of the smallest hurt. And when that *callum, schirrus,* or *incrustation,* drawn over it by nature, and hardened by custom in sin, is once flayed off, the conscience becomes so pliant and supple, that the least imaginable touch is painful unto it.

TIM. What is the fourth reason?

PHIL. The folly of the patient; who being stung, hath not the wisdom to look up to Christ, the brazen serpent, but torments himself with his own activity. It was threatened to Pashur,

I will make thee a terror to thyself: so fares it Jer. xx. 4. with God's best saint during the fit of his perplexed conscience; he hears his own voice, — he thinks, this is that which so often hath sworn, lied, talked vainly, wantonly, wickedly; his voice is a terror to himself. He sees his own eyes in a glass, — he presently apprehends, these are those which shot forth so many envious, covetous, amorous glances; his eyes are a terror to himself. Sheep are observed to fly without cause, scared (as some say) with the sound of their own feet: their feet knack because they fly, and they fly because their feet knack: an emblem of God's children in a wounded conscience, self-fearing, self-frightened.

TIM. What is the fifth reason which makes the pain so great?

PHIL. Because Satan rakes his claws in the reeking blood of a wounded conscience. Beelzebub, the Devil's name, signifies in Hebrew the Lord of flies, which excellently intimates his nature and employment; flies take their felicity about sores and galled backs, to infest and inflame them: so Satan no sooner discovers (and that bird of prey hath quick sight) a soul terror-struck, but thither he hastes, and is busy to keep the wound raw, — there he is in his throne to do mischief.

TIM. What is the sixth and last reason why a wounded conscience is so great a torment?

PHIL. Because of the impotency and in-validity of all earthly receipts to give ease thereunto. For there is such a gulf of dis-proportion betwixt a mind-malady and body-medicines, that no carnal, corporal comforts can effectually work thereupon.

TIM. Yet wine in this case is prescribed in Scripture; Give wine to the heavy-hearted, that they may remember their misery no more.

Prov. xxxi. 6.

PHIL. Indeed, if the wound be in the spirits, those cursitors betwixt soul and body, to recover their decay or consumption, wine may usefully be applied: but if the wound be in the spirit, in Scripture phrase, all carnal, corporal comforts are utterly in vain.

TIM. Methinks merry company should do much to refresh him.

PHIL. Alas! a man shall no longer be wel-come in merry company than he is able to sing his part in their jovial concert. When a hunted deer runs for safeguard amongst the rest of the herd, they will not admit him into their com-pany, but beat him off with their horns, out of principles of self-preservation, for fear the hounds, in pursuit of him, fall on them also. So hard it is for man or beast in misery, to find a faithful friend. In like manner, when a set of bad-good-fellows perceive one of their society dogged with God's terrors at his heels, they will forsake him as soon as they can, preferring his room, and declining his company, lest his sadness prove infectious to themselves. And now, if all six reasons be put together, so heavy a hand, smiting with so sharp a sword on so tender a part of so foolish a patient, whilst Satan seeks to widen, and no worldly plaster can cure the wound, it sufficiently proves a wounded conscience to be an exquisite torture.

TIM. Give me, I pray, an example thereof.

PHIL. When Adam had eaten the forbidden fruit, he tarried a time in paradise, but took no contentment therein. The sun did shine as bright, the rivers as clear, as ever before, birds sang as sweetly, beasts played as pleasantly, flowers smelt as fragrant, herbs grew as fresh, fruits flourished as fair, no punctilio of pleasure was either altered or abated. The objects were the same, but Adam's eyes were otherwise; his nakedness stood in his light; a thorn of guiltiness grew in his heart before any thistles sprang out of the ground; which made him not to seek for the fairest fruits to fill his hunger, but the biggest leaves to cover his nakedness. Thus a wounded conscience is able to unparadise paradise itself.

TIM. Give me another instance.

PHIL. Christ Jesus, our Saviour, he was blinded, buffeted, scourged, scoffed at, had his hands and feet nailed to the cross, and all this while said nothing. But no sooner apprehended he his Father deserting him, groaning under the burden of the sins of mankind imputed unto him, but presently the Lamb (who hitherto was dumb before his shearer, and opened not his mouth) for pain began to bleat, My God, my God, why hast thou forsaken me?

TIM. Why is a wounded conscience by David
Psalm xxxviii. 2. resembled to arrows, Thine arrows stick fast in me?

PHIL. Because an arrow, especially if barbed, rakes and rends the flesh the more, the more metal the wounded party hath to strive and struggle with it: and a guilty conscience pierces the deeper, whilst a stout stomach with might and main seeks to outwrestle it.

TIM. May not a wounded conscience also work on the body to hasten and heighten the sickness thereof?

PHIL. Yes, verily, so that there may be em-
Col. iv. 14. ployment for Luke, the beloved physician, (if the same person with the Evangelist,) to exercise both his professions: but we meddle only with the malady of the mind, abstracted from any bodily indisposition.

DIALOGUE V.

Sovereign Uses to be made of the Torment of a wounded Conscience.

TIMOTHEUS.

SEEING the torture of a wounded conscience is so great, what use is to be made thereof?

PHIL. Very much : and first, it may make men sensible of the intolerable pain in hell fire. If the mouth of the fiery furnace into which the children were cast was so hot that it burnt those which approached it, how hot was the furnace itself! If a wounded conscience, the suburbs of hell, be so painful, O how extreme is that place where the worm never dieth, and the fire is never quenched !

TIM. Did our roaring boys (as they call them) but seriously consider this, they would not wish God damn them, and God confound them, so frequently as they do.

PHIL. No, verily: I read in Theodoret of the ancient Donatists, that they were so ambitious of martyrdom (as they accounted it), that many of them, meeting with a young gentleman, requested of him, that he would be pleased to kill them. He, to confute their folly, condescended to their desire, on condition, that first they would submit to be fast

27

bound: which being done, he gave order that they should be severely scourged, and then saved their lives. In application: when I hear such riotous youths wish that God would damn or confound them, I hope God will be more merciful than to take them at their words, and to grant them their wish; only I heartily desire that he would be pleased sharply to scourge them, and soundly to lash them with the frights and terrors of a wounded conscience. And I doubt not but that they would so ill like the pain thereof, that they would revoke their wishes, as having little list, and less delight to taste of hell hereafter.

TIM. What other use is to be made of the pain of a wounded conscience?

PHIL. To teach us seasonably to prevent what we cannot possibly endure. Let us shun the smallest sin, lest, if we slight and neglect it, it by degrees fester and gangrene into a wounded conscience. One of the bravest spirits * that ever England bred, or Ireland buried, lost his life by a slight hurt neglected, as if it had been beneath his high mind to stoop to the dressing thereof, till it was too late. Let us take heed the stoutest of us be not so served in our souls. If we repent not presently of our sins

* Sir Thomas Norris, President of Munster, *ex levi vulnere neglecto sublatus.* Camden's Elizab. An. 1641.

committed, but carelessly contemn them, a scratch may quickly prove an ulcer; the rather, because the flesh of our mind, if I may so use the metaphor, is hard to heal, full of choleric and corrupt humours, and very ready to rankle.

TIM. What else may we gather for our instruction from the torture of a troubled mind.

PHIL. To confute their cruelty who, out of sport or spite, willingly and wittingly wound weak consciences: like those uncharitable Co-¹ ^{1 Cor. viii. 12.} rinthians, who so far improve their liberty in things indifferent, as thereby to wound the consciences of their weaker brethren.

TIM. Are not those ministers to blame, who, mistaking their message, instead of bringing the Gospel of peace, frighten people with legal terrors into despair?

PHIL. I cannot commend their discretion, yet will not condemn their intention herein. No doubt their desire and design ·is pious, though they err in the pursuit and prosecu- · tion thereof, casting down them whom they cannot raise, and conjuring up the spirit of bondage which they cannot allay again: wherefore, it is our wisest way to interweave promises with threatenings, and not to leave open a pit of despair, but to cover it again with comfort.

TIM. Remaineth there not, as yet, another use of this point?

PHIL. Yes, to teach us to pity and pray for those that have afflicted consciences, not like Psalm lxix. 26. the wicked, who persecute those whom God hath smitten, and talk to the grief of such whom he hath wounded.

TIM. Yet Eli was a good man, who, notwithstanding, censured Hannah, a woman of sorrowful spirit, to be drunk with wine. 1 Sam. 1. 13, 14.

PHIL. Imitate not Eli in committing, but amending his fault. Indeed, his dim eyes could see drunkenness in Hannah where it was not, and could not see sacrilege and adultery in his own sons, where they were. Thus, those who are most indulgent to their own, are most censorious of others' sins. But Eli afterwards, perceiving his error, turned the condemning of Hannah into praying for her. In like manner, if in our passion we have prejudiced or injured any wounded consciences, in cold blood let us make them the best amends and reparation.

DIALOGUE VI.

That in some Cases more Repentance must be preached to a wounded Conscience.

TIMOTHEUS.

SO much for the malady, now for the remedy. Suppose you come to a wounded conscience, what counsel will you prescribe him?

PHIL. If, after hearty prayer to God for his direction, he appeareth unto me, as yet, not truly penitent, in the first place I will press a deeper degree of repentance upon him.

TIM. O miserable comforter! more sorrow still! Take heed your eyes be not put out with that smoking flax you seek to quench, and your fingers wounded with the splinters of that bruised reed you go about to break.

PHIL. Understand me, sir. Better were my tongue spit out of my mouth, than to utter a word of grief to drive them to despair who are truly contrite. But on the other side, I shall betray my trust, and be found an unfaithful dispenser of divine mysteries, to apply comfort to him who is not ripe and ready for it.

TIM. What harm would it do?

PHIL. Raise him for the present, and ruin him, without God's greater mercy, for the future. For comfort daubed on, on a foul soul, will not stick long upon it; and, instead of pouring in, I shall spill the precious oil of God's mercy. Yea, I may justly bring a wounded conscience upon myself, for dealing deceitfully in my stewardship.

TIM. Is it possible one may not be soundly humbled, and yet have a wounded conscience?

PHIL. Most possible: for a wounded conscience is often inflicted as a punishment for lack of true repentance: great is the difference betwixt a man's being frightened at, and humbled for, his sins. One may passively be cast down by God's terrors, and yet not willingly throw himself down as he ought at God's footstool.

TIM. Seeing his pain is so pitiful as you have formerly proved, why would you add more grief unto him?

PHIL. I would not add grief to him, but alter grief in him; making his sorrow, not greater, but better. I would endeavour to change his dismal, doleful dejection, his hideous and horrible heaviness, his bitter exclamations, which seem to me much mixed in him with pride, impatience, and impenitence, into a willing submission to God's pleasure, and into a kindly, gentle, tender Gospel repentance for his sins.

TIM. But there are some now-a-days who maintain that a child of God after his first conversion needs not any new repentance for sin all the days of his life.

PHIL. They defend a grievous and dangerous error. Consider what two petitions Christ couples together in his prayer: when my body, which every day is hungry, can live without God's giving it daily bread, then and no sooner

shall I believe that my soul, which daily sin-
neth, can spiritually live without God's forgiving it its trespasses.

TIM. But such allege, in proof of their opinion, that a man hath his person justified before
God, not by pieces and parcels, but at once and
forever in his conversion.

PHIL. This being granted doth not favour
their error. We confess God finished the creation of the world, and all therein, in six days,
and then rested from that work, yet so that his
daily preserving of all things by his Providence
may still be accounted a constant and continued
creation. We acknowledge in like manner, a
child of God justified at once in his conversion,
when he is fully and freely estated in God's
favour. And yet seeing every daily sin by him
committed is an aversion from God, and his
daily repentance a conversion to God, his justification in this respect may be conceived entirely continued all the days of his life.

TIM. What is the difference betwixt the
first repentance, and this renewed repentance?

PHIL. The former is as it were the putting
of life into a dead man, the latter, the recovering of a sick man from a dangerous wound:
by the former, sight to the blind is simply
restored, and eyes given him; in the latter,
only a film is removed, drawn over the eyes,

and hindering their actual sight.   By the first, we have a right title to the kingdom of Heaven ; by our second repentance, we have a new claim to Heaven, by virtue of our old title.   Thus these two kinds of repentance may be differenced and distinguished, though otherwise they meet and agree in general qualities : both having sin for their cause, sorrow for their companion, and pardon for their consequent and effect.

TIM. But do not God's children after committing of grievous sins, and before their renewing their repentance, remain still heirs of Heaven, married to Christ, and citizens of the New Jerusalem?

PHIL. Heirs of Heaven they are, but disinheritable for their misdemeanour.   Married still to Christ, but deserving to be divorced for their adulteries.   Citizens of Heaven, but yet outlawed, so that they can recover no right, and receive no benefit, till their outlawry be reversed.

TIM. Where doth God in Scripture enjoin this second repentance on his own children?

PHIL. In several places.   He threatens the
Rev. ii. 5.   Church of Ephesus (the best of the seven) with removing the candlestick from them, except they repent: and Christ tells his own disciples, true converts before, but then guilty

of ambitious thoughts, that except ye be con- _{Matth.} verted ye shall not enter the kingdom of Heav- en. Here is conversion after conversion, being a solemn turning from some particular sin; in relation to which it is not absurd to say, that there is justification after justification : the lat- ter as following in time, so flowing from the former.

DIALOGUE VII.

Only Christ is to be applied to Souls truly contrite.

TIMOTHEUS.

BUT suppose the person in the minister's apprehension heartily humbled for sin, what then is to be done?

PHIL. No corrosives, all cordials; no vin- egar, all oil; no law, all Gospel must be pre- sented unto him. Here, blessed the lips, yea, beautiful the feet of him that bringeth the tid- ings of peace. As Elisha, when reviving the son of the Shunamite, laid his mouth to the mouth of the child; so the gaping orifice of Christ's wounds must spiritually, by preaching, be put close to the mouth of the wounds of a conscience : happy that skilful architect that can show the sick man that the head-stone of his spiritual building must be laid with shouts, crying, Grace, grace.

Tim. Which do you count the head-stone of the building, that which is first or last laid?

Phil. The foundation is the head-stone in honour, the top stone is the head-stone in height. The former the head-stone in strength, the latter in the stature. It seemeth that God's Spirit, of set purpose, made use of a doubtful word, to show that the whole fabric of our salvation, whether as founded, or as finished, is the only work of God's grace alone. Christ is the alpha and omega thereof, not excluding all the letters in the alphabet interposed.

Tim. How must the minister preach Christ to an afflicted conscience?

Phil. He must crucify him before his eyes, lively setting him forth; naked, to clothe him; wounded, to cure him; dying, to save him. He is to expound and explain unto him the dignity of his person, preciousness of his blood, plenteousness of his mercy, in all those loving relations wherein the Scripture presents him: a kind father to a prodigal child, a careful hen to a scattered chicken, a good shepherd that bringeth his lost sheep back on his shoulders.

Tim. Spare me one question: why doth he not drive the sheep before him, especially seeing it was lively enough to lose itself?

Phil. First, because though it had wildness too much to go astray, it had not wisdom

enough to go right. Secondly, because probably the silly sheep had tired itself with wandering ; Habakkuk ii. 13, " the people shall weary
themselves for very vanity," and therefore the
kind shepherd brings it home on his own shoulders.

TIM. Pardon my interruption, and proceed,
how Christ is to be held forth.

PHIL. The latitude and extent of his love,
his invitation without exception, are powerfully to be pressed ; every one that thirsteth, all
ye that are heavy laden, whosoever believeth,
and the many promises of mercy, are effectually
to be tendered unto him.

TIM. Where are those promises in Scripture ?

PHIL. Or rather, where are they not? for
they are harder to be missed than to be met
with. Open the Bible (as he who drew his ¹ Kings
xxii. 34.
bow in battle) at a venture. If thou lightest
on an historical place, behold precedents; if on
doctrinal, promises of comfort. For the latter,
observe these particulars: Gen. iii. 15 ; Exo.
xxxiv. 6 ; Isa. xl. 1 ; Isa. liv. 11 ; Mat. xi. 28 ;
xii. 20 ; 1 Cor. x. 13 ; Heb. xiii. 5, &c.

TIM. Are these more principal places of consolation than any other in the Bible ?

PHIL. I know there is no choosing, where
all things are choicest. Whosoever shall select
some pearls out of such a heap, shall leave be-

hind as precious as any he takes, both in his own and others' judgment; yea, which is more, the same man at several times may in his apprehension prefer several promises as best, formerly most affected with one place, for the present more delighted with another: and afterwards, conceiving comfort therein not so clear, choose other places as more pregnant and pertinent to his purpose. Thus God orders it, that divers men (and perchance the same man at different times) make use of all his promises, gleaning and gathering comfort, not only in one furrow, land, or furlong, but as it is scattered clean through the whole field of Scripture.

TIM. Must ministers have variety of several comfortable promises?

PHIL. Yes, surely: such masters of the assembly being to enter and fasten consolation in an afflicted soul, need have many nails provided beforehand, that if some for the present chance to drive untowardly, as splitting, going awry, turning crooked or blunt, they may have others in the room thereof.

TIM. But grant Christ held out never so plainly, pressed never so powerfully, yet all is in vain, except God inwardly with his Spirit persuade the wounded conscience to believe the truth of what he saith.

PHIL. This is an undoubted truth, for one

may lay the bread of life on their trencher, and cannot force them to feed on it. One may bring them down to the spring of life, but cannot make them drink of the waters thereof: and therefore, in the cure of a wounded conscience, God is all in all, only the touch of his hand can heal this king's evil: I kill ^{Deut.} and make alive, I wound and I heal, neither _{xxxii. 39} is there any that can deliver out of my hand.

DIALOGUE VIII.

Answers to the Objections of a wounded Conscience, drawn from the Grievousness of his Sins.

TIMOTHEUS.

GIVE me leave now, sir, to personate and represent a wounded conscience, and to allege and enforce such principal objections wherewith generally they are grieved.

PHIL. With all my heart, and God bless my endeavours in answering them.

TIM. But first I would be satisfied how it comes to pass, that men in a wounded conscience have their parts so presently improved. The Jews did question concerning our Saviour, How knoweth this man letters, being never ^{John vii.} learned? But here the doubt and difficulty _{15.} is greater. How come simple people so subtle on a sudden, to oppose, with that advantage and vehemence, that it would puzzle a good and grave divine to answer them?

PHIL. Two reasons may be rendered thereof. 1. Because a man in a distemper is stronger than when he is in his perfect health. What Samsons are some in the fit of a fever? Then their spirits, being raised by the violence of their disease, push with all their power. So it is in the agony of a distressed soul, every string thereof is strained to the height, and a man becomes more than himself to object against himself in a fit of despair.

TIM. What is the other reason?

PHIL. Satan himself, that subtle sophister, assists them. He forms their arguments, frames their objections, fits their distinctions, shapes their evasions; and this discomforter (aping God's Spirit, the Comforter, John xiv. 26) bringeth all things to their remembrance, which they have heard or read, to dishearten them. Need, therefore, have ministers, when they meddle with afflicted men, to call to Heaven aforehand to assist them, being sure they shall have hell itself to oppose them.

TIM. To come now to the objections which afflicted consciences commonly make; they may be reduced to three principal heads; either drawn from the greatness and grievousness

of their sins, or from the slightness and lightness of their repentance, or from the faintness
and feebleness of their faith; I begin with the
objections of the first form.

PHIL. I approve your method; pray proceed.

TIM. First, sir, even since my conversion, I
have been guilty of many grievous sins; and,
which is worse, of the same sin many times
committed. Happy Judah, who, though once ^{Gen.}
committing incest with Thamar, yet the text ^{xxxviii. 26.}
saith, that afterwards he knew her again no
more. But I, vile wretch, have often re-fallen
into the same offence.

PHIL. All this is answered in God's promise
in the prophet, Though your sins be as scar- ^{Isaiah i. 18.}
let, I will make them as snow. Consider how
the Tyrian scarlet was dyed, not superficially
dipped, but thoroughly drenched in the liquor
that coloured it, as thy soul in custom of sinning. Then was it taken out for a time and
dried, put in again, soaked and sodden the second time in the fat; called therefore δίβαφον,
twice dyed; as thou complainest thou hast been
by relapsing into the same sin. Yea, the colour
so incorporated into the cloth, not drawn over,
but diving into the very heart of the wool, that
rub a scarlet rag on what is white, and it will
bestow a reddish tincture upon it; as perchance
thy sinful practice and precedent have also in-

fected those which were formerly good, by thy badness.   Yet such scarlet sins, so solemnly and substantially coloured, are easily washed white in the blood of our Saviour.

TIM. But, sir, I have sinned against most serious resolutions, yea, against most solemn vows, which I have made to the contrary.

PHIL. Vow-breaking, though a grievous sin, is pardonable on unfeigned repentance.   If thou hast broken a vow, tie a knot on it to make it hold together again.   It is spiritual thrift, and no misbecoming baseness, to piece and joint thy neglected promises with fresh ones.   So shall thy vow in effect be not broken when new mended: and remain the same, though not by one entire continuation, yet by a constant successive renovation thereof.   Thus Jacob renewed his neglected vow of going to Bethel; and this must thou do, reinforce thy broken vows, if of moment and material.

Compare Gen. xxviii. 20, with Gen. xxxv. 1.

TIM. What mean you by the addition of that clause, if of moment and material?

PHIL. To deal plainly, I dislike many vows men make, as of reading just so much and praying so often every day, of confining themselves to such a strict proportion of meat, drink, sleep, recreation, &c.   Many things may be well done, which are ill vowed.   Such particular vows men must be very sparing how they make.

First, because they savour somewhat of will-worship. Secondly, small glory accrues to God thereby. Thirdly, the dignity of vows is disgraced by descending to too trivial particulars. Fourthly, Satan hath ground given him to throw at us with a more steady aim. Lastly, such vows, instead of being cords to tie us faster to God, prove knots to entangle our consciences: hard to be kept, but oh! how heavy when broken! Wherefore, setting such vows aside, let us be careful, with David, to keep that grand and general vow: I have sworn, and I will perform it, that I will keep thy righteous judgments. ^{Psalm cxix. 106.}

TIM. But, sir, I have committed the sin against the Holy Ghost, which the Saviour of mankind pronounceth unpardonable, and therefore all your counsels and comforts unto me are in vain.

PHIL. The Devil, the father of lies, hath added this lie to those which he hath told before, in persuading thee thou hast committed the sin against the Holy Ghost. For that sin is ever attended with these two symptoms. First, the party guilty thereof never grieves for it, nor conceives the least sorrow in his heart for the sin he hath committed. The second, which followeth on the former, he never wishes or desires any pardon, but is de-

28

lighted and pleased with his present condition.
Now, if thou canst truly say that thy sins are
a burden unto thee, that thou dost desire forgiveness, and wouldest give anything to compass and obtain it, be of good comfort, thou
hast not as yet, and by God's grace never
shalt, commit that unpardonable offence. I
will not define how near thou hast been
unto it. As David said to Jonathan, there is
not a hair's breadth betwixt death and me;
so it may be thou hast missed it very nar-
rowly, but assure thyself thou art not as yet
guilty thereof.

DIALOGUE IX.

*Answers to the Objections of a wounded Conscience
drawn from the Slightness of his Repentance.*

TIMOTHEUS.

I BELIEVE my sins are pardonable in themselves, but alas! my stony heart is such, that
it cannot relent and repent, and therefore no
hope of my salvation.

PHIL. Wouldst thou sincerely repent? thou
dost repent. The women that came to embalm
Christ did carefully forecast with themselves
who shall roll away the stone from the door of
the sepulchre? Alas! their frail, faint, feeble

Mark xvi. 3.

arms were unable to remove such a weight. But what follows? And when they looked, they saw that the stone was rolled away, for it was very great. In like manner, when a soul is truly troubled about the mighty burden of his stony heart interposed, hindering him from coming to Christ; I say, when he is seriously and sincerely solicitous about that impediment, such desiring is a doing, such wishing is a working. Do thou but take care it may be removed, and God will take order it shall be removed.

TIM. But, sir, I cannot weep for my sins; my eyes are like the pit wherein Joseph was put; there is no water in them, I cannot squeeze one tear out of them.

PHIL. Before I come to answer your objection, I must premise a profitable observation. I have taken notice of a strange opposition betwixt the tongues and eyes of such as have troubled consciences. Their tongues some have known (and I have heard) complain that they cannot weep for their sins, when at that instant their eyes have plentifully shed store of tears : not that they spake out of dissimulation, but distraction. So sometimes have I smiled at the simplicity of a child, who being amazed, and demanded whether or no he could speak, hath answered, No. If in like manner, at the sight of such a contradiction betwixt the words and deeds of one in the agony of a wounded conscience, we should chance to smile, know us not to jeer, but joy, perceiving the party in a better condition than he conceiveth himself.

Tim. This your observation may be comfortable to others, but is impertinent to me. For, as I told you, I have by nature such dry eyes that they will afford no moisture to bemoan my sins.

Phil. Then it is a natural defect, and no moral default, so by consequence a suffering, and no sin which God will punish. God doth not expect the pipe should run water where he put none into the cistern. Know also, their hearts may be fountains whose eyes are flints, and may inwardly bleed, who do not outward-

Isaiah li. 3. ly weep. Besides, Christ was sent to preach comfort, not to such only as weep, but mourn in Zion. Yea, if thou canst squeeze out no liquor, offer to God the empty bottles; instead of tears, tender and present thine eyes unto him. And though thou art water-bound, be not wind-bound also; sigh where thou canst not sob, and let thy lungs do what thine eyes cannot perform.

Tim. You say something, though I cannot weep, in case I could soundly sorrow for my sins. But alas! for temporal losses and crosses, I am like Rachel, lamenting for her children, and would not be comforted. But my sorrow for my sins is so small that it appears none at all in proportion.

PHIL. In the best saints of God, their sorrow for their sins being measured with the sorrow for their sufferings, in one respect will fall short of it, in another must equal it, and in a third respect doth exceed and go beyond it. Sorrow for sins falls short of sorrow for sufferings, in loud lamenting or violent uttering itself in outward expressions thereof; as in roaring, wringing the hands, rending the hair, and the like. Secondly, both sorrows are equal in their truth and sincerity, both far from hypocrisy, free from dissimulation, really hearty, cordial, uncounterfeited. Lastly, sorrow for sin exceeds sorrow for suffering, in the continuance and durableness thereof: the other like a land-flood, quickly come, quickly gone; this is a continual dropping or running river, keeping a constant stream. My sins, saith David, are ever before me; so also is the sorrow for sin in the soul of a child of God, morning, evening, day, night, when sick, when sound, feasting, fasting, at home, abroad, ever within him. This grief begins at his conversion, continues all his life, ends only at his death.

TIM. Proceed, I pray, in this comfortable point.

Phil. It may still be made plainer by comparing two diseases together, the toothache and consumption. Such as are troubled with the former shriek and cry out, troublesome to themselves, and others in the same and next roof: and no wonder, the mouth itself being plaintiff, if setting forth its own grievances to the full. Yet the toothache is known to be no mortal malady, having kept some from their beds, seldom sent them to their graves; hindered the sleep of many, hastened the death of few. On the other side, he that hath an incurable consumption saith little, cries less, but grieves most of all. Alas! he must be a good husband of the little breath left in his broken lungs, not to spend it in sighing, but in living; he makes no noise, is quiet and silent; yet none will say but that his inward grief is greater than the former.

Tim. How apply you this comparison to my objection?

Phil. In corporal calamities, thou complainest more like him in the toothache, but thy sorrow for thy sin, like a consumption, which lies at the heart, hath more solid heaviness therein. Thou dost take in more grief for thy sins, though thou mayest take on more grievously for thy sufferings.

Tim. This were something, if my sorrow for

sin were sincere, but alas! I am but a hypocrite. There is mention in the prophet of God's besom Isaiah xiv. 23. of destruction; now the trust of a hypocrite, Job viii. 14, is called a spider's web; here is my case, when God's besom meets with the cobwebs of my hypocrisy, I shall be swept into hell-fire.

PHIL. I answer, first in general: I am glad to hear this objection come from thee, for self-suspicion of hypocrisy is a hopeful symptom of sincerity. It is a David that cries out, As for me, I am poor and needy; but lukewarm Laodicea that brags, I am rich, and want nothing.

TIM. Answer, I pray, the objection in particular.

PHIL. Presently, when I have premised the great difference betwixt a man's being a hypocrite, and having some hypocrisy in him. Wicked men are like the apples of Sodom, Solinus Polyhistor in Judæa. seemingly fair, but nothing but ashes within. The best of God's servants are like sound apples, lying in a dusty loft (living in a wicked world),. gathering much dust about them, so that they must be rubbed or pared before they can be eaten. Such notwithstanding are sincere, and by the following marks may examine themselves.

TIM. But some in the present day are utter enemies to all marks of sincerity, counting it needless for preachers to propound, or people to apply them.

PHIL. I know as much; but it is the worst sign, when men of this description hate all signs: but no wonder if the foundered horse cannot abide the smith's pincers.

TIM. Proceed, I pray, in your signs of sincerity.

PHIL. Art thou careful to order thy very thoughts, because the Infinite Searcher of the heart doth behold them? Dost thou freely and fully confess thy sins to God, spreading them open in his presence, without any desire or endeavour to deny, dissemble, defend, excuse, or extenuate them? Dost thou delight in an universal obedience to all God's laws, not thinking with the superstitious Jews, by over keeping the fourth commandment, to make reparation to God for breaking all the rest? Dost thou love their persons and preaching best, who most clearly discover thine own faults and corruptions unto thee? Dost thou strive against thy revengeful nature, not only to forgive those who have offended thee, but also to wait an occasion with humility to render a suitable favour to them? Dost thou love grace and goodness even in those who differ from thee in point of opinion and civil controversies? Canst thou be sorrowful for the sins of others, no whit relating unto thee, merely because the glory of a good God suffers by their profaneness?

TIM. Why do you make these to be the signs of sincerity?

PHIL. Because there are but two principles which act in men's hearts, namely, nature and grace; or, as Christ distinguishes them, flesh and blood, and our Father which is in Heaven. Now seeing these actions, by us propounded, are either against or above nature, it doth necessarily follow, that where they are found, they flow from saving grace. For what is higher than the roof and very pinnacle, as I may say, of nature, cannot be lower than the bottom and beginning of grace.

TIM. Perchance, on serious search, I may make hard shift to find some one or two of these signs, but not all of them, in my heart.

PHIL. As I will not bow to flatter any, so I will fall down, as far as truth will give me leave, to reach comfort to the humble, to whom it is due. Know to thy further consolation, that where some of these signs truly are, there are more, yea all of them, though not so visible and conspicuous, but in a dimmer and darker degree. When we behold violets and primroses fairly to flourish, we conclude the dead of the winter is past, though as yet no roses or July flowers appear, which long after lie hid in their leaves, or lurk in their roots; but in due time will discover themselves. If some of these signs be above ground in thy sight, others are under ground in thy heart, and though the former started first, the other will follow in order; it being plain that thou art passed from death unto life, by this hopeful and happy spring of some signs in thy heart.

DIALOGUE X.

Answers to the Objections of a wounded Conscience drawn from the Feebleness of his Faith.

TIMOTHEUS.

BUT faith is that which must apply Christ unto us, whilst (alas!) the hand of my faith hath not only the shaking, but the dead palsy; it can neither hold nor feel anything.

PHIL. If thou canst not hold God, do but touch him, and he shall hold thee, and put feel-
Phil. iii. 12. ing into thee. Saint Paul saith, If that I may apprehend that for which also I am apprehended of Christ Jesus. It is not Paul's apprehending of Christ, but Christ apprehending of Paul, doth the deed.

TIM. But I am sure my faith is not sound, because it is not attended with assurance of salvation. For I doubt (not to say despair) thereof. Whereas divines hold, that the essence of saving faith consists in a certainty to be saved.

PHIL. Such deliver both a false and dangerous doctrine ; as the careless mother killed her little infant, for she over-laid it : so this opinion would press many weak faiths to death, by laying a greater weight upon them than they can bear, or God doth impose ; whereas to be assured of salvation is not a part of every true faith, but only an effect of some strong faiths, and that also not always, but at some times. [1 Kings iii. 19.]

TIM. Is not certainty of salvation a part of every true faith?

PHIL. No, verily, much less is it the life and formality of faith, which consists only in a recumbency on God in Christ, with Job's resolution, Though he slay me, yet will I trust in him. Such an adherence, without an assurance, is sufficient, by God's mercy, to save thy soul. Those that say that none have a sincere faith without a certainty of salvation, may with as much truth maintain, that none are the king's loyal subjects but such as are his favourites. [Job xiii. 15.]

TIM. Is then assurance of salvation a peculiar personal favour, indulged by God, only to some particular persons?

PHIL. Yes, verily: though the salvation of all God's servants be sure in itself, yet is only assured to the apprehensions of some select people, and that at some times; for it is too fine fare for the best man to feed on every day.

Tim. May they that have this assurance afterwards lose it?

Phil. Undoubtedly they may; God first is gracious to give it them, they for a time careful to keep it; then negligently lose it, then sorrowfully seek it. God again is bountiful to restore it; they happy to recover it; for a while diligent to regain it, then again foolish to forfeit it, and so the same changes in one's lifetime, often over and over again.

Tim. But some will say, If I may be infallibly saved without this assurance, I will never endeavour to attain it.

Phil. I would have covered my flowers, if I had suspected such spiders would have sucked them. One may go to heaven without this assurance, as certainly, but not so cheerfully, and therefore prudence to obtain our own comfort, and piety to obey God's command, obliges us all to give diligence to make our calling and election sure, both in itself and in our apprehension.

DIALOGUE XI.

God alone can satisfy all Objections of a wounded Conscience.

TIMOTHEUS.

B UT, sir, these your answers are no whit satisfactory unto me.

PHIL. An answer may be satisfactory to the objection, both in itself and in the judgment of all unprejudiced hearers, and yet not satisfactory to the objector, and that in two cases: First, when he is possessed with the spirit of peevishness and perverseness. It is lost labour to seek to feed and fill those who have a greedy horseleech of cavilling in their heart, crying, Give, give.

TIM. What is the second case?

PHIL. When the bitterness of his soul is so great and grievous, that he is like the Israelites Exod vi. 9. in Egypt, who hearkened not to Moses, for anguish of spirit, and for cruel bondage. Now as those who have meat before them, and will not eat, deserve to starve without pity; so such are much to be bemoaned, who through some impediment in their mouth, throat, or stomach, cannot chew, swallow, or digest comfort presented unto them.

TIM. Such is my condition; what then is to be done unto me?

PHIL. I must change my precepts to thee
Psalm xc. into prayers for thee, that God would satisfy
thee early with his mercy, that thou mayest
rejoice. Ministers may endeavour it in vain:
whilst they quell one scruple, they start another; whilst they fill one corner of a wounded
conscience with comfort, another is empty.
Only God can so satisfy the soul, that each
chink and cranny therein shall be filled with
spiritual joy.

TIM. What is the difference betwixt God's
and man's speaking peace to a troubled spirit?

PHIL. Man can neither make him to whom
he speaks to hear what he says, or believe what
he hears. God speaks with authority, and doth
both. His words give hearing to the deaf, and
faith to the infidel. When, not the mother of
Christ, but Christ himself, shall salute a sick
soul with Peace be unto thee, it will leap for
joy, as John the babe sprang, though imprisoned in the dark womb of his mother.
Thus the offender is not comforted, though
many of the spectators and under officers tell
him he shall be pardoned, until he hears the
same from the mouth of the judge himself who
hath power and place to forgive him; and then
his heart revives with comfort.

TIM. God send me such comfort: in the
mean time, I am thankful unto you for the
answers you have given me.

PHIL. All that I will add is this. The Lacedemonians had a law, that if a bad man, or one disesteemed of the people, chanced to give good counsel, he was to stand by, and another, against whose person the people had no prejudice, was to speak over the same words which the former had uttered. I am most sensible to myself of my own wickedness and how justly I am subject to exception. Only my prayer shall be, that whilst I stand by, and am silent, God's Spirit, which is free from any fault, and full of all perfection, would be pleased to repeat in thy heart the self-same answers I have given to your objections: and then, what was weak, shallow, and unsatisfying, as it came from my mouth, shall and will be full, powerful, and satisfactory, as re-inforced in thee by God's Spirit.

DIALOGUE XII.

Means to be used by wounded Consciences for the recovering of Comfort.

TIMOTHEUS.

ARE there any useful means to be prescribed, whereby wounded consciences may recover comfort the sooner?

PHIL. Yes, there are.

TIM. But now in the present day, some condemn all using of means. Let grace alone (say they) fully and freely do its own work: and thereby man's mind will in due time return to a good temper of its own accord: this is the most spiritual serving of God, whilst using of means makes but dunces and truants in Christ's school.

PHIL. What they pretend spiritual will prove airy and empty, making lewd and lazy Christians: means may and must be used with these cautions. 1. That they be of God's appointment in his word, and not of man's mere invention. 2. That we still remember they are but means, and not the main. For to account of helps more than helps is the highway to ~~make~~ them hinderances. Lastly, that none rely barely on the deed done; which conceit will undo him that did it, especially if any opinion of merit be affixed therein.

TIM. What is the first means I must use; for I re-assume to personate a wounded conscience?

PHIL. Constantly pray to God, that in his due time he would speak peace unto thee.

TIM. My prayers are better omitted than performed; they are so weak they will but bring the greater punishment upon me, and Jer xlviii. involve me within the prophet's curse, to 10.

those that do the work of the Lord negligently.

PHIL. Prayers negligently performed draw
a curse, but not prayers weakly performed.
The former is when one can do better, and
will not; the latter is when one would do
better, but, alas! he cannot: and such failings,
as they are his sins, so they are his sorrows
also: pray therefore faintly, that thou mayest
pray fervently; pray weakly, that thou mayest
pray strongly.

TIM. But in the law they were forbidden to
offer to God any lame sacrifice, and such are ^{Deut. xv.} my prayers.   ^{21.}

PHIL. 1. Observe a great difference betwixt
the material sacrifice under the law, and spiritual sacrifices (the calves of the lips) under
the Gospel. The former were to be free from
all blemish, because they did typify and resem-
ble Christ himself. The latter (not figuratively
representing Christ, but heartily presented unto
him) must be as good as may be gotten, though
many imperfections will cleave to our best performances, which by God's mercy are forgiven.
2. Know that that in Scripture is accounted
lame which is counterfeit and dissembling, (in
which sense hypocrites are properly called halt- ^{1 Kings}
ers,) and therefore if thy prayer, though never ^{xviii. 21.}
so weak, be sound, and sincere, it is acceptable
with God.   29

TIM. What other counsel do you prescribe me?

PHIL. Be diligent in reading the word of God, wherein all comfort is contained; say not that thou art dumpish and indisposed to read, but remember how travellers must eat against their stomach; their journey will digest it; and though their palate find no pleasure for the present, their whole body will feel strength for the future. Thou hast a great journey to go, a wounded conscience has far to travel to find comfort, (and though weary, shall be welcome at his journey's end,) and therefore must feed on God's word, even against his own dull disposition, and shall afterwards reap benefit thereby.

TIM. Proceed in your appointing of wholesome diet for my wounded conscience to observe.

PHIL. Avoid solitariness, and associate thyself with pious and godly company: O the blessed fruits thereof! Such as want skill or boldness to begin or set a psalm, may competently follow tune in concert with others: many houses in London have such weak walls, and are so slightly and slenderly built, that, were they set alone in the fields, probably they would not stand an hour; which now ranged in streets, receive support in themselves, and mutually return it to others; so mayest thou in good society, not only be reserved from much mischief, but also be strengthened and confirmed in many godly exercises, which solely thou couldst not perform.

TIM. What else must I do?

PHIL. Be industrious in thy calling: I press this the more, because some erroneously conceive that a wounded conscience cancels all indentures of service, and gives them (during their affliction) a dispensation to be idle. The inhabitants of the bishopric of Durham pleaded a privilege, that King Edward the First had no power, although on necessary occasion, to press them to go out of the country, because, forsooth, they termed themselves holy-work-folk, only to be used in defending the holy shrine of St. Cuthbert. Let none in like manner pretend that (during the agony of a wounded conscience) they are to have no other employment than to sit moping to brood their melancholy, or else only to attend their devotion; whereas a good way to divert or assuage their pain within, is to take pains without in their vocation. I am confident, that happy minute which shall put a period to thy misery shall not find thee idle, but employed, as ever some secret good is accruing to such who are diligent in their calling.

Camd. Brit. in Durham.

TIM. But though wounded consciences are not to be freed from all work, are they not to be favoured in their work?

PHIL. Yes, verily. Here let me be the advocate to such parents and masters, who have sons, servants, or others, under their authority, afflicted with wounded consciences. O, do not, with the Egyptian taskmasters, exact of them the full tale of their brick! O, spare a little till they have recovered some strength! Unreasonable that maimed men should pass on equal duty with such soldiers as are sound.

TIM. How must I dispose myself on the Lord's day?

PHIL. Avoid all servile work, and expend it only in such actions as tend to the sanctifying thereof. God, the great landlord of all time, hath let out six days in the week to man to farm them; the seventh day he reserves as a demesne in his own hand: if therefore we would have quiet possession, and comfortable use of what God hath leased out to us, let us not encroach on his demesne. Some Popish people * make a superstitious almanac of the Sunday, by the fairness or foulness thereof. guessing of the weather all the week after. But I dare boldly say, that, from our well or

* If it rains on Sunday before mess, it will rain all the week more or less. A Popish old rhyme.

ill spending of the Lord's day, a probable conjecture may be made how the following week
will be employed.   Yea, I conceive we are
bound (as matters now stand in England) to
a stricter observation of the Lord's day than
ever before.   That a time was due to God's
service, no Christian in our kingdom ever did
deny : that the same was weekly dispersed in
the Lord's day, holy days, Wednesdays, Fridays,
Saturdays, some have earnestly maintained :
seeing therefore all the last are generally neglected, the former must be more strictly observed ; it being otherwise impious, that our
devotion, having a narrower channel, should
also carry a shallower stream.

TIM. What other means must I use for expedition of comfort to my wounded conscience ?

PHIL. Confess that sin or sins, which most 2 Sam. xii.
perplexes thee, to some godly minister, who by Matth. iii.
absolution may pronounce and apply pardon 6.
unto thee.

TIM. This confession is but a device of
divines, thereby to screw themselves into other
men's secrets, so to mould and manage them
with more ease to their own profit.

PHIL. God forbid they should have any other
design but your safety, and therefore choose
your confessor, where you please, to your own
contentment ; so that you may find ease, fetch

it where you may ; it is not our credit, but your cure, we stand upon.

Tim. But such confession hath been counted rather a rack for sound, than a remedy for wounded consciences.

Phil. It proves so, as abused in the Romish Church, requiring an enumeration of all mortal sins, therein supposing an error, that some sins are not mortal, and imposing an impossibility, that all can be reckoned up. Thus the conscience is tortured, because it can never tread firmly, feeling no bottom, being still uncertain of confession, (and so of absolution,) whether or no he hath acknowledged all his sins. But where this ordinance is commended as convenient, not commanded as necessary, left free, not forced, in cases of extremity sovereign use may be made, and hath been found thereof, neither magistrate nor minister carrying the sword or the keys in vain.

Tim. But, sir, I expected some rare inventions from you for curing wounded consciences : whereas all your receipts hitherto are old, stale, usual, common, and ordinary ; there is nothing new in any of them.

Phil. I answer first, if a wounded conscience had been a new disease, never heard of in God's word before this time, then perchance we must have been forced to find out new remedies. But it is an old malady, and therefore old physic is best applied unto it. Secondly, the receipts indeed are old, because prescribed by him who is the Ancient of Days. Dan. vii. 9. But the older the better, because warranted by experience to be effectual. God's ordinances are like the clothes of the children of Israel, Deut. xxix. 5. during our wandering in the wilderness of this world, they never wax old, so as to have their virtue in operation abated or decayed. Thirdly, whereas you call them common, would to God they were so, and as generally practised as they are usually prescribed. Lastly, know we meddle not with curious heads, which are pleased with new-fangled rarities, but with wounded consciences, who love solid comfort. Suppose our receipts ordinary and obvious; if Naaman counts the cure too cheap and easy, 2 Kings v. 12. none will pity him if still he be pained with his leprosy.

TIM. But your receipts are too loose and large, not fitted and appropriated to my malady alone. For all these (pray, read, keep good company, be diligent in thy calling, observe the Sabbath, confess thy sins, &c.) may as well be prescribed to one guilty of presumption, as to me, ready to despair.

PHIL. It doth not follow that our physic is not proper for one, because it may be profitable for both.

Tim. But despair and presumption, being contrary diseases, flowing from contrary causes, must have contrary cures.

Phil. Though they flow immediately from contrary causes, yet originally from the common fountain of natural corruption : and therefore such means as I have propounded, tending towards the mortifying of our corrupt nature, may generally, though not equally, be useful to humble the presuming, and comfort the despairing; but to cut off cavils, in the next dialogue we will come closely to peculiar counsels unto thee.

DIALOGUE XIII.

Four wholesome Counsels, for a wounded Conscience to practise.

TIMOTHEUS.

PERFORM your promise ; which is the first counsel you commend unto me ?

Phil. Take heed of ever renouncing thy filial interest in God, though thy sins deserve that he should disclaim his paternal relation to thee. The prodigal, returning to his father, did not say, I am not thy son, but I am no more worthy to be called thy son. Beware of bastardizing thyself, being as much as Satan desires,

Luke xv. 21.

and more than he hopes to obtain. Otherwise thy folly would give him more than his fury. could get.

TIM. I conceive this a needful caution.

PHIL. It will appear so if we consider what the Apostle saith, that we wrestle with princi- Ephes. vi. palities and powers. Now wrestlers in the ¹² Olympian games were naked, and anointed with oil to make them sleek and glibbery, so to afford no holdfast to such as strove with them. Let us not gratify the Devil with this advantage against ourselves, at any time to disclaim our sonship in God: if the Devil catches us at this lock, he will throw us flat, and hazard the breaking of our necks with final despair. Oh no! still keep this point: a prodigal son I am, but a son, no bastard; a lost sheep, but a sheep, no goat; an unprofitable servant, but God's servant, and not absolute slave to Satan.

TIM. Proceed to your second counsel.

PHIL. Give credit to what grave and godly persons conceive of thy condition, rather than what thy own fear (an incompetent judge) may suggest unto thee. A seared conscience thinks better of itself, a wounded worse, than it ought: the former may account all sin a sport, the latter all spórt a sin: melancholy men, when sick, are ready to conceit any cold to be the cough of the lungs, and an ordinary pustule no less than the plague sore. So wounded consciences conceive sins of infirmity to be of presumption, sins of ignorance to be of knowledge, apprehending their case more dangerous than it is indeed.

Tim. But it seems unreasonable that I should rather trust another saying, than my own sense of myself.

Phil. Every man is best judge of his own self, if he be his own self; but during the swoon of a wounded conscience, I deny thee to be come to thy own self: whilst thine eyes are blubbering, and a tear hangs before thy sight, thou canst not see things clearly and truly, because looking through a double medium of air and water; so whilst this cloud of pensiveness is pendent before the eyes of thy soul, thine estate is erroneously represented unto thee.

Tim. What is your third counsel?

Phil. In thy agony of a troubled conscience, always look upwards unto a gracious God to keep thy soul steady; for looking downward on thyself thou shalt find nothing but what will increase thy fear, infinite sins, good deeds few and imperfect: it is not thy faith, but God's faithfulness, thou must rely upon; casting thine eyes downwards on thyself to behold the great distance betwixt what thou deservest and what thou desirest, is enough to make thee giddy, stagger, and reel into despair : ever therefore lift up thine eyes unto the hills, from whence ^{Psalm cxxi. 1.} cometh thy help, never viewing the deep dale of thy own unworthiness, but to abate thy pride when tempted to presumption.

TIM. Sir, your fourth and last counsel.

PHIL. Be not disheartened, as if comfort would not come at all, because it comes not all at once, but patiently attend God's leisure ; they are not styled the swift, but the sure mer-^{Isaiah lv. 3, and lviii. 8.} cies of David : and the same prophet says, the glory of the Lord shall be thy reward : this we know comes up last to secure and make good all the rest : be assured, where grace patiently leads the front, glory at last will be in the rear. Remember the prodigious patience of Elijah's servant.

TIM. Wherein was it remarkable ?

PHIL. In obedience to his master : he went several times to the sea ; it is tedious for me to tell what was not troublesome for him to do, one, two, three, four, five, six, seven times^{1 Kings xviii. 43.} sent down steep Carmel, with danger, and up it again with difficulty, and all to bring news of nothing, till his last journey, which made recompense for all the rest, with the tidings of a cloud arising. So thy thirsty soul, long parched with drought for want of comfort, though late, at last shall be plentifully re- freshed with the dew of consolation.

Tim. I shall be happy if I find it so.

Phil. Consider the causes why a broken leg is incurable in a horse, and easily curable in a man : the horse is incapable of counsel to submit himself to the farrier, and therefore, in case his leg be set, he flings, flounces, and flies out, unjointing it again by his misemployed mettle, counting all binding to be shackles and fetters unto him ; whereas a man willingly resigns himself to be ordered by the surgeon, preferring rather to be a prisoner for some days, than Psalm a cripple all his life. Be not like a horse or xxxii. 9. mule, which have no understanding : but let James 1.3. patience have its perfect work in thee. When Isa. lxi. 1. God goes about to bind up the broken-hearted, tarry his time, though ease come not at an instant, yea, though it be painful for the present, in due time thou shalt certainly receive comfort.

DIALOGUE XIV.

Comfortable Meditations for wounded Consciences to muse upon.

TIMOTHEUS.

FURNISH me, I pray, with some comfortable meditations ; whereon I may busy and employ my soul when alone.

Phil. First, consider that our Saviour had

not only a notional, but an experimental and meritorious knowledge of the pains of a wounded conscience when hanging on the cross. If Paul conceived himself happy being to answer for himself, before King Agrippa, especially because he knew him to be expert in all the customs and questions of the Jews; how much more just cause has thy wounded conscience of comfort and joy, being in thy prayers to plead before Christ himself, who hath felt thy pain, and deserved that in due time by his stripes thou shouldst be healed?

TIM. Proceed, I pray, in this comfortable subject.

PHIL. Secondly, consider that herein, like Elijah, thou needest not complain that thou art left alone, seeing the best of God's saints in all ages have smarted in the same kind: instance in David: indeed, sometimes he boasts how he lay in green pastures, and was led by still waters; but after he bemoans that he sinks in deep mire, where there was no standing. What is become of those green pastures? parched up with the drought. Where are those still waters? troubled with the tempest of affliction. The same David compares himself to an owl, and in the next Psalm resembles himself to an eagle. Do two fowls fly of more different kind? The one the

Psalm xxiii. 2.

Psalm lxix. 2.

Compare Psalm cii. 6, with Psalm ciii. 5.

362 THE CAUSE AND CURE OF

scorn, the other the sovereign; the one the slowest, the other the swiftest; the one the most sharp-sighted, the other the most dim-eyed of all birds. Wonder not, then, to find in thyself sudden and strange alterations. It fared thus with all God's servants, in their agonies of temptation; and be confident thereof, though now run aground with grief, in due time thou shalt be all afloat with comfort.

Tim. I am loath to interrupt you in so welcome a discourse.

Phil. Thirdly, consider that thou hast had, though not grace enough to cure thee, yet enough to keep thee, and conclude that he whose goodness hath so long held thy head above water from drowning, will at last bring thy whole body safely to the shore. The wife of Manoah had more faith than her husband, and thus she reasoned: If the Lord were pleased to kill us, he would not have received a burnt and a meat offering at our hands. Thou mayest argue in like manner: If God had intended finally to forsake me, he would never so often have heard and accepted my prayers, in such a measure as to vouchsafe unto me, though not full deliverance from, free preservation in, my affliction. Know God hath ‚done great things for thee already, and thou mayest conclude, from his grace of supporta-

Judg. xiii. 23.

tion hitherto, grace of ease, and relaxation hereafter.

TIM. It is pity to disturb you ; proceed.

PHIL. Fourthly, consider that, besides the private stock of thy own, thou tradest on the public store of all good men's prayers, put up to heaven for thee. What a mixture of languages met in Jerusalem at Pentecost, — Parthians, Medes, and Elamites, &c. But conceive, to thy comfort, what a medley of prayers, in several tongues, daily centre themselves in God's ears in thy behalf, English, Scotch, Irish, French, Dutch, &c., insomuch, that perchance thou dost not understand one syllable of their prayers, by whom thou mayest reap benefit. ^{Acts ii.}

TIM. Is it not requisite, to entitle me to the profit of other men's prayers, that I particularly know their persons which pray for me ?

PHIL. Not at all, no more than it is needful that the eye or face must see the backward parts, which is difficult, or the inward parts of the body, which is impossible ; without which sight, by sympathy they serve one another. And such is the correspondency by prayers betwixt the mystical members of Christ's body, corporally unseen one by another.

TIM. Proceed to a fifth meditation.

PHIL. Consider, there be five kinds of consciences on foot in the world ; first, an ignorant

conscience, which neither sees nor saith anything, neither beholds the sins in a soul, nor
reproves them. Secondly, the flattering conscience, whose speech is worse than silence
itself, which, though seeing sin, soothes men
in the committing thereof. Thirdly, the seared
conscience, which hath neither sight, speech, nor
sense, in men that are past feeling. Fourthly,
a wounded conscience, frighted with sin. The
last and best is a quiet and clear conscience,
pacified in Christ Jesus. Of these, the fourth
is thy case, incomparably better than the three
former, so that a wise man would not take a
world to change with them. Yea, a wounded
conscience is rather painful than sinful, an affliction, no offence, and is in the ready way, at
the next remove, to be turned into a quiet conscience.

Ephes. iv. 19.

TIM. I hearken unto you with attention and
comfort.

PHIL. Lastly, consider the good effects of a
wounded conscience, privative for the present,
and positive for the future. First, privative,
this heaviness of thy heart (for the time being)
is a bridle to thy soul, keeping it from many
sins it would otherwise commit. Thou that
now sittest sad in thy shop, or walkest pensive
in thy parlour, or standest sighing in thy chamber, or liest sobbing on thy bed, mightest per-

chance at the same time be drunk, or wanton,
or worse, if not restrained by this affliction.
God saith in his prophet to Judah, I will hedge Hos. ii. 6.
thy way with thorns, namely to keep Judah
from committing spiritual fornication. It is
confest that a wounded conscience, for the
time, is a hedge of thorns (as the messenger
of Satan, sent to buffet St. Paul, is termed a
thorn in the flesh). But this thorny fence 2 Cor. xii.
keeps our wild spirits in the true way, which 7.
otherwise would be straggling: and it is better
to be held in the right road with briers and
brambles, than to wander on beds of roses in
a wrong path, which leads to destruction.

Tim. What are the positive benefits of a
wounded conscience?

Phil. Thereby the graces in thy soul will be
proved, approved, improved. Oh, how clear
will thy sunshine be, when this cloud is blown
over! And here I can hardly hold from envy-
ing thy happiness hereafter. Oh that I might
have thy future crown, without thy present
cross; thy triumphs, without thy trial; thy
conquest, without thy combat! But I recall
my wish, as impossible, seeing what God hath
joined together, no man can put asunder.
These things are so twisted together, I must
have both or neither.

DIALOGUE XV.

*That is not always the greatest Sin whereof a Man
is guilty, wherewith his Conscience is most pained
for the present.*

TIMOTHEUS.

IS that the greatest sin in man's soul, wherewith his wounded conscience, in the agony
thereof, is most perplexed?

PHIL. It is so commonly, but not constantly.
Commonly, indeed, that sin most pains and
pinches him, which commands as principal in
his soul.

TIM. Have all men's hearts some one paramount sin, which rules as sovereign over all the
rest?

PHIL. Most have. Yet, as all countries are
not monarchies governed by kings, but some
by free states, where many together have equal
power; so it is possible (though rare) that one
man may have two, three, or more sins, which
jointly domineer in his heart, without any dis-
cernible superiority betwixt them.

TIM. Which are the sins that most generally
wound and afflict a man, when his conscience
is terrified?

PHIL. No general rule can exactly be given
herein. Sometimes, that sin in acting whereof

he took most delight; it being just, that the
sweetness of his corporal pleasure should be
sauced with more spiritual sadness. Sometimes,
that sin which (though not the foulest) is the
most frequent in him. Thus his idle words
may perplex him more than his oaths, or
perjury itself. Sometimes that sin (not which
is most odious before God, but) most scandalous
before men does most afflict him, because drawing greatest disgrace upon his person and profession. Sometimes, that sin which he last committed, because all the circumstances thereof
are still firm and fresh in his memory. Sometimes that sin which (though long since by him
committed) he hath heard very lately powerfully reproved; and no wonder, if an old gall
new rubbed over smart the most. Sometimes,
that sin which formerly he most slighted and
neglected, as so inconsiderably small that it was
unworthy of any sorrow for it, and yet now it
may prove the sharpest sting in his conscience.

TIM. May one who is guilty of very great
sins sometimes have his conscience much troubled only for a small one?

PHIL. Yes, verily: country patients often
complain, not of the disease which is most
dangerous, but most conspicuous. Yea, sometimes they are more troubled with the symptom
of a disease (suppose an ill colour, bad breath,

weak stomach) than with the disease itself. So in the soul, the conscience ofttimes is most wounded, not with that offence which is, but appears, most; and a sin incomparably small to others, whereof the party is guilty, may most molest for the present, and that for three reasons.

TIM. Reckon them in order.

PHIL. First, that God may show in him, that as sins are like the sands in number, so they are far above them in heaviness, whereof the least crumb taken asunder, and laid on the conscience by God's hand, in full weight thereof, is enough to drive it to despair.

TIM. What is the second reason?

PHIL. To manifest God's justice, that those should be choked with a gnat-sin, who have swallowed many camel-sins, without the least regret. Thus some may be terrified for not fasting on Friday, because indeed they have been drunk on Sunday: they may be perplexed for their wanton dreams, when sleeping, because they were never truly humbled for their wicked deeds, when waking. Yea, those who never feared Babylon the great, may be frightened with little Zoar; I mean, such as have been faulty in flat superstition may be tortured for committing or omitting a thing in its own nature indifferent.

Tim. What is the third reason?

Phil. That this pain for a lesser sin may occasion his serious scrutiny into greater offences. Any paltry cur may serve to start and put up the game out of the bushes, whilst fiercer and fleeter hounds are behind to course and catch it. God doth make use of a smaller sin, to raise and rouse the conscience out of security, and to put it up, as we say, to be chased, by the reserve of far greater offences, lurking behind in the soul, unseen and unsorrowed for.

Tim. May not the conscience be troubled at that which in very deed is no sin at all, nor hath truly so much as but the appearance of evil in it?

Phil. It may. Through the error of the understanding, such a mistake may follow in the conscience.

Tim. What is to be done in such a case?

Phil. The party's judgment must be rectified, before his conscience can be pacified. Then is it the wisest way to persuade him to lay the axe of repentance to the root of corruption in his heart. When real sins in his soul are felled by unfeigned sorrow, causeless scruples will fall of themselves. Till that root be cut down, not only the least bough and branch of that tree, but the smallest sprig,

twig, and leaf thereof, yea, the very empty
shadow of a leaf (mistaken for a sin, and
created a fault by the jealousy of a misin-
formed judgment) is sufficient intolerably to
torture a wounded conscience.

DIALOGUE XVI.

*Obstructions hindering the speedy flowing of Comfort
into a troubled Soul.*

TIMOTHEUS.

HOW comes it to pass, that comfort is so
long a coming to some wounded consciences ?

PHIL. It proceeds from several causes: either
from God, not yet pleased to give it; or the
patient, not yet prepared to receive it; or the
minister, not well fitted to deliver it.

TIM. How from God not yet pleased to give
it ?

PHIL. His time to bestow consolation is not
yet come: now no plummets of the heaviest
human importunity can so weigh down God's
clock of time, as to make it strike one minute
before his hour be come. Till then, his mother
John ii. 4. herself could not prevail with Christ to work
a miracle, and turn water into wine: and till
that minute appointed approach, God will not

in a wounded conscience convert the water of affliction into that wine of comfort which makes glad the heart of the soul.

Tim. How may the hinderance be in the patient himself?

Phil. He may as yet not be sufficiently humbled, or else God perchance in his providence foresees, that as the prodigal child, when he had received his portion, riotously misspent it, so this sick soul, if comfort were imparted unto him, would prove an unthrift and ill husband upon it, would lose and lavish it. God therefore conceives it most for his glory, and the other's good, to keep the comfort still in his own hand, till the wounded conscience get more wisdom to manage and employ it.

Tim. May not the sick man's too mean opinion of the minister be a cause why he reaps no more comfort by his counsel?

Phil. It may. Perchance the sick man hath formerly slighted and neglected that minister, and God will now not make him the instrument for his comfort, who before had been the object of his contempt. But on the other side, we must also know, that perchance the party's over-high opinion of the minister's parts, piety, and corporal presence (as if he cured where he came, and carried ease with him) may hinder the operation of his advice. For God grows jealous of so suspicious an instrument, who probably may be mistaken for the principal. Whereas a meaner man, of whose spirituality the patient hath not so high carnal conceits, may prove more effectual in comforting, because not within the compass of suspicion to eclipse God of his glory.

TIM. How may the obstructions be in the minister himself?

PHIL. If he comes unprepared by prayer, or possessed with pride, or unskilful in what he undertakes; wherefore in such cases, a minister may do well to reflect on himself (as the disciples did when they could not cast out the Devil), and to call his heart to account, what may be the cause thereof: particularly whether some unrepented for sin in himself hath not hindered the effects of his counsels in others.

Matth.
xvii. 19.

TIM. However, you would not have him wholly disheartened with his ill-success.

PHIL. O no; but let him comfort himself with these considerations. First, that though the patient gets no benefit by him, he may gain experience by the patient, thereby being enabled more effectually to proceed with some other in the same disease. Secondly, though the sick man refuses comfort for the present, yet what doth not sink on a sudden may soak in by degrees, and may prove profitable afterwards. Thirdly, his unsucceeding pains may notwithstanding facilitate comfort for another to work in the same body, as Solomon built a temple with most materials formerly provided and brought thither by David. Lastly, grant his pains altogether lost on the wounded conscience, yet his labour is not in vain in the Lord, who without respect to the event will reward his endeavours. [1 Cor. xv. 58.]

TIM. But what if this minister hath been the means to cast this sick man down, and now cannot comfort him again?

PHIL. In such a case, he must make this sad accident the more matter for his humiliation, but not for his dejection. Besides, he is bound, both in honour and honesty, civility and Christianity, to procure what he cannot perform, calling in the advice of others more able to assist him, not conceiving, out of pride or envy, that the discreet craving of the help of others is a disgraceful confessing of his own weakness: like those malicious midwives, who had rather that the woman in travail should miscarry, than be safely delivered by the hand of another more skilful than themselves.

DIALOGUE XVII.

What is to be conceived of their final Estate who die in a wounded Conscience without any visible Comfort.

TIMOTHEUS.

WHAT think you of such, who yield up their ghost in the agony of an afflicted spirit, without receiving the least sensible degree of comfort ?

PHIL. Let me be your remembrancer to call or keep in your mind what I said before, that our discourse only concerns the children of God : this notion renewed, I answer. It is possible that the sick soul may receive secret solace, though the standers-by do not perceive it. We know how insensibly Satan may spirt and inject despair into a heart, and shall we not allow the Lord of heaven to be more dexterous and active with his antidotes than the Devil is with his poisons ?

TIM. Surely, if he had any such comfort, he would show it by words, signs, or some way, were it only but to comfort his sad kindred, and content such sorrowful friends which survive him ; were there any hidden fire of consolation kindled in his heart, it would sparkle in his looks and gestures, especially seeing no

obligation of secrecy is imposed on him, as
on the blind man, when healed, to tell none Mark viii.
thereof. 26.

PHIL. It may be he cannot discover the comfort he hath received, and that for two reasons:
First, because it comes so late, when he lies in
the marshes of life and death, being so weak,
that he can neither speak, nor make signs with
Zechariah, being at that very instant when the
silver cord is ready to be loosed, and the golden
bowl to be broken, and the pitcher to be broken
at the fountain, and the wheel to be broken at
the cistern.

TIM. What may be the other reason?

PHIL. Because the comfort itself may be in-
communicable in its own nature, which the
party can take and not tell; enjoy, and not
express; receive, and not impart: as by the
assistance of God's Spirit, he sent up groans Rom. viii.
which cannot be uttered, so the same may from 26.
God be returned with comfort which cannot
be uttered; and as he had many invisible and
privy pangs, concealed from the cognizance of
others, so may God give him secret comfort,
known unto himself alone, without any other
men's sharing in the notice thereof. The heart Prov. xiv.
knoweth his own bitterness, and a stranger doth 10.
not intermeddle with his joy. So that his comfort may be compared to the new name given .

Rev. ii. 17. to God's servants, which no man knoweth, save he that receiveth it.

Tim. All this proceeds on what is possible or probable, but amounts to no certainty.

Phil. Well, then, suppose the worst, this is most sure, though he die without tasting of any comfort here, he may instantly partake of everlasting joys hereafter. Surely many a despairing soul, groaning out his last breath with fear and thought to sink down to hell, hath presently been countermanded by God's goodness to eternal happiness.

Tim. What you say herein, no man alive can confirm or confute, as being known to God alone, and the soul of the party. Only I must confess that you have charity on your side.

Phil. I have more than charity, namely, Matth. v. 4. God's plain and positive promise, Blessed are such as mourn, for they shall be comforted. Now though the particular time when be not expressed, yet the latest date that can be allowed must be in the world to come, where such mourners, who have not felt God in his comfort here, shall see him in his glory in heaven.

Tim. But some who have led pious and godly lives have departed, pronouncing the sentence of condemnation upon themselves, having one foot already in hell by their own confession.

PHIL. Such confessions are of no validity, wherein their fear bears false witness against their faith. The fineness of the whole cloth of their life must not be thought the worse of, for a little coarse list at the last. And also their final estate is not to be construed by what was dark, doubtful, and desperate at their deaths, but must be expounded by what was plain, clear, and comfortable in their lives.

TIM. You then are confident, that a holy life must have a happy death.

PHIL. Most confident. The logicians hold, that, although from false premises a true conclusion may sometimes follow ; yet from true propositions nothing but a truth can be thence inferred ;* so, though sometimes a bad life may be attended with a good death, (namely, by reason of repentance, though slow, sincere, though late, yet unfeigned, being seasonably interposed,) but where a godly and gracious life hath gone before, there a good death must of necessity follow ; which, though sometimes doleful (for want of apparent comfort) to their surviving friends, can never be dangerous to the party deceased. Remember what St. Paul saith, Our life is hid with Christ in God. Col. iii. 3.

TIM. What makes that place to your purpose ?

* Ex veris possunt, nil nisi vera sequi.

PHIL. Exceeding much. Five cordial observations are couched therein. First, that God
sets a high price and valuation on the souls
of his servants, in that he is pleased to hide
them : none will hide toys and trifles, but what
is counted a treasure. Secondly, the word hide,
as a relative, imports, that some seek after our
souls, being none other than Satan himself, that

1 Peter v. 8.

roaring lion, who goes about seeking whom he
may devour. But the best is, let him seek, and
seek, and seek, till his malice be weary, (if that
be possible,) we cannot be hurt by him whilst
we are hid in God. Thirdly, grant Satan find
us there, he cannot fetch us thence : our souls
are bound in the bundle of life, with the Lord
our God. So that, be it spoken with reverence,
God first must be stormed with force or fraud,
before the soul of a saint sinner, hid in him,
can be surprised. Fourthly, we see the reason
why so many are at a loss, in the agony of a
wounded conscience, concerning their spiritual
estate : for they look for their life in a wrong
place, namely, to find it in their own piety,
purity, and inherent righteousness. But though
they seek, and search, and dig, and dive never so
deep, all in vain. For though Adam's life was
hid in himself, and he intrusted with the keeping his own integrity, yet, since Christ's coming,
all the original evidences of our salvation are

kept in a higher office, namely, hidden in God himself. Lastly, as our English proverb saith, he that hath hid can find ; so God (to whom belongs the issues from death) can infallibly find out that soul that is hidden in him, though it may seem, when dying, even to labour to lose itself in a fit of despair. ^{Psalm lxviii. 20.}

TIM. It is pity but that so comfortable a doctrine should be true.

PHIL. It is most true : surely as Joseph and Mary conceived that they had lost Christ in a crowd, and sought him three days sorrowing, till at last they found him, beyond their expectation, safe and sound, sitting in the temple : so many pensive parents, solicitous for the souls of their children, have even given them for gone, and lamented them lost, (because dying without visible comfort,) and yet, in due time, shall find them, to their joy and comfort, safely possessed of honour and happiness, in the midst of the heavenly temple and church triumphant in glory. ^{Luke ii. 48.}

DIALOGUE XVIII.

Of the different Time and Manner of the coming of Comfort to such who are healed of a wounded Conscience.

TIMOTHEUS.

HOW long may a servant of God lie under the burden of a wounded conscience ?

Acts i. 7.   PHIL. It is not for us to know the times and the seasons, which the Father hath put in his own power. God alone knows whether their grief shall be measured unto them by hours, or days, or weeks, or months, or many years.

TIM. How then is it that St. Paul saith, that 1 Cor. x. 13. God will give us the issue with the temptation, if one may long be visited with this malady ?

PHIL. The Apostle is not so to be understood, as if the temptation and issue were twins, both born at the same instant ; for then no affliction could last long, but must be ended as Acts ix. 33. soon as it is begun ; whereas we read how Æneas, truly pious, was bedridden of the palsy eight Matth. ix. 2. years ; the woman diseased with a bloody issue Luke xiii. 11. twelve years; another woman bowed by infirmity John v. 5. eighteen years ; and the man lame thirty-eight years at the pool of Bethesda.

TIM. What then is the meaning of the Apostle ?

PHIL. God will give the issue with the temptation; that is, the temptation and the issue
bear both the same date in God's decreeing
them, though not in his applying them: at the
same time wherein he resolved his servants
shall be tempted, he also concluded of the
means and manner how the same persons should
infallibly be delivered. Or thus: God will
give the issue with the temptation; that is, as
certainly, though not as suddenly. Though
they go not abreast, yet they are joined successively, like two links in a chain; where one
ends, the other begins. Besides, there is a two-
fold issue; one, through a temptation; another,
out of a temptation. The former is but mediate, not final; an issue to an issue, only support-
ing the person tempted for the present, and
preserving him for a future full deliverance.
Understand the Apostle thus, and the issue is
always both given and applied to God's children, with the temptation, though the temptation
may last long after, before fully removed.

TIM. I perceive, then, that in some a wounded conscience may continue many years.

PHIL. So it may. I read of a poor widow, Melchior
in the land of Limburgh, who had nine chil- Adamus in
vitâ Theo-
dren, and for thirteen years together was mis- logorum
Exterorum,
erably afflicted in mind, only because she had p. 198.
attended the dressing and feeding of her little

31

ones before going to mass. At last it pleased God to sanctify the endeavours of Franciscus Junius, that learned godly divine, that, upon true information of her judgment, she was presently and perfectly comforted.

TIM. Doth God give ease to all in such manner, on a sudden?

PHIL. O no: some receive comfort suddenly, and in an instant they pass from midnight to bright day, without any dawning betwixt. Others receive consolation by degrees, which is not poured, but dropped into them by little and little.

TIM. Strange, that God's dealing herein should be so different with his servants.

PHIL. It is to show, that, as in his proceedings there is no variableness, such as may import him mutable or impotent, so in the same there is very much variety, to prove the fulness of his power, and freedom of his pleasure.

James I. 17.

TIM. Why doth not God give them consolation all at once?

PHIL. The more to employ their prayers, and exercise their patience. One may admire why Boaz did not give to Ruth a quantity of corn more or less, so sending her home to her mother, but that rather he kept her still to glean; but this was the reason, because that is the best charity which so relieves another's

Ruth ii. 8.

poverty, as still continues their industry. God, in like manner, will not give some consolation all at once, he will not spoil their (painful but) pious profession of gleaning; still they must pray and gather, and pray and glean, here an ear, there a handful, of comfort, which God scatters in favour unto them.

TIM. What must the party do when he perceives God and his comfort beginning to draw nigh unto him?

PHIL. As Martha, when she heard that John xi. 20 Christ was coming, stayed not a minute at home, but went out of her house to meet him; so must a sick soul, when consolation is coming, haste out of himself and hie to entertain God with his thankfulness. The best way to make a homer of comfort increase to an ephah (which is ten times as much), is to be heartily grateful Exod. xvi. 36. for what one hath already, that his store may be multiplied. He shall never want more, who is thankful for and thrifty with a little: whereas ingratitude doth not only stop the flowing of more mercy, but even spills what was formerly received.

DIALOGUE XIX.

*How such who are completely cured of a wounded
Conscience are to demean themselves.*

TIMOTHEUS.

GIVE me leave now to take upon me the
person of one recovered out of a wounded conscience.

PHIL.   In the first place, I must heartily con-
gratulate thy happy condition, and must rejoice
at thy upsitting, whom God hath raised from
the bed of despair : welcome David out of the
deep, Daniel out of the lion's den, Jonah from
the whale's belly, welcome Job from the dung-
hill, restored to health and wealth again.

TIM.   Yea, but when Job's brethren came to
visit him after his recovery, every one gave him
Job xlii 11. a piece of money, and an ear-ring of gold : but
the present I expect from you, let it be, I pray,
some of your good counsel for my future deportment.

PHIL.   I have need to come to thee, and com-
est thou to me?   Fain would I be a Paul, sitting at the feet of such a Gamaliel, who hath
been cured of a wounded conscience in the
height thereof : I would turn my tongue into
ears, and listen attentively to what tidings he
brings from hell itself.   Yea, I should be worse

than the brethren of Dives, if I should not believe one risen from the dead, for such in effect I conceive to be his condition.

TIM. But waiving these digressions, I pray proceed to give me good advice.

PHIL. First thankfully own God thy principal restorer, and comforter paramount. Remember that, of ten lepers, one only returned Luke xvii. 17. to give thanks, which shows, that by nature, without grace overswaying us, it is ten to one if we be thankful. Omit not also thy thankfulness to good men, not only to such who have been the architects of thy comfort, but even to those who, though they have built nothing, have borne burthens towards thy recovery.

TIM. Go on, I pray, in your good counsel.

PHIL. Associate thyself with men of afflicted minds, with whom thou mayest expend thy time to thine and their best advantage. O how excellently did Paul comply with Aquila and Priscilla! As their hearts agreed in the general profession of piety, so their hands met in the trade of tent-makers, they abode and wrought Acts xviii. 3. together, being of the same occupation. Thus I count all wounded consciences of the same company, and may mutually reap comfort one by another; only here is the difference; they (poor souls) are still bound to their hard task and trade, whilst thou (happy man) hast thy indentures cancelled, and, being free of that profession, art able to instruct others therein.

Tim. What instructions must I commend unto them?

2 Cor. i. 4. Phil. Even the same comfort wherewith thou thyself wast comforted of God : with David, tell them what God hath done for thy soul ; Luke xxii. 32. and with Peter, being strong, strengthen thy brethren : conceive thyself like Joseph, therefore, sent before, and sold into the Egypt of a wounded conscience, (where thy feet were hurt in the stocks, the irons entered into thy soul,) that thou mightest provide food for the famine of others, and especially be a purveyor of comfort for those thy brethren, which afterwards shall follow thee down into the same doleful condition.

Tim. What else must I do for my afflicted brethren?

Phil. Pray heartily to God in their behalf: when David had prayed, Psalm xxv. 2, O my God, I trust in thee, let me not be ashamed ; in the next verse, (as if conscious to himself, that his prayers were too restrictive, narrow, and niggardly,) he enlarges the bounds thereof, and builds them on a broader bottom : Yea, let none that wait on thee be ashamed. Let charity in thy devotions have Rehoboth, room enough:

beware of pent petitions confined to thy private good, but extend them to all God's servants, but especially all wounded consciences.

Tim. Must I not also pray for those servants of God, which hitherto have not been wounded in conscience?

Phil. Yes, verily, that God would keep them from, or cure them in, the exquisite torment thereof. Beggars, when they crave an alms, constantly use one main motive, that the person of whom they beg may be preserved from that misery whereof they themselves have had woful experience. If they be blind, they cry, Master, God bless your eyesight; if lame, God bless your limbs; if undone by casual burning, God bless you and yours from fire. Christ, though his person be now glorified in heaven, yet he is still subject, by sympathy of his saints on earth, to hunger, nakedness, imprisonment, and a wounded conscience, and so may stand in need of feeding, clothing, visiting, comforting, and curing. Now when thou prayest to Christ for any favour, it is a good plea to urge, edge, and enforce thy request withal, Lord, grant me such or such a grace, and never mayest thou, Lord, in thy mystical members, never be tortured and tormented with the agony of a wounded conscience, in the deepest distress thereof.

Tim. How must I behave myself for the time to come?

PHIL. Walk humbly before God, and carefully avoid the smallest sin, always remembering Christ's caution : Behold, thou art made whole; sin no more, lest a worse thing come unto thee.

John v. 14.

DIALOGUE XX.

Whether one cured of a wounded Conscience be subject to a Relapse.

TIMOTHEUS.

MAY a man, once perfectly healed of a wounded conscience, and for some years in peaceable possession of comfort, afterwards fall back into his former disease?

PHIL. Nothing appears in Scripture or reason to the contrary, though examples of real relapses are very rare, because God's servants are careful to avoid sin, the cause thereof; and being once burnt therewith, ever after dread the fire of a wounded conscience.

TIM. Why call you it a relapse? .

PHIL. To distinguish it from those relapses more usual and obvious, whereby such who have snatched comfort before God gave it them, on serious consideration that they had usurped that to which they had no right, fall back again into the former pit of despair; this is improp-

erly termed a relapse, as not being a renewing, but a continuing of their former malady,
from which, though seemingly, they were never
soundly recovered.

TIM. Is there any intimation in Scripture of
the possibility of such a real relapse in God's
servants ?

PHIL. There is ; when David saith, Psalm
lxxxv. 8, I will hear what God the Lord will
speak, for he will speak peace unto his people,
and to his saints, but let them not turn again to
folly : this imports that if his saints turn again
to folly, which by woful experience we find too
frequently done, God may change his voice, and
turn his peace, formerly spoken, into a warlike
defiance to their conscience.

TIM. But this methinks is a diminution to
the majesty of God, that a man, once completely cured of a wounded conscience, should
again be pained therewith : let mountebanks
palliate, cures break out again, being never
soundly, but superficially healed : He that is all
in all never doth his work by halves, so that
it shall be undone afterwards.

PHIL. It is not the same individual wound in
number, but the same in kind, and perchance a
deeper in degree : nor is it any ignorance or
falsehood in the surgeon, but folly and fury in
the patient, who, by committing fresh sins,
causes a new pain in the old place.

TIM. In such relapses, men are only troubled for such sins which they have run on score since their last recovery from a wounded conscience.

PHIL. Not those alone, but all the sins which they have committed, both before and since their conversion, may be started up afresh in their minds and memories, and grieve and perplex them, with the guiltiness thereof.

TIM. But those sins were formerly fully forgiven, and the pardon thereof solemnly sealed, and assured unto them; and can the guilt of the same recoil again upon their consciences?

PHIL. I will not dispute what God may do in the strictness of his justice. Such seals, though still standing firm and fast in themselves, may notwithstanding break off, and fly open in the feeling of the sick soul: he will be ready to 1 Kings ii. conceive with himself, that as Shimei, though 44. once forgiven his railing on David, was afterwards executed for the same offence, though upon his committing of a new transgression, following his servants to Gath, against the positive command of the king; so God, upon his committing of new trespasses, may justly take occasion to punish all former offences; yea, in his apprehension, the very foundation of his faith may be shaken, all his former title to heaven brought into question, and he tormented with the consideration that he was never a true child of God.

TIM. What remedies do you commend to such souls in relapses?

PHIL. Even the self-same receipts which I first prescribed to wounded consciences, the very same promises, precepts, comforts, counsels, cautions. Only as Jacob, the second time ^{Gen. xliii.} that his sons went down into Egypt, commanded them to carry double money in their hands; so I would advise such to apply the former remedies with double diligence, double watchfulness, double industry, because the malignity of a disease is riveted firmer and deeper in a relapse.

DIALOGUE XXI.

Whether it be lawful to pray for, or to pray against, or to praise God for, a wounded Conscience.

TIMOTHEUS.

IS it lawful for a man to pray to God to visit him with a wounded conscience?

PHIL. He may and must pray to have his high and hard heart truly humbled, and bruised with the sight and sense of his sins, and with unfeigned sorrow for the same: but may not explicitly and directly pray for a wounded conscience, in the highest degree and extremity thereof.

Tim. Why interpose you those terms explicitly and directly?

Phil. Because implicitly and by consequence, one may pray for a wounded conscience: namely, when he submits himself to be disposed by God's pleasure, referring the particulars thereof wholly to his infinite wisdom, tendering, as I may say, a blank paper to God in his prayers, and requesting him to write therein what particulars he pleases; therein generally and by consequence, he may pray for a wounded conscience, in case God sees the same for his own glory, and the parties' good; otherwise, directly he may not pray for it.

Tim. How prove you the same?

Phil. First, because a wounded conscience is a judgment, and one of the sorest, as the resemblance of the torments of hell. Now it is not congruous to nature, or grace, for a man to be a free and active instrument, purposely to pull down upon himself the greatest evil that can befall him in this world. Secondly, we have neither direction nor precedent of any saint, recorded in God's word, to justify and warrant such prayers. Lastly, though praying for a wounded conscience may seemingly scent of pretended humility, it doth really and rankly savour of pride, limiting the Holy One of Israel. It ill becoming the patient to prescribe to his heavenly physician what kind of physic he shall minister unto him.

TIM. But we may pray for all means to increase grace in us, and therefore may pray for a wounded conscience, seeing thereby at last piety is improved in God's servants.

PHIL. We may pray for and make use of all means whereby grace is increased : namely, such means as by God are appointed for that purpose ; and therefore, by virtue of God's institution, have both a proportionableness and attendency in order thereunto. But properly, those things are not means, or ordained by God, for the increase of piety, which are only accidentally overruled to that end by God's power against the intention and inclination of the things themselves. Such is a wounded conscience, being always actually an evil of punishment, and too often occasionally an evil of sin ; the bias whereof doth bend and bow to wickedness: though overruled by the aim of God's eye, and strength of his arm, it may bring men to the mark of more grace and goodness. God can and will extract light out of darkness, good out of evil, order out of confusion, and comfort

32

out of a wounded conscience: and yet darkness, evil, confusion, &c. are not to be prayed
for.

TIM. But a wounded conscience, in God's
children, infallibly ends in comfort here, or
glory hereafter, and therefore is to be desired.

PHIL. Though the ultimate end of a wounded conscience winds off in comfort, yet it brings
with it many intermediate mischiefs and mal-
adies, especially as managed by human corruption : namely, dulness in divine service,
impatience, taking God's name in vain, despair
for the time, blasphemy ; which a saint should
decline, not desire ; shun, not seek ; not pursue,
but avoid, with his utmost endeavours.

TIM. Is it lawful positively to pray against a
wounded conscience ?

PHIL. It is, as appears from an argument
taken from the lesser to the greater. If a man
may pray against pinching poverty, as wise
Prov. xxx. Agur did; then may he much more against a
8.
wounded conscience, as a far heavier judgment.
Secondly, if God's servants may pray for ease
under their burdens, whereof we see divers
1 Kings particulars in that worthy prayer of Solomon ;
viii. 33.
I say, if we pray to God to remove a lesser
judgment by way of subvention, questionless
we may beseech him to deliver us from the
great evil of a wounded conscience, by way
of prevention.

Tim. May one lawfully praise God for visiting him with a wounded conscience?

Phil. Yes, verily. First, because it is agreeable to the will of God, in everything to be thankful: here is a general rule, without limitation.ᶜ Secondly, because the end, why God makes any work, is his own glory; and a wounded conscience being a work of God, he must be glorified in it, especially seeing God shows much mercy therein, as being a punishment on this side of hell-fire, and less than our deserts. As also, because he hath gracious intentions towards the sick soul for the present, and when the malady is over, the patient shall freely confess that it is good for him that he was so afflicted. Happy then that soul, who, in the lucid intervals of a wounded conscience, can praise God for the same. Music is sweetest near
or over rivers, where the echo thereof is
best rebounded by the water. Praise
for pensiveness, thanks for tears,
and blessing God over the
floods of affliction, makes
the most melodious
music in the ear
of Heaven.

1 Thes. v. 18. Ephes. v. 20. Psalm clii. 22, and cxlv. 10.

THE CONCLUSION OF THE AUTHOR
TO THE READER.

AND now God knows how soon it may be said unto me, Physician, heal thyself, and how quickly I shall stand in need of these counsels, which I have prescribed to others. Herein I say with Eli to Samuel, It is the Lord, let him do what seemeth him good: with David to Zadok, Behold, here am I, let him do to me as seemeth good unto him. With the disciples to Paul, The will of the Lord be done. But oh how easy it is for the mouth to pronounce, or the hand to subscribe these words! But how hard, yea, without God's grace, how impossible, for the heart to submit thereunto! Only hereof I am confident, that the making of this treatise shall no ways cause or hasten a wounded conscience in me, but rather on the contrary (especially if, as it is written by me, it were written in me) either prevent it, that it come not at all, or defer it, that it come not so soon, or lighten it, that

1 Sam. iii.
18.
2 Sam. xv.
26.

Acts xxi.
14.

it fall not so heavy, or shorten it, that it last not
so long.   And if God shall be pleased hereafter
to write bitter things against me, who have Job xiii. 26.
here written the sweetest comforts I could for
others, let none insult on my sorrows: But
whilst my wounded conscience shall lie like Acts iii. 2.
the cripple, at the porch of the temple, may
such as pass by be pleased to pity me, and per-
mit this book to beg in my behalf the charitable prayers of well-disposed people ;
till Divine Providence shall send
some Peter, some pious minister, perfectly to restore
my   maimed   soul
to her former
soundness.
Amen.

www.ingramcontent.com/pod-product-compliance
Lightning Source LLC
Chambersburg PA
CBHW020237110726
47898CB00004B/1299